Honeymoon

Mary J Howell

Mary J Howell

Honeymoon

First published in 2017
Mary J Howell

Copyright © Mary J Howell, 2017
Cover Image © Lateefa Spiker

The rights of the author have been asserted in accordance with Sections 77 and 78 of the Copyright Designs and Patents Act, 1988.

ISBN No. 978-1979403252

All rights reserved.
No part of this book may be reproduced (including photocopying or storing in any medium by electronic means and whether or not transiently or incidentally to some other use of this publication) without the written permission of the copyright holder except in accordance with the provisions of the Copyright, design and Patents Act 1988. Applications for the Copyright holder's written permission to reproduce any part of this publication should be addressed to the publishers.

This book is a work of fiction. Names, characters, businesses, organisations, places and events other than those clearly in the public domain, are either the product of the author's imagination or are used fictitiously. Any resemblance to actual persons, living or dead, events or locales is entirely coincidental.

For Denis

I often wish that I could rid the world of the tyranny of facts. What are the facts, but compromises? A fact merely marks the point where we have agreed to let investigation cease.

BLISS CARMAN

ONE

Fact: A thing that is definitely known to be true.
Fact: Our mother was long gone before we knew her.
Fact: There are no photographs of her known to exist.
If the facts were distinguishable from the myths, it would be easy.
Check the facts.
Gone: no longer presented, available, or in existence.
Your point being?
Point: the most important or relative part of what is being discussed.
Comes after
Poignant: arousing a feeling of sadness or regret.

No it doesn't, poinsettia comes next. Look, is there any point, or not?

I'm trying to establish the facts but it's

Hopeless: feeling or causing despair, very bad or incompetent.

No, there isn't any point.

You always interrupt when I'm just starting to get somewhere.

You could ask Granda again. One day he might give in and answer you.

Mystique: an air of secrecy surrounding an activity or subject, making it impressive or baffling to those people not involved in it.

The cat, whose name was Mystique, had lived with Granda, for as long as anyone could remember, including Granda.

No.

The cat had lived with Granda for as long as he could remember and they both had the same mystique.

Which do you think sounds better?

I think it's pointless. It doesn't need looking up because it's stupid.

You've no mystique at all.

Shut up, shut up.

Honeymoon

Rain hammered to be let in and our roof, feeling magnanimous, let it. It didn't matter what day of the week it was, as far as the roof was concerned, it was open-house. It didn't matter who was clamouring to be let in, the roof wanted to oblige. 'Isn't it your duty to provide shelter?' Granda asked, shaking his fist and scowling. The roof didn't reply; it never did. Another tile clattered to the ground, its splinters narrowly missing the cat who was as old and scowling as Granda. As the roof became more open and the birds of the air took more liberties, Granda, who was a stickler for duty, had even more reason to shake his fist.

'No one listens anymore, Mystique,' and he scooped her up in his arms.

You'd better put 'thin arms'.

I hate it when you do that.

What?

Spy on: watch someone secretly.

Comes after

Sputum: mucus coughed up from the throat or lungs.

Does it say if it's normal for old people?

No, that's a different sort of dictionary. Anyway, I think all old people do it.

Spy's next anyway.

Spy: a person employed to collect and report secret information on an enemy.

Who's the enemy?

Myrmidon: a follower or subordinate of a powerful person, especially one who is willing to engage in dishonest activities.

You're a myrmidon yourself with your dishonest dictionary.

DAY ONE

They sat with their backs to the lichen-spattered wall that surrounded the churchyard where lush grass made a cushion and delayed looking at graves. A wicket fence was all that kept them from tumbling into the glittering sea that undulated over the horizon all the way to America. Birds flew with wild cries starting into the sky in majestic arcs from the squalor and stench of their nesting sites below. With every puff of breeze a soft, low keening set up, like angelic humming, a melancholic, restful sound. It was the breeze playing on the hollow bars of the gate, Rosie decided. Presumably, when any sort of wind blew at all, the gate might change its tune and howl.

'Happy, Mrs Pierce?' Fergal kissed Rosie again, grazing her shoulders in her thin dress against the warm stone, and she sighed.

'Ecstatic thank you, Mr Pierce.' It was almost a game they needed to play as they got to know each other.

Honeymoon

'We should go in, do you think?' Fergal said, rising and pulling her to her feet. He opened the gate. Cinder paths crisscrossed the walled field that tapered to a blunt end. Grass grew taller than the gravestones in places, strewn with wild flowers. In others, the grass was shorn, clipped close to the earth as if grazed by sheep or goats, giving it all an unkempt wild feel. They wandered among the hotchpotch of gravestones, stopping again and again to look for names that would mean something, slowly drifting apart till Fergal's outline blurred with sun glancing off him and the shimmering sea. There was that special summer feel, heat with a hint of insects, and a sense of dislocation.

You don't have to go through with it you know – her mother's devastating final assault on her resolve had made Rosie want to cry and not for the first time in the weeks leading up to the wedding. Her brother Hugo, had swung his head round the bedroom door and the delight of seeing him so handsome in his morning suit made her smile.

'You're not filling her with last minute advice, are you mother?' And he'd stuck out his elbows for Rosie and their mother to link and had bundled them out.

The sweet-sour smell of grass cuttings heaped against the wall filled the air and a vivid splash of pink flowers caught her eye. A headstone covered in lichen like exploding fireworks read Margaret Pierce, loving wife and mother, beloved daughter of Colonel and Lady Gopsill, as if the parents' grief reached this grave. Their names were a surprise. She had not expected grandparents. Also Aidan Pierce, devoted husband and father and their son Lorcan, aged 7 years. What a terrible thing! She found it hard to catch her breath in so much sadness, picturing a stiff little body laid out in a white suit, Pavane for a Dead Infanta playing softly and old ladies dabbing their eyes and supporting one another.

She raised her hand, wanting to let Fergal know that here in the lovingly tended grave lay his past but let it hang in the air and did not call out. Words seemed too brutal. Fergal stretched his back, leaning back as if to ease a stiffness, then waved from across the graveyard, his face brightening on seeing her as it had on their wedding day when he waited at the altar.

Fergal made his way slowly towards her and the startling patch of flowers. 'It's here then,' he said, planting a kiss and his hand on her bare neck and her body quickened with desire.

'Well,' Fergal said and stopped. Again he brushed her neck with his lips, before delicately tracing over his brother's name with his fingers. A couple of times he drew in breath as if he would speak, but still he was silent. She wondered how she would cope if she stood beside Hugo's grave and felt a nauseous, dull ache in the pit of her stomach. It didn't bear thinking of. Rosie leaned into him wanting to be close as when a child she yearned to be close to Hugo. She wondered if Hugo was as good a lover if he was gentle if the musk of his body excited the girl in his arms.

Whenever she'd been losing the battle for her

family's blessing, Hugo had spoken up for him, 'I like him; he's solid as a rock and a good lawyer for the firm.' Fergal had appeared from nowhere, their mother was right, but Hugo's approval was enough for her. Hugo loved Fergal too and that was comforting, loving the same person he loved.

Fergal crumpled to his knees, his white neck poking forward as if waiting to be guillotined. She touched his back tentatively, feeling the juddering breath, aware of his bones under her hand, and wanted to protect him. 'I'm so sorry, Fergal.' She had never seen a grown man cry. She thought of Hugo, stoic under their father's rigid gaze, her mother floating behind him, a frightened wisp. She'd cried often, dissolving under that glare, running to Hugo to be comforted. Hugo the intellectual, their mother called him, whose opinion she sought on nearly every subject, whose good opinion of her mattered above all.

Fergal sniffed and wiped his eyes with his thumb as if to punish them, acknowledging his weakness with a sheepish grin. 'I only wanted to see what's left of the house and, well,' he reached for her hand, his fingers cold and soft and clammy. He had been so angry with her for suggesting the graveyard. Perhaps this was his apology, his explanation of why. Perhaps it was her fault after all, for interfering and he had not wanted this emotion to resurface. A darling butterfly was what her mother called her, to console her after various failed attempts at a career as if being a butterfly was adequate aspiration for her.

'That's why we all love you,' she'd said. She had modelled herself on butterflies; gatekeeper, common blue, red admiral, silver-washed fritillary, flitting from flower to flower, taking nectar where she found it. It could explain why Fergal had been so angry.

Fergal turned back to the grave and again touched his fingers lightly over his brother Lorcan's name. 'Not such a bad place to lie,' he whispered.

'You must miss them terribly,' she said, 'especially your brother.'

'Not really,' Fergal said, 'it's too long ago.'

'But you must,' she insisted. 'How old were you when?'

'Didn't Hugo tell you?' Fergal shrugged. 'We were twins.'

'Oh, Fergal.' Somehow this made the loss worse and she was near tears herself, mortified that she hadn't known and annoyed with Hugo for not telling her since he had told her most of what she knew about Fergal. Struck with the thought that perhaps there was someone left and wanting to be of practical use she asked, 'I wonder who brings the flowers.' She ran a finger over the names of Fergal's grandparents. 'What about them?'

Fergal stared blankly at her till she wished she hadn't spoken at all, then he folded her in his arms and kissed the top of her head. 'I don't know.' His words vibrated through her.

'Pity,' Rosie said. Solid dependable names of the sort her parents would have wished her to marry, a colonel and a lady, but perhaps they were dead too.

Honeymoon

'I've never been here,' Fergal continued, 'I must have been sent away even before the funeral.' He jabbed his thumb at the last date on the gravestone. 'I do know that was the day we were found. Only my grandfather and I were left alive.'

'God!' She took in the enormity of what he said and turned to look at the date. She hadn't noticed the date. It sent a shiver like an electric shock. The very week of their wedding, the very week of this honeymoon, twenty years before. Her mind grasped dully at the possibility that Fergal had planned meticulously for their whirlwind romance that to her had seemed so impetuous and thrilling and remembered again his flare of rage when she suggested the village graveyard was a good place for family trees.

'I'm not here to do my family tree,' spoken with such disgust. Was there a connection she was missing? His face gave nothing away and yet seemed closed to all questioning.

He took her hand and slowly they walked away, closing the gate behind them with its angelic hum. They lay for a long while in each other's arms on the lush ground beside the cemetery wall, Rosie's head on Fergal's chest listening to the strong lub dub of his heart and the distant, crashing sea. He stroked her forehead with his fingers smoothing away questions that bubbled up and she decided to wait and let Fergal speak in his own good time; that would be her best way to help him recover his past.

A footpath led away along the edge beyond the

graves and Fergal suggested they take a look, bounding up with energy and pulling a face at her when she was sluggish. They followed it aimlessly for a while, stopping frequently to kiss and to gaze out to sea. They went to peer through windows of a ruined cottage, forlorn and sad, its tin roof staved in, and saw nothing, just an empty room and a few pieces of broken china on the flagged floor. 'No one comes here now.' Eventually, Fergal said he was too hot and suggested they make their way to the sea.

A dizzying slope fell away to the beach. Fergal went first and held out his hand when Rosie lost her nerve. He seemed to have no difficulty, surefooted and confident even when the path was vertical.

'I'm glad we've seen it.' His voice drifted up as she concentrated on grasping tufts of grass that came away from the earth in her sweating hands. 'That sort of thing has never bothered me. I mean once you're dead nothing matters, does it? I know it's important to some people, but that isn't why I've come. What interests me is the house.'

Rosie was breathless from the descent and did not answer. To her, death and the graveyard seemed the most important and most logical place to start. Families buried their dead. Hadn't he collapsed with grief, however briefly, at the grave, what her father would, with disdain, have called 'making a display'. She thought of all the houses they had lived in growing up. There were so many, they lost importance. Every school holiday, it seemed, she came home to a different house, a different country even, till they went mostly to their grandparents. Hugo was her home. She had not thought of that till now. When Hugo was there, she'd felt safe and all the upheaval and her dwindling treasures, survivors of the latest removal, packed up for her in ever-smaller boxes, didn't seem to matter.

'I don't believe in an afterlife,' Fergal said. She thought she was pretty near finding out, one slip and she would have the answer.

'Rosie?' he was there beneath her. 'I suppose you don't like heights?'

'Nor descents.' The effort of speaking sent sparks of fear through her and bathed her with sweat. At the very least, she might lose her shoes.

'We're nearly there.' Fergal was conciliatory. He reminded her of Hugo relenting after merciless teasing.

They walked for miles, hand in hand, skittering along, delighting in each other and thinking only of the moment. They imagined they could see past the huge boulders protecting the bay, all the way to America and they laughed at the thunder of the Atlantic Ocean petering to a clickety-clack in the pebbles at their feet. A coast for pirates and smugglers, not the gentle safe-to-swim coast of Rosie's childhood, her grandparents' coast. The wildness was new to her. 'I love it here,' she said. Fergal stood behind her wrapping her in his arms and swaying gently.

'We used to come,' he murmured, 'after Mass. I'm sure of it.'

She turned to look at him, his arms still encircling her, 'That must be a very early memory.' He kept his eyes on the horizon and she laid her head on his chest and he rested his chin on it. Then, as if he had been giving it much thought, he said, 'My father used to say if we went to Mass at all it was for my mother's sake because he had no belief left.' Rosie looked up at him, still staring at the horizon and wondered if he minded her asking. 'Heavens Rosie,' and he tightened his arms, swung her round and put her back on her feet with a kiss. She didn't press him further.

'Don't look now,' he said, 'but there's a face in the dunes. Someone's watching us.'

'Sinister,' she said without thinking.

'Not quite,' Fergal was still watching, 'anyway, they've disappeared now.'

'Like a leprechaun then?' And she raced off, calling over her shoulder for him to catch her. Fergal caught up easily and pirouetted with her, wrestling her to the ground, making sure she landed on top of him, helpless with laughter.

'There was someone in the dunes.'

'Perhaps just someone out walking a dog.'

'You didn't see them.'

'Perhaps visitors are rare.'

They fetched towels from the rented cottage and lazed on the beach. Rosie swam in the rough sea, lingering to play in the breath-taking waves. Fergal stood at the edge and would not be persuaded to go deeper than his knees. Seeing Fergal, slight and pale at the water's edge, she could not help but compare him with Hugo, a rugby player, thick-set and full of adventure. She felt a twinge of disappointment but laughed it away because she was in love and the day was hot and the sea was delicious. She came and lay beside him dripping cold water on his skin till he rolled over with her, covering her with sand and she protested, 'Stop, Fergal. Now I'll have to go and wash this off.'

Later Rosie lay in Fergal's arms in the soft white bed, her hair still damp from the sea. He licked her arm, 'Hmm salty!' Then he bit her gently on the pad of her shoulder as if it tempted him. 'I'm starving and we've not touched the picnic. I'll get it,' he said and he leaped from the bed grinning at her when she protested. His buttocks and the tops of his thighs glowed white in the early evening light as he disappeared down the stairs that opened straight into the bedroom.

She propped herself on the pillows and sighed contentedly. Fergal climbed in beside her and placed the basket on his knees and the gingham cloth on hers. The basket released meaty smells and she was hungry too. There was a bottle of homemade lemonade. The lid loosened with a hiss of fizz and Rosie drank deeply. 'This is lovely,' she said.

'Well, save some for me.' Fergal did not look up, concentrating on opening foil parcel after foil parcel: beef sandwiches on thick white bread, Brie with a strong, ripe smell, fruit cake, even a little jar of pickles. 'Fit for a king.' He helped himself to a sandwich, 'and a queen.' He offered them to Rosie but she shook her head. She toyed with baby tomatoes. Fergal clicked his tongue, 'It's hours since breakfast, Rosie. Eat something.'

She tore a beef sandwich in half, thinking she would not possibly finish it but she was wrong, once she'd started she could have eaten them all. 'These are lovely too.' Fergal laughed at her. 'Food critic Rosie Pierce gives the thumbs up to the picnic.'

'That's unfair.' She felt peeved. 'I never claimed to be clever.'

'Get a grip. It was only a tease.' Fergal spoke with his mouth full. She watched the food slosh around his mouth. She hadn't ever noticed before, when they had been out with Hugo and all his gang, that Fergal did not close his mouth when he ate. He bent and licked her shoulder but this time it was not in the least sensuous. She glanced at her skin where his tongue had left a spittle trail of soggy white bread crumbs.

'That's disgusting,' and she wiped her shoulder on the gingham serviette. She wanted to accuse him, 'You're disgusting,' and make a huge fuss and tear the day to shreds like some pampered princess. But Fergal put his hand over hers.

'I love you, Rosie Pierce,' and just as suddenly everything was all right again. 'Shall we stay in tonight? Build a fire, shut out the world?' Fergal made it sound romantic, but somehow she knew it would be a mistake.

'I don't think there's a fireplace, is there?'

Fergal sighed an exaggerated sigh, 'Do you know that you wrinkle up your nose when it's something you don't want to do? Hugo didn't warn me about that.'

'Oh, and what did Hugo warn you about?'

'The mad maiden aunt you take after and an over fondness for chocolate. Loads of things.'

'Skeletons? You're a fine one to talk.' She whacked him with one of the pillows till he begged for a truce. 'Or, we could go for a meal in that nice pub in the village. Do you think we need to book?'

'Doubt it,' Fergal said, 'They'll just be glad of the custom.'

~*~

Joe Kelly flung his suitcase open on the bed and considered unpacking it. Instead, he took only the book lying on top and settled back beside it to read. A small photograph marked his place, and he studied this for a while. Tuneful whistling drifting through the open window distracted him and he got up to look. Dermot, the boy who had driven him from the airport, polished the gleaming black taxi in the pub courtyard, leaning in to rub and then stepping back to admire his handiwork, willowy and graceful as if he were dancing and finally threw down his cloths and set off with a swagger back inside.

Joe laughed then leaned against the window, pursing his lips, uncertain now what to do with the day, the first of four he'd booked off to mark his fortieth birthday and to keep a promise he'd made himself. His preparations had been meticulous for the impression he hoped to give, almost a false trail that would put anyone off his scent if need be, but now that he was here he felt a reluctance to actually do anything as if he'd wound himself like a spring to get himself here but had slowly unwound and lost all impetus. Perhaps coming back after twenty years was still too soon and already too late. One thing was certain, though. Nothing would be achieved by staying in his room. He retrieved the small photograph from his book and placed it in his wallet and set off. In the doorway of the pub, wind blowing in off the sea hit Joe Kelly like a slap, awakening a long-forgotten sense of his youth, warm days with nothing to do but hope for a semblance of life to begin.

'Anything I can get for you, Mr Kelly?' Dermot was behind him.

'Why not?' Joe Kelly, affable and polite delayed his decision, 'I'll have a coffee.'

He waited as Dermot sprinkled the frothed milk with tiny chocolate teardrops through a heart-shaped stencil. At first, Joe assumed Dermot must be in hope of a fat tip, but remembered the same attention to detail, the professionalism when Dermot had met him earlier that day. 'Thanks for picking me up at the airport. That's a grand service.' Joe suppressed a smile when Dermot, pleased with the compliment, puffed out his chest.

'It was all my own idea.'

'Oh?'

'The taxi, the advertising. I just don't own the taxi yet,' Dermot added with a hint of regret. Joe smiled fleetingly, fearing he'd be embroiled in the boy's whole history. He hadn't expected small talk. He stirred sugar into his coffee, and half listened as the boy rattled on.

'Start small my brother-in-law says. It's a good maxim for business, saves overreaching yourself. I could have borrowed the money, but it made more sense to have a sleeping partner. Hennessy, he's quite good like that. He owns the taxi, like everything else round here.'

Already Joe wanted to think of something else or of nothing and carried his cup to an armchair by the window. He collected the newspaper from the stand, turning pages as he stirred his coffee. Volcanoes had made the headlines. Freak weather warning. A volcano in Iceland threatened to disrupt airlines. The name was unreadable. He tried a couple of times, Eyjafjallajökull, breaking it into syllables, before abandoning the attempt. They should get over themselves and their warnings. They were never wise before the event; it always fizzled to nothing or they missed it altogether and reports of damage, flooding and disruption, went on for weeks. When he could no longer concentrate on the paper he watched Jenny, the girl behind the bar, poised and pretty, who had come to join Dermot.

He decided in an instant to ask her. 'Listen,' Joe said, reaching for his wallet, approaching her behind the bar, 'I wondered if you could help?' He flashed the tiny photograph of Louise in school uniform, her cheeks impossibly pink, her hair impossibly curly and was rewarded with smiles and dimples and more attention than he knew what to do with, but not an answer to his question.

'She's very pretty. Can't help I'm afraid.'

Joe had the coffee charged to his room, then approached Dermot with his photograph and blundered on. 'I wonder if you could, how shall I put this? I used to know a girl.' He stopped, catching the look Jenny flashed and Dermot's raised eyebrows and, realising how ridiculous and very old he must sound, was about to replace the small photograph in his wallet. Dermot held his arm and leaned closer for a better view, turning his head sideways and his mouth down at the corners as if considering. Joe shrugged dismissively, 'Ah, never mind, eh?' and pulled his arm away, too embarrassed to see that Dermot burned with curiosity.

'It's such a grand day,' Dermot said, 'Why don't I take you for a drive? You can ask me anything you want then.'

Joe Kelly agreed. 'A couple of hours, maybe, why not?' Then immediately regretted accepting, unable quite to get out of it or imagine what there was to gain by being driven around.

'I'll let himself know you've engaged me then. Anywhere in particular you'd like to see? Or shall I make up a guided tour? We could start at the park and work our way back.'

Barely a moment passed before Dermot was back but Joe Kelly paced like a panther in a zoo as he waited, his spirits sinking, unable to explain his unease. He would have taken himself off had Dermot not returned so quickly.

They were silent in the taxi, driving along narrow lanes with not much view. Joe, still agitated, repeatedly blew his thumbnail against his lips with a slight clicking sound and soon Dermot suggested a diversion. 'Want to walk a while?' It was, after all, a beautiful day. He stopped the taxi at a dirt pull-in. A path meandered ahead towards a clearing and Joe Kelly stepped out obligingly, abandoning himself, finally, to whatever would follow.

The walk was brisk and Joe was breathless. By the time they arrived at the edge where a ruin and an isolated graveyard overlooked a vastness of sea and sky, they had exhausted topics of weather, books and politics and were again tight-lipped and silent. Not once did Joe refer to the photograph or mention what brought him to the village. Not once did Dermot ask, although Joe suspected he was curious, sensing he searched for some clue as he snatched the odd hard look at his profile.

Dermot tried to ease the tension and proposed a circuit of the graveyard, 'I know you'd like it. It's peaceful, and some of the graves are so nicely tended, it's like a park. Then we could drive along the edge.'

Joe stalled, 'I think, after all, it's too good a day to climb in the car. I'll wander back myself.' He reached for his wallet from his back pocket and produced a crisp note and tried to press it on Dermot whose mouth twitched at the corners with mild annoyance. 'Thanks all the same, Mr Kelly,' Dermot said and retraced his steps, slamming the taxi door hard.

Amused the offer of money had given offence – what sort of businessman refuses money? Joe strode toward the edge. Beneath him, on the slope dizzying down to the beach, he heard voices and waited, staring out to sea, high and remote, till all danger of meeting them had gone, then made his way down. He anticipated a long, slow walk and savoured the slope of pebbles, the expanse of sand and the distant sea.

A warm wind blew unpredictably, skimming sand in stinging swirls and Joe folded his arm over his face to protect it. His jacket flapped wildly against his flank with a slapping noise like a flag and his hair was flying. A little way off a couple hunched together, leaning into each other like sandbags, facing the full blast of the ocean. He saw the woman turn and smile and the man kiss her so passionately, so tenderly, that his own lips tingled. He headed away, keeping in the lee of the dunes. Finally, he glimpsed the cottage he was looking for, camouflaged and half buried in sand, protected by giant boulders. More dilapidated than ever, it looked abandoned. He prayed it wasn't, as close as he came to prayers these days. Grateful to step into the porch out of the wind he smoothed his flying hair, feeling sand grains under his fingers.

Polite knocks went unanswered. He tried the door, rattling the handle in escalating disappointment. He walked round the place, peering in at each window wiping away grime and shading his eyes. He expected to see the accumulated stuff of a lifetime; maybe even Driscoll himself slumped in a chair but it was spartan and nearly empty. It was the same in every room. Either there had been a grand clear out or Driscoll no longer lived there.

Joe wandered away from the house, hit again by a gust of wind. He put his back to one of the boulders to be out of it and slid down onto the sand. He tipped his head back, weary with the effort of bringing himself here after all these years. He welcomed the sun on his face and closed his eyes letting visions of that last summer dance rosy under his eyelids.

It didn't seem to matter what time he called at the house then, Driscoll was never in. Louise's mother would answer the door and the welcome would always be the same. 'Come along in. Is it our Louise you've come for?' Lou – ise, belted out like the house was a mansion, and Louise would saunter in as if she had been waiting for him, raise her eyebrows and expect him to follow, which he did.

They went out into the sunshine, to squat beside the house under the open window. In his memory, the house would be full of women, cooing and clucking as Mrs Driscoll held forth. Sometimes she'd come to the window as if she'd known they were there all along or had instructed Louise where to take him. 'You shut your ears now. It's just women's talk, you know, and we don't mean any harm by it.' And they'd listen some more.

'I don't suppose his father gives two hoots where he is, so long as he's not under his feet. I've seen bruises. Well I've heard tell of them and that's more or less the same thing. Poor motherless boy, God love him. His father can't keep from the drink. No wonder, poor man, losing his wife and him with six mouths to feed. The oldest is away in the army. Will you have more tea, Mrs Finucane? And the next two are as likely in prison. Poor Elizabeth. She'd have hated that. Well, what mother wouldn't? Perhaps they wouldn't have gone to the bad if she'd been here. Shoplifting, joyriding and all sorts. This cake you brought is very light, very light. You've a gift, Mrs Finucane.'

On and on it went every time. Mrs Finucane replaced by Mrs Morris or someone else he didn't know until Joe had wondered what it was that women did with their lives, except gossip.

Louise was different. 'I'm not like that. Soon as I can, I'm out of here. University: a teacher maybe, or a lawyer. No way am I staying round here. Isn't that what they all do? Fall for a baby and ruin their lives. Not me.' And then the question he dreaded. 'What about you, Joe, what'll you do?'

Joe never knew. He'd shrug and make up something. His sole ambition was to be where she was but he knew enough never to say that to her. Sometimes he wondered if it was the whole Driscoll family he was in love with for the security they gave him. No one beat him here; teased him, certainly, but he could cope with that. He never ate with them, Louise never asked, Mrs Driscoll never offered. Often though, she would thrust a brown paper parcel in his hands as she pushed him back through the door. 'Time for home, Joe.' Bread, cheese sometimes and once or twice even cake. Maybe she expected him to share it, but it was always gone before he left the beach.

Once, Louise caught sight of a bruise blooming like a black tattoo on his chest. Joe showed her the series of purpling fist prints, but only the once. Louise had cried. She'd put her arms round his neck and actually shed tears for him, warm and wet on his skin as if she wanted to wash the bruises away. There was never anything visible after that. He never asked if she'd told. Perhaps she did. Or some well-meaning parishioner had warned his father off. Maybe his father had shamed himself by the sight of his own handy work, crying and begging forgiveness as he did sometimes. But Joe did not remember ever feeling sorry for his father. He was, he supposed, too busy feeling sorry for himself – the runt, the poor motherless boy.

Something kicked the soles of his boots repeatedly. An animal smell like wet badgers filled the air. He opened his eyes in alarm and a face, dark against the sun, was very close to his.

'Fine watchman you'd make.' Joe reeled away, then stopped when he realised who it was. Driscoll squatted down beside him. 'You looking for me?'

'That's right.'

'Well, you found me.' A look passed over Driscoll's face that Joe could not interpret. 'So, are you coming in or are we staying here, Joe Kelly?' His name was said with an emphasis Joe did not like.

'Here's grand for the moment, thanks.'

'Suit yourself – you'll live longer.'

Sweet air blew away Driscoll's breath that to Joe smelt as if something inside him had died. 'Are you well, Mr Driscoll?'

Driscoll threw back his head and laughed, exposing a row of rotten teeth. His laughter was a blocked drain, something deeply unsavoury about it.

'This a social call?' He dragged a brownish handkerchief from a stiff pocket and applied it to his nose and eyes.

'You could call it that, a social call.'

They sat together awhile, silent in the sun, both with their elbows round their bent knees, side by side, like friends at a picnic. Driscoll stared resolutely in front of him, presenting only his pickled cheek. Joe felt white by comparison, white and weak next to the redoubtable survivor. Finally, Driscoll asked, 'Why are you back now, by the way? Remind me. Is it some anniversary?' He cleared phlegm from his throat and spat with vigour, the gobbet landing in the sand beside Joe and turned to glare with poison enough to paralyse an elephant. 'You don't belong here.' The anger in the old man's voice was like a knife opening old wounds. Then he seemed to relent. 'You belong in a town, Joe Kelly. You were always too soft for the country. It's a savage place.'

Joe shuddered at memories of poaching on moonless nights. The throes of a dying animal released from a trap his father set, always unable to put them out of their misery himself and the quick slash of his father's knife, the swish of the blade, the rip of flesh and the sudden quiet of the release from life, the release from pain.

Driscoll touched a finger on one of Joe's cufflinks. 'Done well for yourself.'

'You think so?' Joe was pleased this fine touch had not gone unnoticed. He had chosen his clothes with care, all new, creases ironed out of the shirts and flash cufflinks that would all be paid for in the coming months.

'Let's get it over with, Joe Kelly.' Driscoll stood up and headed indoors, leaving Joe to follow.

Joe remembered the house almost with affection. Once chaotic and festooned with tackle, bait, hooks, nets, with the reek of the sea depths, it had been magical, his second home, happier with Driscoll than with his own father. He had felt Driscoll treated him like a son, an apprentice at least. In the early days, he'd followed Driscoll round like a puppy, learning the ropes and longing for a glimpse or a smile from Louise. Now it was austere, a hermit's cell.

Driscoll sat with a sigh and pointed to the chairs. 'Sit down, can't you.' Joe sat upright on a hard chair, a stranger, and studied his hands. Driscoll made little sucking noises with his teeth and neither of them spoke. There was so much Joe needed to ask, it was hard to know where to begin. All that he had practised seemed useless now that he was actually here, yet he hoped Driscoll would have the answers. In the end there was no preamble. 'I want to know about that day at the big house,' Joe said.

Driscoll's breath made a whistling sound, 'Sure you do, so why come to me?'

'There's no one else to ask.'

The memory of that day swung between them setting teeth on edge like a pub sign needing oil; a lantern illuminating and casting shadows in the mind, nightmarish ghoulish faces swinging into the light and out. The day that altered his life set him on a path he'd never envisaged. Or perhaps it was a path he'd dreamed of. A few hours of one day that couldn't be taken back, could not be denied or altered, troubled his soul however much it refused to recall. Joe could not be sure who had been there, or how many, or how long he'd stayed. He remembered dragging himself off, running and stumbling blindly and being with Louise too in the dark; small and white and innocent in the sand with the cleansing sound of crashing waves filling his ears. Try as he might there was no waking memory of it all. That was the nightmare, the fallout that haunted him a lifetime.

Driscoll eyed him neutrally, 'It's easy to run away; makes it easier to reconstruct your past.'

Joe was not sure what he meant. 'Perhaps,' he said.

'There's no perhaps about it.' Driscoll was angry. 'Did you never think to ask? To check?'

'I never stopped asking. No one ever answered my letters and I was afraid to.'

Driscoll interrupted, 'That's you, afraid. Your father's son.' He lowered his voice, 'No one ever got any letters.'

'Well, I sent them.' Joe had his head in his hands. 'I gave up writing. I thought it for the best.'

'That's what I always thought.' Driscoll paused. Then, deliberately enunciating each word he said, 'No one ever got your letters because I kept them.'

Joe gasped as if Driscoll had punched him. Suddenly there was nowhere near enough air. The empty room threatened to close in on him, suffocate him. 'I suppose you read them and laughed.'

'What type of a man do you take me for?'

Driscoll produced two fat bundles of letters tied with orange twine from a large chest, thrusting them insistently till Joe stood up to take them from him. Joe studied his handwriting and the name Louise Driscoll and the address of this house in the dunes. He couldn't grasp that his letters had not reached Louise. He had the feeling his head was a dull wooden block to be beaten repeatedly against a wall to get sense from it. All the heartache, the bewildering sense of loss and betrayal that had characterised those first years in England! He stared at Driscoll and imagined a conspiracy, a double betrayal. 'So her mother gave the letters to you?'

'They never even got to the house. I couldn't take the risk of Louise getting hold of them. Not in the circumstances. I picked them up at the post office.'

The injustice seared as if Driscoll had branded him. 'Twenty years,' Joe said, 'that's my youth you've kept shut in your box.'

'It wasn't about you,' Driscoll sucked his teeth. 'What about my daughter?'

Joe's head began to throb. The money he'd sent begging Louise to come, unable to understand why she never replied. His chest tightened with the awful loneliness of those years. One thing made sense, he supposed. He was implicated in the murder of a man and that was not something to allow your only daughter to get mixed up in.

'A child died because of it.' The tension in Driscoll's voice tightened the sinews of his neck like a macabre medical drawing. 'Starved to death.'

Joe dimly remembered that a child had died. He'd seen it on the news along with other atrocities. Children were born and children died; it's what they did. He was nineteen then and children were far-distant things that happened to other people. He hadn't known much about them, still didn't. 'You blaming me for the child?' It occurred to him that Driscoll, any of them, would have been far better placed to save it. Driscoll sucked his teeth and the noise began to grate.

'Suppose I do come with you?' Driscoll got to his feet. 'Let's take a walk down memory lane tomorrow morning, early. Wait outside the pub and I'll find you.' There was a pause. 'Now if you don't mind,' Driscoll turned his back, 'you can see yourself out.'

Joe hesitated, unprepared for the coldness. He eyed Driscoll's scrawny neck, how it seemed now to fold in on itself meekly with his head bent forward and wondered fleetingly how it would feel to have his hands round it. This was not how he'd wanted the meeting to be. Hostility was not what he'd expected.

Honeymoon

Open arms would have been too far perhaps, but somewhere in-between. He wanted to ask after Louise; to hear Driscoll say she was happily married and had presented him with a lapful of bonny grandchildren to brighten his old age. Tomorrow would be soon enough. What was one more day after so many? 'I'll see you tomorrow then,' he said. Driscoll grunted but still did not turn round.

Joe stood for a long time at the water's edge lulled by the secrets of the sea, gradually aware of the dead weight of the letters in his hands. He contemplated casting them unopened into the waves to be free of them and imagined the bundles floating out to sea only to be carried back with the next tide. Besides, they were a link to his past and he was curious to know himself then, so he forced them into his jacket pockets to be dealt with later. Sun was hot on his head. The wind had died. He did not relish sitting in the half-light of the pub for the remains of the day but was at a loss what to do. He bent to select stones and skimmed them along the water's edge as he used to when a boy. Elation as they spun out, five, six, seven hops over the silver water, was short-lived. He could go for a swim, except he hadn't got trunks. Swimming in the sea had not been on his agenda when he'd packed. Eventually, he decided to cut back into the dunes with the sea behind him and climb high and fast beyond Driscoll's. He was soon breathing hard and the underworked muscles of his legs screamed for rest.

The surprise of the shipping container stopped

him. He dropped to his belly, moving forward slowly till he had a better view. At a slight angle, between high dunes and waving marram grass, sat a large, oblong container where no one would ever suspect, heaved up and spat out by the sea. Joe imagined contraband, smugglers, gun runners, although he had always thought this part of the beach was deserted. He pictured a flurry of locals arriving with wheelbarrows to retrieve whatever the sea had donated, going away empty-handed and grumbling that the container was already empty. That's what he would have done then, anyway. He waited flat on his belly as a fly buzzed his face and he waved it away.

Dermot appeared in the entrance, like any man standing at his own front door to enjoy the sun, then disappeared down the far side. Soon a thin curl of white smoke unfurled from behind the container. Joe could not see the fire but a rich smell of sausages mingled with wood smoke and his stomach grumbled. His back began to ache. He rolled over to ease the pain, anxious not to be seen, and waited, warmed by the sun, thinking.

When Joe turned again on his belly, his face close to the sand where ants hurried about, the curl of smoke had dwindled and Dermot was back in view. Joe contemplated dropping down to the container, inviting himself to share the meal, being falsely jovial and asking to be shown round. Dermot had been eager enough to please earlier but here on his own territory, Joe couldn't be sure and he didn't want to be challenged or to have to explain how long he'd been watching. He glanced at his watch, with luck Dermot would be going back for another shift and he could poke about on his own, a far better prize.

Dermot kneeled at a low table and methodically set a place for himself. Joe half expected Dermot would say grace before his meal, make the sign of the cross and bless his food. He suppressed a laugh and chewed a long blade of grass and waited letting his mind drift with the clouds. A deep metallic clang brought him back. The table had been cleared away, the door was shut and Dermot was piling sand against it with his feet in a great soft mound.

When he was sure Dermot was gone, Joe approached, slithering down the incline, feeling sand shift under his feet and sneak inevitably into his shoes. He set about letting himself in. With each tug of the door the mound of sand slid away until with one final heave the door hung open. The effort quelled any sense of compunction. It took some moments for his eyes to adjust but nothing was as Joe had expected. Far from squalid and cold, the container had a solid, permanent feel with valiant attempts to make it a home and keep it tidy. It had been floored with a mix of hardboard and planks. One side of the container was lined floor to ceiling with books on more planks separated with bricks as if Dermot had inherited a whole library. If nothing else, the books would provide good insulation. Joe ran his fingers along the dry spines, some of them paperbacks and some worthy, old tomes and imagined Dermot reading night after night, working his way through the whole lot.

At one end, a double mattress lay on the floor with a large rug beside it. The bedding had been straightened and a brightly coloured patchwork quilt draped over it. His foot nudged a pile of orange and white Penguins next to it and sent them toppling. He did not stoop to pick them up, but noticed amongst the titles, Nineteen Eighty-Four and Brave New World.

Pictures and maps covered the remaining walls. Joe snooped, opening boxes and poking his fingers through Dermot's treasures. If this was how Dermot lived, he was impressed; his own room had been spartan, slovenly, unwelcoming. A photograph album lay open on a low table, its glossy pages glowed dully in light reflected from the open door. Black and white photos revealed grey scenes. Joe flicked through the first few pages. Semi-circles of formally dressed men gazed at the camera. A secret sect or a wedding perhaps, to judge from the clothes, or a christening, no one took pictures at funerals. He wished he had a magnifying glass to help dislodge a memory or two. He might even spot himself. He smiled thinly. He stood till he grew weary, flexing his knees to relieve the pain in his back and retreated to the mattress, squatting on the edge with his knees bent up and the album flat on the floor between them. He lingered over a group of three men in suits. An early picture of Driscoll and his own father before life had defined their features and beside them the priest whose face, so familiar yet totally forgotten, sent a cold stab as if a bony finger from his deep subconscious had poked him hard. Try as he might he could not dredge up a name.

He snapped the album shut, deciding to 'borrow' it. He stood up decisively and tucked the album into the belt of his trousers for want of a better place. His foot nudged a small book jutting out under the mattress. He picked it up, drew his fingers across the dark cover, spoiled with damp and dust and flicked the sparse, handwritten pages. A diary perhaps? He knew immediately he would take this too, to read alone in his room, even take it back to England with him as a souvenir of this trip.

He made no attempt to hide his traces; any detective dusting for fingerprints could have discovered his scattered carelessly on everything he'd touched. He didn't think Dermot would tell the police and besides he would be gone in a day or two, back to England, mission accomplished. He swung the door closed, heaping sand with his foot, as he'd seen Dermot do and half-heartedly scuffled away his own footprints. He set off across the dunes, careful to give Driscoll's house a wide berth.

Safely back on the strand, striding out and swinging his arms, the diary discreetly in his hand, he felt elated. The sea air made him hungry and he thought of what he might eat at the pub. When he reached the village, he slowed down, lingering by the chemist's window as he passed. A jumble of items including a snorkel and fins and fresh eggs, were displayed. Perhaps they sold swimming trunks and he smiled to himself at the same old, sleepy place.

The sign on the window in a halo of gold letters read Louise McCann Pharmacy. His armpits pricked uncomfortably at the coincidence of the Christian name. It would be just like her to have done well, a bright girl, university was what she had wanted. He had wondered for so long after he had given up writing how she had got on with her life. He drifted in realms of possibilities. She could still be the girl of his dreams fossilised, barely changed since he left. A vision resurfaced of himself with Louise and a brood of tousled children. Twice Joe had his hand on the door and twice he faltered. It was probably not his Louise anyway, a married woman; they would be two strangers; he would be just another customer in the shop. As he walked away, the door opened and a woman called out, 'Was there something you wanted?' A handsome woman, small and full-figured with dark curly hair disappearing down her back stood with a hand on one hip. 'Only you were loitering.' Words died on her lips like a last sigh.

The old longing momentarily took Joe's breath, sweeping away the barrier of intervening years. He moved beside her, drawn to her, close enough to smell her perfume and see the fine down on her cheeks. 'I would have known you anywhere, Louise.'

Louise took a step back and studied him, a look of deep scepticism on her face. 'I was a child of fifteen when you left.'

The words struck home hard, wrenching him

fiercely from half-remembered dreams as in the early days when he hardly dared hope he'd survive and, receiving no word, had relinquished the search for her in the face of every stranger, or her handwriting among the letters on the hall table of his digs. She knew him too, then, and he held out his hand in greeting.

'You better come inside,' she said faintly, ignoring the proffered hand.

The clean, clinical smell of disinfectant and herbal remedies and the cold feel of glass jars lining the walls with their labels all the same, intimidated him. Their reflections from many angles off mirrored walls gave the impression they were in a crowded room, and made it impossible to talk. Still they stared. Joe laid his hand on the glass counter for support, displacing some soft toys with his fingers, running his thumb pad along the smoothed glass edge. The small and faded diary, that had seemed so indispensable in the container, lay half hidden and quite forgotten in a moment's inattention under a bear of pale blue fur.

Finally Louise said, 'It's my half day,' and she invited him home; the home that had belonged to her grandparents that now she shared with her husband Pat. Joe followed her the short distance. Waiting beside her as she unlocked the door, he wanted to weep. There were no tears left, just the sadness. Did he really think she had pined all these years and waited for him?

She led him along a corridor. One wall partly replaced by glass revealed a neat, small sitting room.

Their dark reflections made it seem they passed through both somehow, like ghosts. Once in the room he still felt wrong, too large and out of place. He stood by the window staring out at the narrow street and low-roofed houses. A view he had seen all his life, even after he had moved away. Now there were roses at the doors, red geraniums in window boxes, chocolate box images that hid what went before.

'I don't think you even heard me, did you?' Louise said.

'Sorry,' Joe said, casting around for something to latch on to.

'Is that what you came to say?' Joe was not sure if she was angry.

'I shouldn't have come.'

There was a pause as if Louise agreed with him. Finally she said, 'You should so,' and made it sound convincing, as if he had every right to turn up unannounced after so many years. 'You might have given me some warning, that's all.'

'Sorry.'

She frowned at him for apologising again. 'I thought you would've come for your father's funeral.'

'Telepathy, you mean. No one told me he'd even died.' But he did know his father was dead. There had been a small obituary in the paper that he had seen quite by chance many years ago.

'Where would we have written? I thought you might have been in touch with some of the old gang, or one of your brothers.'

'No. Did they come?'

'No.'

Joe nodded, pensive. 'Full military honours, was it?'

'He was cremated and his ashes were scattered down on the strand there. The whole community together; it was moving.'

'Glad to be rid of him?'

'Maybe, for some.'

He thought he should be angry but he couldn't detect any emotion in himself. There was numbness, an enormous emptiness as if he had left his heart somewhere along the way.

'When I was a girl,' she spoke slowly, breathing the words as if she was telling a secret, 'I watched the street, every day. I thought you would come walking back up it. I didn't believe you'd drowned like they said. I couldn't believe you would have left me here. Why didn't you send word? Not even a letter.'

Joe was conscious of the bundles of letters bulging his pockets but didn't give Driscoll away, not yet, at least. 'It wasn't easy.'

'You think it was easy being left behind?' Yes, she was angry.

The sound of laughter and English voices floated in from outside. The couple he had seen before on the beach stepped out through the door of their cottage and made their way towards the sea. Their bodies leaned in to each other, like lovers.

'Visitors,' Louise said. 'They're trying to encourage tourists for the local economy. I could let this place in the summer and live in a caravan or a washed-up container.'

'Are there a lot of them?' Joe asked.

'Visitors?'

He laughed, 'No, I mean washed-up containers.'

And she laughed too. The laughter released the tears and she sobbed, briefly inconsolable. He hugged her then and for a moment she laid her head against his chest and he stroked her hair.

'That's a very nice suit you're wearing,' she said, sniffing and pulling away, smoothing the fine wool lapels between her fingers. 'You're quite the man about town.' He fished in his trouser pocket for his handkerchief and handed it to her. She admired the clean, ironed cloth as she unfolded it and blew into it hard. 'Got a wife, have you?' she said, handing him back his handkerchief. He waved it away.

'No. There was someone once but it didn't work out.' He looked into her eyes for any sign she detected the irony.

'So, no kids then?'

'None that I know of,' he laughed. 'You?'

'God, no,' Louise shook her head.

Joe thought there was sadness in the glib answer. He smiled. There was the whole of their story in a few words. He wasn't sure she even knew she was the girl of his dreams.

'I wouldn't mind a drink, if there's one in the offing.'

'We don't keep much in but I think there's a drop of whisky.'

Honeymoon

'I meant a cup of tea.' He felt drained as if he had been the one sobbing. He followed her along the narrow corridor into the kitchen, a new bright space with a view to the small and curvaceous garden. Louise went in and out of the old scullery waiting for the water to boil and he glimpsed old wallpaper he might have recognised.

'So, why did you come back?'

He hesitated, wondering which version of the truth to risk. There was a story he had woven over the years, modified with the telling of it, the blame differently attributed depending on who the story was for. 'It was time,' he said at last, and Louise seemed to accept that as ample explanation. It was time to do what he had come to do. She belonged to a part of his life he had sealed up long ago like a nuclear reactor with a plug of concrete. He wanted to dismantle it. Perhaps enough years had passed and the fallout would have lost its potency.

'Biscuit?' Louise asked. 'Sugar?'

'No, no thanks,' and he patted his flat belly.

They were silent for a long while, each nursing a china mug of tea, but neither of them looked away. Afternoon shadows lengthened and the sun receded from the neat garden as they sat weaving versions of themselves to wrap one around the other. Joe liked the look that passed over Louise's face as if she was prepared to idolise him. It was a long time since anyone had looked at him like that and he could dimly remember how it felt. Yet, perhaps the dim recollection was of her then, no more than a scrawny kid. He had not expected to find her here and yet in his heart he knew that he hoped he might. He was not sure how things would pan out. He had a plan, but plans were fickle. Louise was his contingency. Getting in touch with long lost friends was a valid excuse for being back. Seeing her reminded him of something indefinable like tawny autumn sunshine, the light in her eyes like a glimmer of hope. It took him back to a time before life was spoilt; a time of innocence that he had thought was no longer part of him.

She broke the silence. 'There was talk when you left.'

He made no reply. She put her hand over his. 'It can't have been easy, Joe. I mean you look like you've...' Joe moved his hand away abruptly to stop her. Suddenly, he could not bear to hear any reference to the incident from her lips. He could not speak. There was too much to say and nothing. Again it was Louise who broke the silence. Words poured from her and he let them wash over him.

'Strange isn't it? All the years I spent longing for you to turn up and now when it's happened – don't take this the wrong way – it's not that I'm not overjoyed to see you. It's just now it's not so important to me. I have a life of my own, Joe. And do you know?' Louise paused for breath but he knew she did not expect a response. 'Before, when you asked if we had children and I gave my usual answer "God no", as if it didn't matter one iota, I lied.' He saw her shiver involuntarily.

Honeymoon

'I know you did,' Joe said, suspecting a longing for children. He stood up to put his arms around her and felt her relax as he hugged her like a child. Louise pulled herself away, smoothed her hair awkwardly and excused herself to use the bathroom.

He heard her trip up the stairs, heard drawers open and close, heard her talking to herself. He slumped at the table and put his head on his arms so that his sleeves would soak up his tears. No tears came but he called himself a fool for ever having come. No way had he expected emotions would surface after so long, at least, not from him. He was tempted to flee, forget the whole sorry business, just as he had done before, as he had always done. If he could just leg it, get a taxi to the airport and sit it out till he could get a flight.

Someone approached the house, boots against stone and the sound of a key in the lock, and the front door swung open. A man walked down the narrow corridor towards him. Too late now, Joe thought, like a rat in a trap. He sprang to his feet, on guard and stood with the back door behind him and he faced the incomer whose soiled workman's clothes smelt of the outdoors. 'You must be Mr McCann,' he said, remembering the name from the shop door and holding out his hand.

'Pat, call me Pat,' automatically shaking Joe's hand as if he was the guest and this was Joe's house. 'You've the advantage of me,'

'I'm Joe Kelly.'

Pat raised his eyebrows but said nothing. He

lowered himself into a chair, leaning on the table and letting his hands take his weight, as if truly weary. He touched the cold china teapot with the back of his forefinger, establishing with one touch that Joe and Louise had idled away the afternoon over a cup of tea. A look of resignation passed across his face and Joe squirmed like a guilty child before a headmaster, conscious the whiff of his aftershave filled the kitchen rather than the meaty aroma of a hearty meal. Or worse, perhaps Pat knew who he was.

They could hear Louise coming down the stairs. She burst into the kitchen, expecting only to see Joe sitting as she had left him and started at the sight of the two of them, 'Pat.'

'Surprised to see me?' Pat said dryly. Louise's shoulders slumped as if a bubble of joy had suddenly burst but she managed a smile. 'Are you not going to introduce us, Louise?' Pat said more gently.

'Sure, Pat, I thought you'd have got acquainted already. This is Joe Kelly. He used to live here ages ago.' And she turned to ask Joe, knowing the answer to the exact day, 'How long ago is it now, Joe?'

Joe took his cue from Louise, 'We used to know each other when we were children.' This was not a lie.

'Well, well,' Pat stood up to shake Joe's hand again. A much smaller man, older looking and more care-worn, he kept hold of the soft manicured hand in his bear's paw, his pale blue eyes quite fierce as if searching for something they might have in common. Finally, Pat demanded, with a semblance of his usual good humour, and suddenly struck with a bright idea.

'You'll stay for a meal, of course. Louise'll rustle up something, she's a grand cook,' then sank into his chair and absently rubbed his face with his hands.

Joe saw a look of consternation cross Louise's face as her eyes ranged an enamel dish on the side that had been there when they came in hours before. Used to catering for himself, Joe recognised that Louise had not even christened the meal and imagined, if their finances were like his, the dish would contain a cheaper cut of meat that needed long, slow cooking to make anything of it.

'Can we not get a meal in the pub? I'd like to treat you,' Joe said, hoping his face was bright. Rustling up something grand would presumably not be a problem for the local pub. Louise accepted graciously and immediately without even consulting Pat.

Joe Kelly walked back to the pub, springing along in easy strides. On the whole, he thought it had gone well. He dismissed what might have been had Louise still been available with a shrug. Better this way with no complications. He had misgivings about the meal together, but once Pat had asked him, what could he do without putting Louise on the spot.

When he reached the pub, he looked up and down the street, a furtive habit, born of his life-long assumption of guilt, before stooping to get under the lintel, his shoes catching on the stone flags. The hunger he felt on leaving the beach had gone but he looked forward to a pint; he deserved a pint. He let his eyes grow accustomed to the gloom and the chill. Even the fire that flickered in a stone grate seemed to turn in on itself and swallow light and heat. Joe leant on the bar, about to put his finger on the shiny bell and summon someone. 'I'm already here,' Jenny said, a disembodied voice near the fire. 'I've been fighting to get this thing going for ages, it's driving me mad.'

'By the time you've poured me a pint and had something for yourself it'll pick up, you'll see.' His jovial tone had the desired effect. Jenny was all dimples and smiles, as if no one ever came to the village, no one interesting or handsome, that is.

'Will you be wanting something to eat later?' she asked him. 'We've fresh fish, just coming in.'

'I will,' he said, falling easily into the accent he had schooled himself away from. 'And I'll be bringing a couple of guests.' He saw her raise her eyebrows but he wasn't going to tell her. 'Is there music tonight?'

'Open mike, they call it. Anyone can sing and play.'

His face must have given him away and she hastened to reassure him, 'We've grand musicians. Anyway, if you don't want to hear it you can always step outside.' She turned to look at the disappointing fire and said with a sigh, 'I knew it would be dying on me. The boss likes it and it brightens up the old place, so I'd better, you know.' She nodded her head towards the grate.

Joe watched her slim hips as she turned away from him and imagined she accentuated the sway for his benefit. He was quite used to the effect he had on women, girls some of them. He could have made some comment. He could have voiced what he was thinking about her provocative round arse, like an apple in the wind just ripe for plucking, but didn't. He was here a few more days and the riper the apple, the sweeter. He had lost count of the encounters he thought would assuage his loneliness. He downed the rest of his pint, barely appreciating the cold liquid in his gullet and wiped his lips hard on the back of his hand to stop himself from feeling maudlin.

He climbed the narrow stairs to his room under the eaves and stretched out on the bed with his hands propped behind his head. Weary from the walk and the long afternoon with Louise. It was only then he thought of the notebook. He cursed, realised he must have left it at the pharmacy and cursed again with disappointment at his carelessness. If he had chosen to ruin the suit and force the notebook into a pocket, he might still have it. He let his anger subside. Tomorrow would have to do. He pulled one of the letters free of its bundle and read with a mixture of acute embarrassment and shame that made his eyes water. The emotion, long since buried and forgotten, hit him full force as if it was only yesterday that the hope Louise would join him had slowly died.

~*~

Louise hummed as she got herself ready. She liked the bedroom in the evening; the way the dying sun cast shadows and illuminated the silver specks of dust to dance before her eyes. Pat's cough sounded in the living room below and she imagined him reading the newspaper, tipping his glasses on the bridge of his nose to see the print better. She checked her watch, plenty of time; it wasn't often they went out for a meal. She leaned in to the dressing table mirror examining the fine lines round her eyes and mouth and wondered what Joe Kelly made of her now. She acknowledged her disloyalty with a grimace and groped for the familiar slouch of her makeup bag in the drawer. Instead, her fingers found the neat velvet dome of a jewel box and she withdrew her hand as if she had been stung. The box was always there; she knew it was, shoved to the back of the drawer and in it a brooch that had been her mother's only treasure, a gewgaw of paste rubies and pearls that she had loved as a child. Once, she can't have been more than six or seven, she'd been in trouble for wearing the brooch to school. She had taken it from her mother's drawer and pinned it to her school uniform where her mother would not see it. School had rung her mother who had come and taken her out of the classroom to stand with her in the corridor. 'Is there anything you want to tell me, Louise?'

'No,' her automatic, bold response. She'd known why her mother was there and had felt the prickling of guilt as they stood together in the quiet corridor. Her mother never demanded, never shouted, rarely scolded. The look of disappointment was usually punishment enough. When she got home after school Louise just slipped the brooch back where she'd found it and the incident was never mentioned.

Louise smiled to think of her mother making her presence felt and pinned the brooch to her throat, turning her head first one way then the other. Memories of her mother fell with the silver motes of dust. The brooch seemed particularly lovely in the dying light as if it really was made of precious stones. Keep it safe, her mother used to say. It's good to know you've got it, Louise. You don't know when you might need it. Louise never did believe it was valuable. How could her mother have kept anything through all the years of hardship but for its sentimental value? She wasn't even sure where it came from, if it was a gift or had been handed down.

Louise pulled the drawer right out, tipped the contents on the bed, scrabbling with the age-mottled lining paper. There was something else her mother had made her keep safe, for just in case. The envelope with its copperplate writing was still where her mother had hidden it with a warning finger to her lips, stuck to the wood with age.

For the best part of twenty years, she'd kept silent and borne the burden of the secret while the proof had lain hidden under the paper that lined the drawer, with the living proof ever before her eyes. The lovely boy with ringlets in his hair who had been passed off as her brother and a 'late surprise' for her parents when there was no such thing as birth control and the place was amok with 'late surprises'. Maybe they were all illegitimate babies born to underage girls and passed off as their mother's 'late surprise'. Who was she to say? The secret she had intended only for Pat's ears that she could not bring herself to tell even after five years of marriage, that she had so nearly let slip hours before.

She held the envelope to her nose and breathed in the painful secret that had gnawed her conscience to an uneasy truce during all the years of marriage. She imagined producing it with a flourish tonight during the meal when the conversation was flagging; get it over with once and for all; unburden herself.

'Here, Pat, take a look at this. I've been meaning to show it you for ages.' How could she say it? 'This is the Joe Kelly I pined for, whose name I could never say out loud for fear of giving the game away, who took my heart, my virginity.' Why not? Straight out and surprise the pair of them when neither of them had any inkling. 'This is the man I made you wait for. The one I believed in for years, my first love, who I thought was the only man for me.' Like a story from Mills and Boon. The sort of story their English teacher at school had warned them not to believe in. Here, at last, was the long-lost Joe barely changed from when he left a lifetime ago just when she'd almost forgotten him. 'Oh, and by the way, Joe, you might as well both find out together.' She smoothed the birth certificate lovingly with her fingers.

'For the love of God, Louise,' Pat called her from downstairs and made her start.

'Ok, Pat, ok.'

It had grown almost dark. She tucked the long, slim envelope back beneath the paper lining, smoothing it with her hands, replaced the contents and closed the drawer with a brisk click.

Honeymoon

Pat was pacing the hallway but when he saw her, he smiled, 'Worth the wait,' he said and kissed her. 'You're even prettier than the day I met you.' And off they went arm in arm to the pub, the local inn they never went to, not for birthdays or high days or even holidays. 'This'll give them something to talk about,' Pat grinned, 'the McCanns stepping out for their evening meal with the rest of them.'

Louise was glad that Pat was in such good humour, taken out of himself and his usual routine, but the prospect of making small talk over steak Diane for a couple of hours in full view with Joe, the handsome stranger in their midst, made her slightly queasy. To say nothing of the lovely boy with ringlets in his hair grown now to a fine young man with close shorn head, believing his mother is his sister, with no idea of his true father, who would be serving them their meal in the pub.

She had lived with the lie for years, battling with it like a silent, slow-growing cancer that threatened to turn malignant and eat her away. Especially after she had accepted Pat, waking in the night with the worry of it, she'd struggled to keep her balance, to keep the sense of herself in the world. She had wondered if the lie was the reason they had never had children of their own: a form of retribution. Five years was a long time to wait. If she produced the birth certificate with a flourish then maybe she would fall pregnant the instant the truth was told.

She tightened her grip on Pat's arm. She would not let that spoil tonight. That was for tomorrow or the next day. Announcing to Pat and letting Joe know were two distinct events that should be kept separate, compartmentalised so they were clear. It was anything but clear. Then there was Dermot.

'Louise. Have you heard a word I've said?'

'No, Pat, I have not. I've been in a world of my own.'

Pat laughed at her honest answer and she laughed too, turning to him with love.

The bar was lively and it put her in good spirits too. She would just go on pretending and not let anything spoil the meal. She was glad for Dermot that he worked here in such a happy atmosphere. She could see he was busy chatting and she did not want to catch his eye. It was Jenny who showed them to a table and asked if she could get them any drinks. Louise said they would wait for their other party but then wished she had a drink in her hand after all, especially when Mr Hennessy came to their table. He bowed very formally and said it was an honour to see them in his pub. Louise was too flustered to suspect him of irony. He insisted loudly that they have a drink, 'On the house, on the house, what will it be?' Straight away Louise whispered it was very kind of him. She knew Pat would be annoyed at Mr Hennessey's largesse, and refusal would mean loud remonstration, not at all, not at all, that would ultimately lead to acceptance anyway. So Jenny was summoned again to bring beer and dry white wine and a little dish of salt nuts. The ice-cold of the wine and sting of salt on her tongue sent a little shiver of pleasure in spite of the knot of worry as they waited for Joe. Oh God! Why had he come back? With Joe Kelly suddenly on the scene it was as if the one line she had been travelling had been hijacked. He'd stayed away for twenty years, why come snooping round now?

An old woman, who was often in the chemist's, stopped by their table. 'Ah hello there, Louise, I didn't recognise you in here.' She looked them up and down, shamelessly scrutinising them both. 'It's unusual to see you in the pub, Louise. And Pat, of course; a rare treat, if I might say.'

Louise remained silent, keeping her eyes downcast after the briefest of smiles, knowing she was being unkind. The odds on making a good impression on any of them were less than even, outside at best. She cringed but was livid that this woman with dyed and faded ginger hair and noticeable tremor and odour of stale sweat, claimed intimacy because she frequented her shop. She supposed film stars must feel this animosity to perfect strangers who claimed friendship because they had seen them on the screen. She forced a thin smile, then frowned a warning to Pat not to encourage her either.

When the woman had gone on to the bar, she could be heard complaining loudly to Jenny. 'Some people about the place are terribly snooty and above themselves.' They did not hear what Jenny said in response, just the strains of her rather gentle voice.

Pat said, 'That was awful harsh, Louise.'

'She's a terrible busybody,' Louise tried to explain.

'The less she knows the better.'

Pat raised his eyebrows. 'You might feel you've gone up in the world because some handsome divil from way back has come to your door.'

Louise opened her mouth to defend herself but closed it without saying anything. Pat's Adam's apple accused her, chafing over the collar of his only decent shirt that was tighter than the last time he had worn it. She had insisted on being smart and Pat had pushed and squeezed into uncomfortable clothes just to please her.

The upright back of the pew, rescued from the church and put to good use, was already causing him to fidget when all he really wanted was his tea and watch the news before he had to settle his animals for the night. Sometimes she went with him when it was fine, like tonight, a lovely night to be walking up the back fields under the wide arching sky and the stars to check the livestock. He never even minded the rain; good honest rain, he called it. Pat would be a misfit anywhere else. She had known that when he proposed and all the long year she kept him waiting for her reply. Before she married she had always hoped, almost like a war bride keeping a candle burning for the airman she feared would never return, that she would run off to find Joe or that Joe would turn up and want her to live with him in London or Dublin or any other big city. She would have a good job with prospects and they would be a proper family. Novelettish, she could see her Irish teacher wrinkle up her nose in disdain; real life never dovetails and is never neat. Louise knew that real life was visceral and messy. The teacher, auburn-haired and coquettish, with aspirations to be an actress, had run off just before Louise should have taken her junior cert. In her class, only the girls whose parents could afford to pay for private tuition ever got to take the exam. Most of them had to repeat or left without qualifications. For her, there were other extenuating circumstances, of course.

Waiting here at the pub and feeling out of place and not knowing what to say to each other in these surroundings she realised would simply reveal what she wanted to hide. A poor farmer and his wife settled to a life of hard work and the threat of poverty because that was what was on offer. 'Next year,' or 'It can only get better,' had begun to sound hollow and Pat had stopped saying it, just as she had stopped hoping month after month for a baby. The large family and comfortable life they had both dreamed of and promised each other was not their lot.

'You better take off the tie, since it's such a trial. I'll put it in my bag,' and she leaned over and tenderly undid Pat's top button to release the struggling Adam's apple. 'It's just the one night, Pat, and they say the steak is to die for.' She reached for his hand and put hers comfortingly on top and watched, smiling as he studied her, waiting for his face to relax into its usual broad smile. He looked so old suddenly and she wondered how long before she would have the same look too, careworn and faded. She decided that she would not, no way, not for ages yet.

Music started; all kinds of instruments tuning up: a guitar, a lute, a fiddle and some she didn't even know the name of, all strumming quietly. She thought the musicians were flicking through black-backed songbooks and any moment they would burst into song, till she realised it was just the menu they looked at. God Louise, she berated herself. Anyone would think you were some poor hick from the country. 'How grand,' she said out loud, 'a few songs to cheer us up. I might sing myself if they ask.'

~*~

It was ten to eight when Joe woke, his arms stiff, almost painful, folded behind his head. There was barely time to shower in the tepid trickle that passed for en suite facilities. As he shaved, scraping his face with a blunt disposable razor, he held his face close to the mirror till his steely reflection was barely recognisable and whispered, 'Don't fuck this up, Joey; not having come this far.'

He put on a clean white shirt and the smart suit he had just taken off, chose a brightly coloured tie, changed it for a more subtle dark blue, then left off a tie altogether and opened his top button. He adjusted his cuffs, smoothed his hair with both hands and with one last glance in the mirror, made his way downstairs.

Joe saw Pat and Louise before they saw him, how their shoulders slumped, how they were not talking, staring away from each other, and was mortified that he was late. He collected himself, fixed a smile and was about to step up when someone gave him an almighty slap on the back. A voice boomed low, 'Well, well. I like to greet the guests myself, at least once during their stay. Joe Kelly, I remember you knee high to a grasshopper.'

A genial face, broad like a potato head, loomed over him. Hennessy, of course! Joe remembered him now. Everyone was knee high compared to Mr Hennessy. Joe had been too preoccupied to even consider who else he might meet again. Nothing about Hennessy had changed, his face so full of character, so determined and decided that change was not a possibility. Or could it be that nothing he had done made any impression on him? Hennessy! Seeing him in the flesh, unleashed a shaft of memories. What should he say to the man who had made him wait out the back when he wanted a beer? Would not even allow him in to wash glasses in return for the Guinness. The Selfish Giant they used to call him because back then, he never let any of them in. Joe held out his hand, 'Mr Hennessy,' and was in danger of having his arm pulled out of its socket while Mr Hennessy's laugh rumbled round the whole room. Even twenty years ago Hennessy had been a force to be reckoned with. Joe glanced towards Pat and Louise who had, of course, turned to see whose entrance was creating such a stir.

'I won't keep you,' Hennessy boomed. 'Your party's waited for you long enough,' and he propelled Joe on his way with an almighty shove from his hand the size of a dinner plate. Joe barely had time to recover before he landed beside Louise and Pat.

He apologised for keeping them waiting. 'What are you drinking Pat? What'll you have Louise? Have you looked at the menu yet? I could kick myself, I'm so sorry. I fell asleep, would you believe it?' He knew he was too loud, making a show of himself and calling attention to them all. He felt desperate to show he knew how things should be done – one of the Kelly gang made good. He saw Pat's jaw clench and struggled to find a topic that would produce more than a one-word answer. He knew nothing of animal husbandry and nothing of their life, except that they had no children. In the end, he told them anecdotes from his life in England and raised a few laughs. Try as he might, he could tell Louise was not enjoying herself. He felt her eyes on his face though he hardly looked at her, keeping his own hooded. He barely knew what he felt, let alone how she must feel, a mistake to have offered the meal, a mistake to be here.

As the food arrived and the candles were lit, Pat seemed to relax and enjoy his steak. A couple of times Joe stifled a yawn and Pat had the grace not to notice. Louise smiled at him. 'It's the sea air, does that to you.'

He smiled back and lied, 'It's grand to see you.' He ate heartily too, there was nothing wrong with the meal or his appetite and when the singing started he actually enjoyed it. The young couple he had seen in the street were in the bar. Newlyweds at a guess, honeymooners. Not a bad voice.

Honeymoon

~ * ~

In the pub, Rosie made the effort to be jovial, although the pub itself was making no such effort. Tired paintwork certainly did the rooms no favours. Painted a vicious blue, a colour to be ashamed of and want to hide, instead of white or cream. Even the fire seemed tired. It glowed dully and failed to make a focal point so she wasn't sure if it was real.

Around the walls, benches of unvarnished oak with upright backs like pews divided the eating area into booths and gave the impression of privacy although there was nothing intimate about the place. Then in the middle of the room, tables and chairs were hemmed in so closely that diners simply would not be able to ignore their neighbours and would even have to pass food along since a waitress could not possibly fit. It was as if a great number of customers were expected but had failed to arrive.

They stood awkwardly at the bar, till Dermot rescued them, two newcomers who did not know the ropes. 'Did you reserve a table, at all?'

'I'm afraid we didn't.' Rosie scanned the near empty room.

Dermot waved a hand expansively as if he ran the place, then showed them to one of the free booths next to another couple and waited as Rosie slid along the bench opposite Fergal before presenting them with menus. 'Can I get you any drinks? Jenny will be back for your order.'

Rosie saw the woman on the nearest table wink at Dermot and suppressed a smile. She thought he was play-acting; he looked too much of a boy to be taken seriously, yet he made a creditable waiter.

They studied the menu, smiling at each other intermittently.

'The steak is to die for,' the woman near them said and Rosie checked to see who she was talking to. It was not, as she first thought, directed at them. The woman had dark, curly hair and a pretty, intelligent face; early thirties perhaps, but the man, quite gnarled by life, seemed much older. His large hands resting on the table beside his plate looked well used. He looked boiled and squeezed into his clothes as if he wasn't quite used to them. It made Rosie uncomfortable just to look at him. She smiled at Fergal, so dark and handsome opposite her. She smoothed the back of her shirt, tucking it into her trousers, pleased to feel the bones of her spine, glad she looked after herself. The couple were whispering now but still Rosie could hear them.

'Give it to me then. I'll put it in my bag.' And the man took off his tie. It did not seem to improve anything at all till the woman reached over to him and undid his top button, releasing the Adam's apple. 'God love you, Pat.' It was such a loving gesture, so private yet so public. Rosie looked down at her hands. Perhaps she and Fergal would grow old together like that. She thought of her own parents behind their barricade of newspapers at breakfast and the silence and tension of meal times and shuddered.

A sonorous voice caused them both to turn and look. A giant of a man, who made Rosie think of

Herman Munster, created a ripple of energy practically shaking someone's arm off. Rosie giggled nervously and continued to stare. The giant and the smaller man seemed to be play-acting and reminded her of a Punch and Judy her father had taken them to as children. All that was missing was a string of sausages and perhaps a cudgel. Joe Kelly and Mr Hennessy. Everyone must have heard them.

Joe Kelly surveyed the room, debonair and at ease as if he was used to an audience, then made his way towards their booth, stepping towards them with a smile as if he recognised them. Rosie thought he must want something and couldn't imagine what it could be. Then at the last moment, he veered as if he hadn't seen them at all and sat with the couple whose conversation they could not help overhearing. He had his back to them, which Rosie was grateful for, a tuft of hair like a comb-over moved as he laughed and gesticulated expansively and his voice was still loud.

Jenny arrived with the food. She served very prettily; all smiles and batted eyelashes for Joe Kelly. No matter how hard Jenny flirted, she had got it wrong if she thought Joe Kelly had eyes for her. The older woman was coquettish in a different way. Rosie could not help but notice how her expression changed as she looked first at the older man and then to Joe Kelly. She imagined Joe Kelly was wistful for her, a lover from her past.

Gradually the room began to fill; faces were rosy and laughing in candlelight. This was the real start of it. Rosie was enjoying herself. Fergal relaxed too. She had been nervous, and awkward alone in his company after barely a week of marriage and the stark warnings from some of her family still in her ears. 'You've only known him five minutes. What's his background?' Here, in the glow of candlelight, she looked at him anew. 'How's your steak?' she whispered to Fergal.

'To die for!' he said with a wink.

As they were finishing their meal, music started. One man played a lute while another sang. Even the woman next to them began to sing. Rosie tapped her foot to the rhythm and Fergal began to hum softly. She did not recognise any of the tunes, which were mournful, sea laments, songs of hardship and loss and struggle. One song followed another, a few words spoken, a few jokes made. Then they were prevailed upon for their turn and she shook her head shrinking back into her seat as if that would make her disappear. Fergal stood up to sing and she was embarrassed for him as he spoke to the musicians. He sang a song of murder and love with a fine tenor voice. Shelagh Doran loves Joe Kelly.

At first, she thought Fergal was being provocative in his choice of song. Everyone would think so. It was your green eyes shining that ever made me stray. She felt her heart race, she would be called on to apologise. Joe Kelly went away. The room was suddenly quiet as everyone listened to Fergal, a new pure voice in their midst. He sang again and the woman at the table near them joined in and began to harmonise, low and lulling. If they hadn't come to Ireland she might never have known that Fergal could sing. It was only a minor revelation but she began to see another Fergal, one that belonged here. He felt at home and she was the outsider. 'It is where I come from,' he'd said on the journey coming over. The way Fergal spoke it had sounded like they would live happily ever after. She thought of the plane landing with a spatter of tiny fields beneath them and rain on the tarmac. It had smelled different. The long taxi ride with Dermot, who didn't look old enough to have a licence and Fergal keeping up a witty and light way of talking so different from the way he usually spoke. She liked to see him throw back his head and let go. She thought of him crying at the graveside. She had been right all along, even though he pretended it didn't matter. What difference did it make? Here were four unreal days to get to know him: Ireland, Pierce, an Irish name and Fergal singing.

The singing died down and instruments played quietly in the background. Comments, some ribald, began bouncing round the room. Then voices were raised, and it was no longer jokes but insults that were traded. Rosie looked at Fergal in alarm, imagining jagged bottles thrust viciously into someone's face. Fergal just shrugged. A chair scraped back and crashed to the floor. 'Ya young eejyot, Dermot, go home.'

And Dermot was rushing red-faced and a door slammed. Immediately a musician plucked pizzicato der der de der de – der der and there was laughter. The woman sitting nearest to them leaned in and confided, 'Ah take no notice. He'll get over it. He usually does.' Rosie smiled but she was sorry for Dermot. She thought she saw it all, Jenny flirting for all she was worth with Joe Kelly and putting Dermot's nose out of joint.

She felt deflated and suddenly could not sit up another minute. She told Fergal she was overcome with tiredness. He walked with her back to the cottage they had rented, and the cool evening air blew gently on her hot cheeks.

'I didn't know you could sing,' she said.

'Something you learn in care,' Fergal said, 'how to entertain each other. Actually, my father sang to us.'

In the soft lighting of the small bedroom that was only just big enough for the double bed, Fergal watched her as she undressed. 'You look different,' he said. She did not know what he meant, and still with the tiredness she had felt in the pub she climbed under the duvet without saying anything. He said it again, 'Your body looks different, its shape. I think you're pregnant.'

'Don't be ridiculous. It's only been a week. What the hell would you know, anyway?' The words were out of her mouth, dismissive and angry.

Fergal was the one who'd wanted to wait respectfully for their wedding night before making love. It should be special, don't you think? The chivalry had impressed her but not the state that followed when neither of them had belonged fully to the other. She'd worried Fergal had something wrong with him and was half tempted to ask Hugo for advice. Thankfully she didn't. She'd had the sense to keep the 'no sex' caveat quiet or there'd have been no end of jibes. Hugo had scoffed enough when she'd told him they were engaged. 'For God's sake, Rosie! Engagements are only to impress parents; he's an orphan so he must want to impress ours. Anyway, real engagements last more than eight weeks.' On and on he teased till she was heartily sick and wished she'd never mentioned it. She'd leapt to Fergal's defence of course. 'He's a romantic, Hugo, or hadn't you realised?' Then one night after a party when the guests had gone, it had been inevitable, reckless, as if they'd broken Fergal's unwritten rule. 'You are so beautiful, make love to me,' his gasp and the feverish claiming of her body had made her want to sing. Now it felt as if he had tricked her. Any normal person would have used precautions. She swung her fist at his head, angry enough to hit him. He caught her fist and held her tight till she calmed down enough to laugh at the absurdity of it.

'See,' he said, 'now you're being irrational. It all fits.'

'What if I am?' suddenly vulnerable, afraid almost, all she wanted was his arms around her.

'Well, that's just fantastic, the most exciting thing that can happen, isn't it?'

And he sounded like he meant it too.

'Let's wait and see. How can we bring someone else into the world when we don't even know who you are.'

His arm went limp and he relaxed his hold on her. 'Maybe you're right.'

'I didn't mean it like that exactly, Fergal, I'm sorry.' She realised how like her mother or her great aunt she sounded. She had taken him for better or worse knowing nothing about him. They had discussed nothing before getting married.

He lay on his back with both hands under his head, not looking at her. She held her breath. It was Hugo who'd told her Fergal had never even been adopted, spending his childhood in care. Fergal was Hugo's best friend so presumably they had spoken of it. She thought of the two of them sitting up late over beers talking seriously, man to man, and then she thought of a smaller, younger version of Fergal looking out between banisters of a huge staircase as other boys were embraced and taken off to loving homes. She could not imagine life in an orphanage. Or was it that she did not want to? How little she'd asked him. She laid a hand on his chest. He covered it with his, then kissed her cheek and rolled off the bed. He opened the curtains revealing walls two feet thick and sat looking out at the velvet sky. A shooting star fell across the window.

'Did you see that?' he asked, 'a shooting star!' The wonder in his voice kept her sleep at bay. 'When I was a boy,' he began. She got up to sit beside him on the bed and he put his arm round her. He had spoken so little of his past. She leaned into him. 'We used to gaze at stars. I think my father and my grandfather must have encouraged us. It wasn't encouraged in the orphanage, definite curfew at bedtime.' She lifted her head a fraction, so she could see him telling his story.

'One bonfire night the home was having a party, which was rare. There was a great fuss with a Catherine wheel that got stuck and our housemother burned her fingers. We were all quite glad – she was a bit of a dragon. Afterwards, when I told a boy I thought the fireworks were a grand disappointment, he blabbed and I was walloped for being ungrateful. There were no more fireworks after that just plenty of wallops. What I had meant to say was, I liked the beauty of the sky more than the razzmatazz of fireworks.' He paused. 'The sky had been full of shooting stars and I felt infinitesimal like a speck of stardust and for the first time since coming to the orphanage, I had a great sense of belonging, a sense of the immense beauty of life and of my place in the universe. It felt like an epiphany, however brief, and that everything would be fine. I think that feeling was a memory or a message from before. Does that make sense?'

'I think so.' Rosie tried to take in what he was saying, measure it against all the paraphernalia of her childhood and wondered if she had a sense of herself at all. Her milestones had been recorded in several albums and catalogued by her mother with neat, often witty captions and precise dates in Roman numerals in silver ink underneath. First tooth, first gymkhana, first ballet exam; endless achievements strung together to fabricate Rosie Hardman. She thought it might have been easy to be an undercover agent with all those misleadingly solid red herrings already established to prove her identity. Now her past was irrelevant, she realised with a moment of clarity. She was a new woman, Rosie Pierce, and she could be anyone she wanted.

'You feel chilly,' he said and they lay down and cocooned the covers round them. Fergal began to confide. 'They told me in the home, well they tried to make me believe, I had an imaginary friend.'

'Lots of children have imaginary friends,' she said.

Her childhood had been so safe, so secure, so normal, she supposed. She rarely thought about it but she realised that Fergal must never stop thinking or wondering. This visit to the house, where his people were from, as he put it, was of deep importance to him and maybe even having a child was his way of establishing roots. Something he desperately needed to do. She ran one hand over her belly just to see if it felt different. It didn't.

There had been no narrative to Fergal when she'd met him, no naked photos on the hearthrug, no memories of school or prizes, no favourite food, barely any possessions, as if he had come to her fully formed, beamed into her dimension suddenly, a colleague and friend of her brother's and always round at theirs for his tea. Her eyes were heavy with sleep and her thoughts returned to their wedding day, remembered as a snapshot in their living room, her immediate family surrounding the happy couple. It had not seemed odd at the time that they were the only guests and her brother had been the best man. Surely Fergal had made some friends of his own before meeting Hugo? Whenever they went out it was always with friends of Hugo's, friends she'd known a long time.

'My friend wasn't imaginary,' Fergal said and she flicked her eyes open. 'They just didn't understand that I still spoke with my twin even though he was dead. I kept his voice in my head.'

'Do you still speak to him?' Rosie's mouth was stiff with sleep. She knew about the close bond between siblings. Hugo was her world. He often joked he knew what she was thinking, even before she did, and perhaps he was right.

'Oh, sometimes,' Fergal said.

The bedroom was suddenly very still and she was aware how important this revelation was. She wondered if by admitting to communing with his dead twin Fergal actually wanted to tell her something else. She wondered too if Hugo knew and had chosen not to tell her. 'That's why we're here on our honeymoon, isn't it? To find the past.'

Fergal kissed her cheek. 'When I'm with you, Rosie, life has meaning and a purpose.' He rolled away and presented his back with the splendid curve of a recumbent cello.

'That's a lovely thing to say,' and she rolled up close to him, one arm round his waist. She almost wished her aunt and the other doubters could see them. The full moon beamed into the room filling the frame of the skylight. Two frills of cloud made a fringe for its perfect face.

~ * ~

Louise lay awake fretting over the day, her heart alternately racing or stopped. She tried to steady it in time to Pat's rhythmic puttering beside her. His head touched the pillow and that was that, tonight especially, with the wine and the heavy meal.

The evening had gone well enough, she thought. She had not given herself away and neither she nor Pat had disgraced themselves. Pat had enjoyed his steak and she had broken her diet and had a pudding, but that was fine because she could always start again. There was always tomorrow. That is what she told herself in those wakeful hours, rehearsing the words boldly in her head, but anywhere else, she was dishonestly silent. Those brave words she knew she would never have the courage to use were always put off for another day. She had let the lie close over her till it was worse than the truth. How to say it out loud? With Joe here, the matter was urgent, but she was as fearful as ever. Pat would be shocked, even though it was not the crime it once was. He might want a divorce.

Why, oh why had Joe Kelly come back now? Why, she wondered then and so many times since, had Joe come to her that night? Why did he not just go, if he was going? He was like a cat marking his territory, except he never came back. She stopped crying and sniffed hard.

She had not intended to relive the night she begot her only son but memories were suddenly intense and vivid. The feel of cold, wet sand grazing her back and closing her eyes deliberately, as if by doing so she could shut out the rest of them, and the sense of wonder on opening them, seeing the myriad possibilities of the universe unfolding in the night sky. And Joe weeping; 'I will come back for you, I will write, wait for me,' to her utter bewilderment.

She steadied her breath, preparing to tell the story she had not told a living soul and nudged Pat half hoping that he would not respond. 'Pat, I need to tell you something.' His lips moved sleepily, and he shifted to face her with his good-natured smile.

'Ok then Louise, fire away.' She was silent. It was Pat who spoke as if sleep had been a pretence and he too had been mulling over the evening. 'That Joe seems ok for a city man. Perhaps it was his childhood saw him right.' Louise took hold of his hand in the darkness, pressing it to her for courage.

'Pat, there's something I should have told you before we got married.'

Pat took a deep breath, bracing himself to support Louise for the telling of the secret he already knew, whose details he did not want from her lips; the age-old story of a young girl taken advantage of. 'Never mind old history, Louise.'

He had heard more than enough from Driscoll when he'd asked for her hand in marriage. A request he'd made out of respect for Louise since he had little time for her father. A bully, he thought, and a bad influence for Dermot; glad they'd had little to do with him. It was not often a man invoked such dislike with little or no provocation. It was a gut feeling and Pat was a believer in gut feelings, visceral, like his love for

Louise. The more she insisted, the more Pat said it didn't matter. She did not take his hint, and Pat gave in to her as he did for most things.

'But I tell you, you don't need to. I know all I need to know. I know that I love you. And I believe you love me.'

In the dark and stillness, her voice sounded so weary. 'Dermot's not my brother, he's my son.'

He took her in his arms and smoothed away the tears that fell silently over the bridge of her nose. He had sensed the burden of the secret between them but had not known till now how heavy she found it, had not thought till now that there was not a single soul she could confide in, except him. 'I know, I know.' What else could he say? The words were out before he realised.

'How did you know?' Louise stiffened, startling him with her hard tone. He attempted to limit the damage of this potentially explosive moment.

'I know it from how you are with him. Maybe he knows it himself in a way. He has a special way with you. Do you not notice? There's a bond. And it doesn't take a genius.' Pat wondered if he should tell her he'd known all along that Dermot was her son, aware now that she had shouldered the burden of it long enough. But honesty is not always the best policy and perhaps he should continue to hold his tongue. 'Life is strange, Louise. It's not really something you can bet on as a certainty, is it?'

'Honest to God, Pat! You're so laid back you're horizontal.' She was not laughing. 'Are you not going to say something, Pat? Don't you want to know who the father is?' Louise sounded aggrieved.

He breathed deeply, almost a sigh. 'Listen, love.'

Louise sat bolt upright and reached for the light. 'I'm all ears.' She had a quick temper. Her father told him that too on the eve of their wedding, man-to-man so he would know what he was letting himself in for. Driscoll had not thought to mention who the father of the baby might be but seeing Joe Kelly in his own living room after all these years had been enough. He had known for sure as if he had always known, as if this day would always come. What he did not know was what Louise would do about it.

'Who told you? That bastard. It was him wasn't it, that bully? This has been between us all these years, and you never once thought to mention it and put me out of my misery,' and sobs wrenched from her, loud and violent. She turned to Pat and beat his chest with her fists. He tried to hold her, to calm her with shushing and patting and stroking. The sound of the sobs rent his heart.

'Louise, Louise.' This woman he loved with all his heart who would never have been his had there been no Joe and no Dermot. This woman who felt betrayed and perhaps would not look at him again.

'I know it must be hard to give away a child and be abandoned by the father. A lover for all I know. But it is in the past. Look what a young man he's grown into, a hard worker and honest. No woman can ask more of her son. He's got his head on – a bit of a dreamer perhaps.'

He let his words trail away and rolled back, exhausted from the unaccustomed emotion wrung from him through the night, foolish and afraid. Afraid of what she might think of him. Afraid she might go back to the swank from the city, driving off into the sunset.

They lay beside each other, unable to sleep, unwilling to touch each other to seek the consolation or oblivion union might bring. There was too much to say already that they were not saying. On into the night with their problem that Pat had taken on as if it were his own because he felt it was.

Louise's story came as a flood; words dammed for nearly twenty years broke free, cascading into the night. He didn't try to stem them, however much he wanted to.

'The night Joe came to me, throwing stones at my bedroom window and I ran with him barefoot in my pyjamas, I was a schoolgirl, two weeks off my fifteenth birthday. It did not seem wrong, not the sin everyone whispered about. It felt glorious, like coming of age, like my destiny.

'My mother was gentle with me when she knew. She made the plan when it was obvious that Joe had gone and something would have to be done. She took over the pregnancy as her own. I think she saw it as her escape. Shortly after, she marched with me and a brown cardboard suitcase over the dunes and up the main street of the village back to this house, her parents' house, and never went back. The official story was the need for mains electricity and running water. For an older woman, it was easy to believe.'

'It can't have been easy to live with a man like Driscoll,' Pat mumbled.

'She should never have married him,' Louise said and Pat tutted in agreement. 'I only remember the silences.' Louise said, 'he was a bully, morose most of the time he was home and drunk most of the time he wasn't. There was little laughter. Except, of course, when my mother had the house full of her women. Then she was almost gay and the others hardly got a word in.'

A wistful silence followed as if Louise was remembering her mother. 'I don't know if she minded giving up her women friends, she never said if she did, but she let them know it was not convenient to have them in this house. I mean she had the pretence to keep up. It was ludicrous, Pat. I could cry about it now if it wasn't so ludicrous. Even then, when I cried all the time, it was ludicrous.'

Pat stroked her hair and let her talk. He listened but did not always hear what she said. His head was full of his own memories of that time. Memories of hard work and the poverty his family had lived and the overriding sense of love and happiness. How grateful he should be to his parents.

'My mother put gussets in my skirts and her own so only she appeared to bloom. Her thickened waistline was a pillow. I was bound with a corset. When we couldn't hide the bump any longer, a plausible story was hinted, finishing her education, broadening her opportunities. All the usual, but because my mother was who she was, no one seemed to question. They spared her blushes if they did. Not a word of it reached my ears, at any rate.'

'So where did you go?' Pat asked, curious.

'A boarding house in England and it was only a matter of weeks. The woman was quite motherly; I think she felt sorry for me. It wasn't such a disgrace in England as it was here. Then when the time came, my mother booked me into a private clinic in England and she came back with Dermot a couple of weeks old, she even chose his name and left me to finish broadening, taking pills for the milk to dry up.

'I had Dermot to myself for two whole weeks and then my mother took him away and passed him off as her own child and my brother. It was as if nothing had happened, yet permanent purgatory. It could have been far worse, I know. If she hadn't stood up to Driscoll, if she hadn't had her family to turn to, who knows where we'd have ended up? We never did go back to Driscoll and the beach house and they never lived together again as man and wife. Life was peaceful without him. We were happy and Dermot was a sweet little boy. When I met you at college, Pat, and my mother was dying, it was like a fresh start. Although I didn't know you loved me, of course.'

Pat squeezed her hand reassuringly then with a sharp intake of breath as if a sudden pain had wounded him he said, 'So, he's no idea that he has a son?'

'Joe? None, I had no way of finding him after he ran off. Half of me thought maybe he was dead when he never got back in touch.'

Pat had a sudden thought. 'Is he one of the Kelly gang, that wild bunch? With brothers in prison?' The memory of someone else's tragedy bobbed to the surface and then sank again leaving worrying ripples. 'Something awful happened here around that time, do you remember, and the father was implicated?'

Louise shrugged.

'Joseph Kelly, that's right. The case went on forever. The suicide they never proved that could have been murder or death by misadventure. Everyone had a theory.' Pat's voice ticked evenly. 'And those small boys trapped in the house with the body. One of them died, I think.' He studied her closely. 'Those were dark days, Louise. Death a common occurrence.' She bit her nail disinterestedly and he reasoned she must have been so taken up with events in her own life all those years ago, that she had not immersed herself in the details of the investigation of sudden unexplained deaths in the neighbourhood.

'One thing's for certain, they never got to the bottom of it.' He yawned. 'It'll be dawn soon and we won't have had a wink of sleep.'

Louise turned her head to look at her husband, 'I thought you said you knew nothing about him?'

'Well,' and Pat shifted his position causing the bed to undulate. 'It has come back to me a little.' He fingered the contours of her face, then felt for her hand and brought it to his lips. 'We never got much of the news in the back of beyond where we lived.

Hardly any signal for the TV or the radio, just picked up the gossip once a week in the town. There was plenty of gossip.' She did not return his smile but he did not let go of her hand and they lay in silence for a while. Then Pat asked, 'Why's he here now, do you think?'

'I don't know Pat. Honest I don't. God knows there were plenty of times I wanted him to come walking down the street and knocking on my door.'

'Perhaps I should box his ears, you were under age, we could prosecute him.' Pat was only half joking.

'What'd be the point? Besides, I don't want you to do that. Dermot might find out.'

'Perhaps it's time to tell him the truth.'

'I always meant to. Just as I meant to tell you, but it's so complicated – his father's his grandfather and his sister's his mother. It's one thing growing up knowing and quite another finding out your whole life's been a lie.'

'He'll have to cope. Better he finds out from you though.'

'True.' Louise pulled her hand away suddenly and swung her legs over the side of the bed. Pat tried to catch hold of her, unsure what she would do, and watched as she put on her dressing gown, tying the belt briskly round her waist. 'Enough,' she said as she left the bedroom.

Pat rolled out of bed too, fished his feet into his slippers and pottered downstairs after her. The sense of pride he usually felt as he ran his hand along the banister that he'd varnished and polished so she could live in as near to a palace as he could provide, had evaporated. He felt the bumps and all the imperfections under his fingertips with each step nearer to her, till he was sure he was a condemned man. But a smile awaited him.

'Let's have that cup of tea after all and then perhaps there'll be some sleep in this house.' Beside her in the kitchen with his arm round her, their kiss was tender. 'Why don't you take the day off?' she asked him, knowing the answer already. 'I'll shut the shop, say it's a funeral or a christening. Give the lot of them something to gossip about.'

'They don't need encouraging. Besides, they'll have seen Joe arrive. His name will set their tongues wagging their brains ticking. They'll be in overdrive.'

TWO

Mystique was largely responsible for Granda's view of the world. They had grown up together with Mystique as role model. Granda thought it noteworthy that a house that threw tiles at his best friend, appearing suddenly and unexpectedly out of nowhere, was not somewhere he could make progress.

Progress: forward movement towards a destination.
Comes after
Programme: planned series of events.

Do you think our Da plans things?
He doesn't have time. He's always at the typewriter making no progress whatsoever.

Why does he do it then?
It's what he calls
Work: the job a person does to earn money.
He says we don't have any money whenever I want some.

I'll have lots when I grow up.
Who says you're going to grow up?
Why shouldn't I if I want to?

Death: the state of being dead, the end of something.
I'm never going to die.
Sure you will. It's easy. You just close your eyes and never open them again.

Comes after:
Dearth: lack or inadequate amount of something.

Granda was of the opinion that before his death he would like to make up for the inadequate amounts of everything that Mystique had been forced to undergo, especially information. He gathered Mystique in his thin arms and travelled. For want of money, he took only the one favourite grandson with him and kept his journey to the house, starting at the bottom floor, the coldest and dampest part of the house needing the most buckets in the rainy season. The rainy season in Ireland was the longest season of the year, a disrespecter of boundaries or limits, always intent on breaking records.

DAY TWO

Joe Kelly woke in a sweat, unsure if he'd cried out or just dreamed that he had. A recurring dream of being chased by men, the thunder of their feet and their hard breathing in his ears, and hiding naked under a cold moon till they passed, always left him drenched in sweat, his own loud cry waking him with an overwhelming sense of relief that all his fear has been released with that cry. Perhaps there'd be a complaint from nearby bedrooms, as from former girlfriends, that he had murdered sleep and earplugs should be issued as standard.

He made himself a miserable cup of tea, grappling with a small travel kettle and plastic thimbles of milk, hoping it would go some way to clear his head and climbed back into bed. He winced with the first mouthful, scalding his furred tongue and ripped open the small but welcome packet of biscuits that had come with the room. Too tense to sleep after last night's meal, he'd spent half the night in the bar with Jenny and half a bottle of whisky. He didn't remember when Jenny had disappeared or who had taken over and helped finish the rest of the bottle. Heaven knows when he'd finally made it to his room.

The bundle of his love letters to Louise, still tied in their orange twine, sat on the bedside table. The sight of his young and vulnerable handwriting caused a nauseating wave of self-pity. Last night he'd contemplated tearing open all the letters, reading at random, taking out all the cheques and money he'd sent. Somehow he'd known, even in his drunken state, undoing the string would unleash too much. He reached instead for the photo album, slowly turning the pages and only half concentrating on the faces of stiff, suited groups standing or occasionally seated at dining tables. He suspected some secret sect but had not expected to find himself. He brushed away biscuit crumbs that had fallen on the page. There he was staring into the camera between his father and Driscoll, standing over a man at a table with an open book in front of him, as if they witnessed something. A series of three, one after the other, taken in a room he did not recognise. Someone else must have taken the photograph, but he could not think who that had been. He looked roughly twenty in the photo, so it must have been taken near the time he left. He shook his head slowly as if that would help him think yet, try as he might, he had no memory of it.

He rested his head back on the pillows and sifted through his memories of the time as they came to him now. Memories of Louise were uppermost. He reached for the passport photo of her, held it beside the picture of him and stroked it with his thumb. He remembered the day the photo was taken as if it were yesterday. Louise in her school uniform, waiting for her outside the booth peering round the half curtain trying to make her laugh. Then with his arm round her waiting for the strip of four photos, three serious and this one with a bright smile and her eyes closed, the last in the line, that she had given to him, turning up her face so he had kissed her nose and she had worried someone might see them. A day of his life preserved in a small photograph.

He looked at his watch and decided to get up, his eyes gritty after so few hours' sleep. He walked through the shower and scraped his face with the disposable razor and tried not to catch his own eye in the mirror.

He dragged on the clothes he had worn last night, crumpled on a chair. They would do. He ignored the stale smell of smoke and sweat that he knew from experience would bate him through the day.

Jenny served him coffee in the empty dining room. Her eyes looked puffy too. Perhaps she'd stayed in the pub overnight; a late finish and an early start. 'Did you stay the night here?' he asked then stammered, seeing her suspicious look, 'I mean, you didn't leave the bar till well after midnight and it's barely seven.'

'My dad picks me up whatever time I finish, he would always rather I came home.'

'Good man.' Joe forced a smile. It sounded the type of reply a father might teach his daughter in order to put off men like him, a reply for odious types. He took his coffee outside. The early morning chill lingered round his neck. He half suspected Driscoll would not come and he would be stood up, like a jilted lover.

Crossing the forecourt, he left the pub for a better view of the street. He felt conspicuous and wished he still smoked – at least that would give him an excuse to be lurking. Then the merest hint of movement, mouse-like, caught his eye. Driscoll showed himself and beckoned with his chin for Joe to follow before disappearing into the shadows and slipping back down an alleyway.

They trudged on and on, first one lane then another till they were striding past open fields, Driscoll leading and Joe struggling to keep up.

'Know where you are yet?' Driscoll asked over his shoulder.

Joe didn't recognise it. The ground was peaty underfoot and wet, and made a mess of his shoes. His suit caught on brambles, sweat dripped off his forehead. Driscoll's pace was difficult to keep up and Joe was breathing hard. 'Can't we slow down?'

'No. We'll stop later,' Driscoll laughed. 'Life's made you soft.'

They went through a gap in a wall and followed a path through dark woods till they came to a clearing and finally Driscoll stopped. He perched on a tree stump, fished for a packet of cigarettes and lit himself one, inhaling deeply, before offering one to Joe.

'I've given up,' Joe said, shaking his head.

'Suit yourself.' Driscoll replaced his cigarettes.

They sat in silence. Joe was grateful for the breather. He stared in dismay at his feet and the bottoms of his trousers now speckled with mud and wished for the second time that day that he hadn't given up smoking. Driscoll inhaled deeply taking a satisfying drag down to his lungs before releasing the smoke to rise provocatively in rings.

'I don't remember the house was so far from the village,' Joe said.

'It isn't.' Driscoll's lip curled. 'We're coming the long way. I wanted to bring you here first to be sure what's on your mind.'

'What do you mean?'

'You've seen Louise then?' Driscoll's voice was soft but dangerous. Joe grimaced, caught off guard. He had forgotten how hard it was to breathe in the village without everyone knowing. Driscoll pinched the end of his cigarette then flicked the stub into the undergrowth. 'Leave her alone, if you know what's good for you.'

Joe Kelly almost laughed. 'Is that a threat?'

'Don't be ridiculous. What do you think this is? The eighties? I'm her father, remember. She has a good man and a good life. Don't go stirring up trouble.'

Joe Kelly did not say anything. He thought of the afternoon spent with Louise, of the uncomfortable evening in the pub, and of the stash of unopened letters in his bedroom. Perhaps Driscoll had kept them simply because he did not want his daughter to go away.

'You can sigh all you want, it won't change the way things are, or the way they were,' Driscoll said. Joe didn't even realise he'd been sighing. Perhaps he'd spent his life sighing, fretting over what might have been. Not anymore. 'So, Joe Kelly, are you ready now, do you think?' Driscoll did not sound so mocking. He set off at a pace, expecting Joe to follow.

Almost immediately they were behind the house, coming up to it through thick undergrowth. The house was boarded up at all the lower windows and looked condemned, a surprise for Joe to see the dilapidation.

'There were rumours of money from Europe to do up the place and for a while, it looked as if it would survive.' Driscoll sounded like a councillor or a businessman. 'It could do with finishing off.'

'Where would that money come from?' Joe asked, not really interested. He stood back as Driscoll began to remove wooden slats from a side door with a practised hand, leaning them against the wall in a neat pile.

'I don't mean repairing.' Driscoll coughed, rasping

breathlessly with a sound like blocked drains. 'Insuring and burning. It needs a good bonfire to lay it to rest once and for all.' He bent almost double through the low entrance he had made and growled from inside, 'Come on then if you're coming.' Joe struggled through. Driscoll let the dull beam of a torch linger on Joe's face then flashed it ahead allowing Joe a glimpse of a grand staircase deep inside. He issued instructions to keep close to the wall before bounding ahead, sprightly and light in the bobbing torchlight, his shadow inordinately large up the wall. Joe lumbered after him, banging his shoulders as he tried to keep up with Driscoll.

Driscoll swung doors open, announcing each room; the drawing room, the sitting room, swinging the torch wildly for Joe to take a look, pointing out where the ceiling was down, or damp had destroyed the floor. Joe reeled. A chandelier twinkled. 'It used to be a grand place, remember?' Driscoll sounded almost wistful.

When they got to the kitchen, Joe stopped him. 'Wait, I want to see it.'

Down three steps to a large room, the beam of the torch laid on a vast dresser made a triangle of light across the floor. Joe strained his eyes but the torch was not bright. This had been where he'd come as a boy. He had waited with his father beside the black range, smelly, scruffy and out of place, dirty boots on the clean flagged floor. He didn't recall what it was they had been waiting for, standing for hours inside that house. Handouts, perhaps? Or were they in trouble? It had seemed a long wait; he remembered that.

In his memory, his childhood was compartmentalised, ring-fenced as an innocent time, unaffected by his father's exploits, unaffected by his jagged memories of that last night. It was only standing here with Driscoll the thought occurred to him that his mother's death must have marked a dividing line. There had been a time when he was happy.

'You're very quiet,' Driscoll said. Joe' s mouth was dry and he didn't feel like answering. He didn't feel anything much, just the odd, déjà vu of having stood there with his father. 'Ready?' Driscoll asked. The staircase loomed in front of them. Driscoll led him up the first flight and turned as they reached a wide mezzanine, his face made ghoulish by the torchlight. 'I wouldn't do this for just anybody, I hope you know,' Driscoll said.

'I couldn't ask anybody else.'

'That's not what I meant,' Driscoll said.

'Do you want me to thank you?' Joe realised he had missed the point in the moment's hesitation and now it was too late. Driscoll turned away and warned again of rotten floors. He led the way up the last flight, stopping several times to flash the torch where a tread was missing altogether.

On the landing, several doors faced them. Driscoll swung the last door, flinging it back to crash against the plaster. It opened onto the room in the photograph. Bright sunlight poked across half rotten timbers where the windows were not boarded. Light penetrated a very dark place. It happened suddenly, the terror, the memory of it and the certainty that he had been there and had done nothing to stop it. 'I need air,' Joe said, breathing hard, his heart thudding like hooves, and he began to grope his way out.

'Easy,' Driscoll said. 'Let's finish what we've started. You wanted to see where they left him.' He had a way of sneering Joe didn't like.

Joe shrank back against the wall, reliving that day and heard fists punch flesh, the dull thud of a boot against skin, the loud crack of bone breaking and the groans of an injured man. He wretched and the bitter taste of coffee mixed with bile filled his mouth and he spat it out, wiping drools on the cuff of his jacket. Driscoll laughed at him then hawked himself. 'You were there,' Joe said. The photograph and his memory of that time merged. He could see clearly the person behind the camera and the name of the priest came to him out of the fog, Malachi.

'To my shame,' Driscoll said. 'So were a few of us.'

'Was it me?' Joe's voice a hoarse whisper, his throat burning with rising bile.

'No. Of course not,' Driscoll clicked his tongue. 'You were supposed to be watchman. You were through the door like a frightened rabbit and I never saw you from that day till yesterday. Want me to tell you who?' Driscoll's voice echoed in the empty room.

But Joe knew. Finally, a memory came, a memory of hiding, cold and afraid and when a voice had shouted run, he had run. Those men in the dream were not chasing him. They were running with him and he happened to be out in front. The memory came as a release; he had not issued any blows or been there at the end, he had been outside hiding. Perhaps he had always known. 'It wasn't my fight, I didn't want to be there.' He knew he sounded pitiful. He wanted to believe this, yet in the photograph he'd been full of confidence, smiling at whatever was happening in the room. Not the same day surely? He groaned. 'Why didn't you stop him?'

'Why didn't we stop him, you mean,' Driscoll hesitated. 'Same reason as you? Fear? Or was it we wanted some damage done? Murder was not the intention.' He looked slyly at Joe. 'Unless maybe your father was told something different.' Joe reeled, stumbling from the room lurching into the door, in his hurry to get out. 'What could you have done, anyway?' Driscoll called after him, 'What could any of us have done?'

Joe fled, taking stairs two at a time, his back grazing the damp plaster of the wall. His mind merged his first fleeing with this in a confusion of fear and revulsion. Outside, he blinked in the sunshine and staggered towards the jungle of the grounds. Breaking into a run, he kept running till he could run no more and finding himself in a secluded spot slid slowly to the ground, grazing his back down a dying tree. He gasped for air, his face wet with sweat and tears. He did not want to be found. He heaved violently and lurched to one side to void the contents his stomach. When he was sure it was over he leaned his head back against the trunk, rubbing it from side to side on the rough bark to find a comfortable resting place, drew up his knees and leaned his elbows on them. What a mess. He probed the knowledge that he was a coward, prodding painfully like picking at a scab, justifying himself and his actions. Then, as his heart slowed, his head began to clear. So what if he'd been there? He hadn't been involved, he'd run away; better a coward than a murderer. But it hadn't been like that. His limbs jerked involuntarily as with a sudden pain. Malachi. Bile rose again with the tobacco and sweat smell of the man. He was the bottomless pit of Joe's dreams.

Sunlight poked through the trees that hid him and played on his face. He opened his eyes and the insects of the jungle floor came into focus. He must have slept, catching up on the wretched few hours of the night before, but he had not woken with his usual cry. All these years he'd feared he was guilty of the most terrible crime, but he had not been there at the end, not involved. It had not been his fight. By running away, he had released himself – and by coming back.

His next thought was of Louise. All these years he'd felt rejected, that she had weighed what he had to offer and decided against, that her memory of that night under the stars differed from his and she had rejected him. What if she had received his letters? What if she had come to him? Who knows if he and Louise would ever have married? What if he'd stayed? What of his life then between Malachi and his father? He'd have made even less of himself if he'd stayed. Maybe his body would have washed up along the strand or down the coast, tossed into the sea and carried with the tide alongside his father's. He shook his head to dispel that possibility and searched again for that momentary bright sense of release he'd had on first waking.

He stood up and stretched, dusted down his suit and smoothed his hair with both hands and began to walk back along winding overgrown paths, unsteady at first then gradually more at ease than he'd felt for years. He tested this new feeling, letting his mind find peace. He was Joe Kelly, jack of all trades, from the East Midlands with hardly a trace of his old accent, his old troubles all sloughed off as if he'd been shriven. He would be out of this, next plane back, to his own flat away in England.

~ * ~

Fergal woke Rosie with a kiss. 'Breakfast for the woman I love who is carrying my child?'

'Two out of three,' she said. 'Yes to the breakfast, yes to being loved but only a maybe for the baby.'

'If not this time, the next,' he said.

'Is it so very important to you?' She already knew the answer, but it was another thing they hadn't talked about and maybe they should have. She had assumed children would come later when they were ready and settled.

'You know it is, don't you?' and he opened his lashes wide enough to show her how desperate he was to be loved and she knew then why she loved him. She felt strong in his presence, and earthy, not an ephemeral thing blown hither by any changing wind. 'Ok,' he said. 'Let's have breakfast in the pub and then we'll see what the day brings.'

A long lie in was all Rosie wanted but she hauled

herself out of bed, checking her waistline in the mirror on the way to the bathroom, smiling at the smooth skin, confident she could not be pregnant, but if she was, she wanted to know about Fergal, not of any black sheep necessarily, but a past, a foundation to build on. 'Maybe we should look for the house today,' she called from the bathroom, forgetting already that she was going to let Fergal decide.

They walked with their arms around each other the short way to the pub, past the few houses with matching window boxes. They sat at a table outside and Fergal went to order breakfast. There was a dreamlike quality to the day; another reality or perhaps she was just light-headed. Small birds flitted to and from a bird table hung with an array of feeders with their sudden flash of blues and greens. Then a woodpecker surprised them, ungainly and almost garish, clinging to the mesh possessively and unable to feed, as if it bullied away the smaller birds. 'Dog in a manger,' Rosie said, 'he should feed on what the others drop on the ground.'

Fergal kissed her hand. 'He might be too young to know that yet.'

Jenny brought a picnic basket and rolls still warm from the oven, which Fergal began to wolf down with hardly time for the butter to melt. 'By the way,' Jenny said, watching him, 'you can have breakfast delivered if you'd like.'

Rosie was all smiles. 'Thanks. We'll do that tomorrow.' She handed Fergal the basket with its red gingham cloth and linked his arm knowing they made an ideal couple, lovers out for a day's ramble.

It was a trudge to the house along quiet walled lanes. They barely spoke except for Fergal saying he was sure it was nearer and Rosie saying it was a pity the taxi wasn't about. The muscles in his arm were tense, almost painful against hers and his eyes were doggedly on the ground as if he expected potholes and dangers she could not conceive of, a lone explorer burdened by the enormity of his exploit. Overhanging trees blotted out the warmth of the sun so it felt clammy and cold.

The house had been in Fergal's family for generations. Rosie knew because Hugo had told her. She'd imagined a stately home, a pale Palladian mansion, with parterres and elegant lawns, a sweeping drive, an avenue of trees, grounds enough to ride in, and thought it romantic. Fergal must have felt as if a wicked stepmother had cast a spell. To lose home and family and end up in an orphanage in England was quite a descent.

They came to a gap in the wall where ornate wrought iron gates hung off their hinges and leaned into a hedge. 'This is it, Rosie.' Fergal sounded nervous. They followed the long sweep of the drive in silence but for the crunch of gravel under their feet. When the house came into view Fergal stopped dead and Rosie lurched into him. The vast frontage was boarded up as if to prevent memories scattering to the four winds like photographs charred and damaged from a bonfire. Plants grew in the greening walls; trees grew where the roof had fallen at one end. He let go of her arm and let the basket drop to the ground with a thud and a ting of crockery against glass. 'The house is condemned,' he said. She looked at him tenderly wanting to absorb his disappointment.

Together they peered between wooden slats into gloomy rooms with rotten timbers that would not hold their weight, doors hanging loose with no lintel and nothing beyond. To Rosie, it cried out of unhappiness and secrets. She was afraid the last strength of the house would collapse around them, swallowing Fergal up in its dust. She persuaded him to give up; telling him there would surely be some other way to find what he wanted. He looked betrayed but relented, he said for her sake. She knew she was right. They sat on a low, wide wall with their backs to the house. Fergal lay on his back and folded his arms under his head with his eyes firmly shut, lashes curling darkly against the alabaster of his cheek as if he had fallen asleep instantly like a small child. Even the fly crawling on his elbow did not disturb him. Perhaps he wanted her to lie down beside him. She thought of stone effigies on ancient tombs, a knight and his lady condemned forever to lie side by side in stony silence. 'Fergal why don't you go and take a look on your own? I'd be rubbish on those rotten joists.'

In an instant, Fergal sat up and smiled at her. 'You mean it?' And he was on his feet and almost gone when he turned back and called out, 'See you back here. Half an hour say?' Sun glanced off him as he bounded towards the house and her heart contracted as she remembered the beauty of him naked. He disappeared purposefully down the side of the house as if he knew exactly where he was going. Why didn't he ever just say?

She eyed the basket, turned back the red cloth, opened up several interestingly shaped foil parcels, garlic sausage, a meat terrine, earthy surprises whose savoury smell slightly revolted her. She closed them up and got to her feet determined to explore the garden for herself. Perhaps she should leave an arrow and a trail of olive stones for Fergal to follow.

~ * ~

Louise stepped from the house, felt the sun warming her, and knew she'd made the right decision. Her resolve to take the day off as firm as Pat's to go to work. Lack of sleep had left her light-headed but she wondered if relief didn't play a part. There was a feeling of calm. This was the start of a new life without guilt. She convinced herself that the next step would be easier. Telling Pat had been the hard part. She shook her hair back from her face as if to dispel a niggle of anger that Pat had known all along. Perhaps Dermot knew too without having to hear the words. Besides, there was no urgency. She fingered a square of chocolate in her pocket, sniffed it, and ate it anyway. A disappointing stale taste lingered on her tongue. He had lived the best part of twenty years without needing to know. She would tell him certainly before he was twenty-one.

She clambered up the mound of pebbles and zigzagged down the drop on the other side, trusting the shift of the smooth round stones under her feet, then headed barefoot for the log, her favourite place, slapping her feet on cool sand, enjoying the graze against her skin, till she was almost breathless. The sea had abandoned the log one high spring tide in a wild deserted place and had never reclaimed it. The wood felt dry and permanent beneath her and held memories of long summers spent with Dermot paddling the rock pools sheltered by boulders scattered like marbles from a giant hand. Here she had fretted over Dermot's nappy rash, new teeth, playground scraps. Here she had mourned the loss of her mother. Joe Kelly had missed it all. One thing Louise knew for sure, she owed Joe Kelly nothing, that was plain now, not even a meal in the pub. She convinced herself that he wouldn't stay long and she'd let him disappear out of their lives for decades to come. Joe Kelly did not have to know. She turned her face up to the sun then gazed on the beauty of the place.

She saw Dermot way off, running full pelt down the beach and glanced at her watch, thinking he must be late for his shift. His outline, so dear she would know it anywhere, gradually taking shape as he got nearer to her. Behind him, the squalid shanty just visible at the far end puffed a little trail of white smoke from the chimney. Her childhood home, no longer safe or feasible for anyone to live in, was a blot on this otherwise perfect view that she tried never to notice, never to think of but was never far from her thoughts. Try as anyone might Driscoll could not be shifted, insisting on living in the shambles of stone, wood and corrugated iron that withstood the worst of the wildest winters right there in the shifting sand. She could almost see the wild tufts growing from the roof. Still, not every beach could boast its own old man of the sea. When Joe had disappeared her first thought was he was hiding somewhere near. Surely Driscoll would have helped him? But Driscoll had never said and she'd never dared mention it.

'I was coming to find you,' Dermot called breathlessly, 'you're not in the shop then?' He did not stop for an answer. 'What do you think? I've been burgled. Someone broke into my home.' When Louise did not jump up or even react, he flopped beside her on the log, 'Thanks for your concern.'

'It was probably a fox.'

'Would a fox steal a photograph album?' Dermot sounded near tears.

'I don't know who'd be breaking into your container round here?'

'The village is full of strangers. Snooping around all over the place.'

'I thought you were all for the tourist trade.'

'Not if they burgle my place. It feels like a personal attack, rape even.'

'Get a hold of yourself Dermot. What would you know what rape feels like?'

'I expect it feels a lot like I do after the break-in.'

Louise sighed and studied the fine down on his top lip and the beautiful long lashes. 'Is anything else taken, apart from photographs? Perhaps you should get a lock.'

'No perhaps about it.' Dermot stared back. 'There's books strewn all over. Who knows what else taken? I didn't sleep a wink, last night, what was left of it. It could happen again anytime.' He dug his hands deep into his trouser pockets and shuddered, then glared at the sea. Moments passed before he said, 'So, why aren't you at the shop?'

'Oh, you know. I've taken the day off.'

'Get you.' Then he turned towards her with a grin and added, 'That fellow you and Pat were having your steak with.'

'Who? Joe Kelly?' She kept her voice flat.

'I think he's your long-lost sweetheart.' Dermot looked sideways at Louise glad to see this time he'd provoked some reaction. 'Only joking with you, Louise, I know Pat McCann is the only man for you. But he was flashing your photograph around the bar yesterday, you as a young girl. I came to find you in the shop to tell you but you didn't answer.'

Louise felt pale. Typical Joe Kelly! He ruined her life by running off and now he seemed determined to ruin it by coming back. Dermot would work it out for himself before she ever got to tell it her way. It was hard to keep her voice steady. 'What did he say?'

'Not too much.' Louise started to breathe normally, but Dermot was warming to his tale. 'He showed it to Jenny, who knew it was you straight off but kept her trap shut. She can be quite discreet when she wants. She just said God, wasn't she pretty? Then she only talked about herself, I think she had the bit between her teeth. She gave it to him straight, her own philosophy of life. There's no way she's going to be buried alive here with some two-bit job and married to some old farmer. She has more self-respect; she's off to the university.'

Dermot mimicked Jenny's simpering then added, 'I could tell he wasn't interested in her one little bit, only Jenny couldn't see that, she was so full of herself and her own plans.'

Louise was not laughing. She saw her own life in the one described by Jenny as she would have described it herself in the old days but now would fiercely defend. Pat was not any old farmer. She thought of the dimple in his chin flecked with grey stubble try as he might to shave it away. Jenny was too young to know there were more ways to love a man than fancy the pants off him, but it was the dismissal of her job as two-bit that really rankled. Louise looked at her feet in the sand and thought of the threat Joe Kelly posed. He was forcing her hand, forcing her to speak out before she was ready. She made her voice bright, 'What time do you finish tonight, Dermot? Why don't you come for a meal?'

Dermot accepted with delight and no idea of what Louise had in store. 'That's grand. Should be able to slip away.' He stood up. 'I'd better go. Jenny covered for me this morning.' He started to bound towards the village but turned, still moving backwards and called out, 'What shall I bring?' Louise would have said, just your lovely self, but Dermot said it for her, 'Just my lovely self, is it?'

She repeated the words almost in a daze watching the retreating Dermot, so like the Joe Kelly she remembered. It was a wonder everybody hadn't put two and two together already. 'Wait,' she shouted after him. 'Wait, I'll come with you.'

He turned, some way off now. 'What? I can't hear you.'

'For God's sake, Dermot,' she said, then picked up her shoes and began to run after him. The day off she had given herself after the long night of talking now cancelled altogether. Dermot began walking back towards her, all smiles, 'Let's be late together.'

'I'm not late. And you can tell that Jenny that I do not have a two-bit job.' Dermot laughed, 'Sure you don't and neither do I.'

Louise linked arms, 'What will I make for your tea?'

'Anything you want, so long as it's filling.'

Louise made him wait for her as she put on her shoes and took his arm again to help her up the pebbles. 'You know, a job's only two-bit if you don't enjoy it or if it gets you nowhere.'

'It's not me you have to convince, Louise. But maybe Jenny's beyond convincing.'

As they reached the shop, Dermot stooped to let Louise kiss his cheek. 'See you later.' He turned back to smile at her, touching his hairline with a two-finger salute like some Yank in a film. Louise couldn't help but laugh. She thought wistfully of the time Dermot had been in trouble and wondered how easily he might fall into his old ways should he have a setback, something to throw him off balance. She hoped he'd had enough good times to see him through, the sort of good times Pat insisted on stacking up in preparation for the bad. Pat had been a steadying influence altogether for Dermot because on her own, she would be the first to admit, she had not been doing such a grand job.

She gazed on the quiet morning through the gold letters of the shop window, her mind alternately on the difficulty of telling Dermot and the possible consequences. Would she tell him when he got there? Would they wait till after the pudding? Would she already be too late and he'd have put two and two together now Joe Kelly was in town and flashing her photograph?

She straightened her certificates on the wall and dusted them with her cuff although they shone already. She was proud of her achievements. She'd worked hard for them. When the babies had not come for her and Pat and the months of waiting and hoping slowly turned to years she'd come up with a different plan. The instant the idea of having a career had surfaced the sadness lessened and when the opportunity at the chemist's shop came up she'd grabbed it. Hadn't she always been good at science at school? She had trained herself, night school, that sort of study. She loved the shop and it was good for the community to have their own pharmacy but today, she decided, would be better spent making the meal for tonight which would need careful preparation and besides she was finding it hard to concentrate.

She put up her half-day closing sign just as Mrs Macready was about to come in. 'But Louise it isn't Wednesday.'

'I've an emergency, Mrs Macready,' she said. 'Will it wait till tomorrow?'

'Sure Louise, I only wanted something for the pain, you know.'

Honeymoon

Louise was unrepentant. 'A good stiff walk or even a whiskey will sort that out for one day.'

Mrs Macready's eyes and mouth opened a little wider then narrowed to mere slits as Louise continued to lock the door. There would be talk, Louise supposed. She often overheard gobbets of gossip from some of her customers in the safety of the shop with the stock in its familiar neat rows. It made her think that like the Lady of Shallot, life happened beyond her glass frontage and she had it all second hand. She worried this lull was a temporary reprieve and her life was about to enter a new, but not necessarily better, phase.

She rang Pat, imagining his face as she waited for him to answer and left him a message when he didn't. 'I've asked Dermot for tea tonight. Shall we tell him together?'

~ * ~

Dermot loved it when Jenny was angry, the way her mood reflected in her eyes, which became darker the angrier she was. Was it this that first attracted him? he wasn't sure now. Or, perhaps it was her infectious laugh when he caught her looking at him that had encouraged him enough to hope. Over some things, though, she was unmovable and he liked that about her too. 'Ah go on it's not often my own sister invites me for a meal.'

'Actually, Dermot,' she changed her tune from the brusque no. 'My dad has forbidden me after that late night. He'll make me give up the job altogether if I'm not careful. He says I've to study and he's got a point. It doesn't matter for you. You're going nowhere.' And

Jenny turned on her heel and was gone, leaving Dermot with his mouth hanging open.

He gulped for air, wounded and more downcast than he had ever felt in his life. He sloped off to the yard where the sight of the gleaming taxi usually worked its magic. He buffed it half-heartedly then leaned on it, arms folded, and considered driving off somewhere, or simply retreating to his container. Jenny and her ideas of two-bit jobs and her assertion that he was going nowhere had upset him more than the break-in. It was more than wounded pride, almost an epiphany, not that he knew yet. It was more a premonition, a sobering thought, that adulthood would not be when life blossomed but rather when possibilities slowly dwindled. His life and his vision of himself in the world had changed profoundly. His ambitions, his dreams and his hopes especially in regard to Jenny no longer amounted to much.

Rather than slip along to Louise's shop, as he normally would, he decided to ring Pat and let him tell her that he couldn't come for tea. He dialled from the pay phone near the bar, keeping his voice low so Jenny would not hear him.

'Not to worry, Dermot, the meal will keep or I'll enjoy it.' Pat's voice was so steady Dermot was comforted. 'What'll you do, eat at the pub? Not a bad meal at all. Not as good as one of Louise's, mind you. We'll see you the next time and let's make it soon.'

Dermot listened, sorry that he would not now be seeing Pat, but said nothing. Although he was in the habit of visiting Louise at odd hours in the shop, it was unusual for him to contact Pat these days.

'Are you sure you're all right now, Dermot? You're awful quiet.'

'I've been burgled, Pat, has Louise not told you?'

'She never mentioned it, Dermot. Not a word. She only said to expect you for tea and I was looking forward to it. Any damage done? Well, that's something. Who would do a thing like that round here? Some chancer, I suppose. Get yourself some locks and I'll help you fit them. Was much taken? You can come home for the night if you're worried, anytime.'

'Thanks, Pat, I'll bear it in mind.'

By the time he rang off, Dermot felt better; the Pat Effect, he called it. When Pat said something, it meant something. His word was firm as his handshake. That first touch and you felt perhaps you were tapping into a life force. If he could bottle it, all the parents of all the teenagers in the country would want to buy it and he'd make a fortune.

He hadn't liked Pat, not at all, not at first. He'd been too strict when Dermot had a mind to run wild. At thirteen, when Pat was first on the scene, he'd known it all. Pat had brought him back from the brink. Lucky Pat was more a mechanic than a holy-Joe or by now he'd probably be studying for the priesthood instead of driving the taxi.

Of all the pleasurable aspects of his current job, driving for Mr Hennessy was Dermot's absolute favourite. It was as if Mr Hennessy invented errands simply to give Dermot an excuse to drive the taxi. Apart from as yet very occasional trips to the airport there were essentials Hennessy simply could not do without that Dermot must pick up or drop off for him that necessitated the taxi in tiptop condition. Luckily, Dermot's second most favourite activity was tinkering with the engine and polishing the bodywork. He went back to the yard and set to with his cloth, buffing the bodywork till he was satisfied he could see himself in it.

'You certainly love that thing, Dermot.' Jenny was leaning in the doorway watching him. He smiled, glad to see her smile back. 'Did I hear you've been burgled, sure that's awful. Who'd do that to you? Did they take much stuff?'

Dermot did not take her to task for listening in to his conversation, rather he was glad of her concern. 'I don't have much stuff to take, Jenny, and I can think of only one person for sure,' and Dermot let his eyes rise to the window of the bedroom where Joe Kelly was staying. 'It was personal stuff. I can't think why an outsider would be interested in it unless it was for kicks or something, but then he's a bit old for that.'

Jenny nodded as if she agreed wholeheartedly. 'The boss wants you anyway,' she said, 'he's an errand for you.'

Dermot threw down the cloth he'd been using and managed, for Jenny's sake, to keep his delight low key. 'I better go and see what he wants. By the way, I'm sorry I was late this morning, Jenny, you know that.'

'Sure, I do. I was just grouchy. My dad was getting at me and I hadn't enough sleep, staying up all hours with himself there,' and she gestured over her shoulder back into the pub. 'I'm sorry too, about tonight, but really my dad would kill me. I'll make it up to you.'

'Actually, Jenny, there is something you could do.' It came to him in a flash and Dermot lowered his voice, conspiratorially and whispered, mouthing the words clearly. She was incensed, stepping back from him and hissing, 'I'm not doing your dirty work for you.'

'All I'm asking is for you to keep your eyes open while you're cleaning the room. Is that so much to ask?'

'Yes. It is. I'm not a spy.'

'Ok, I'll have to do it myself. But if I'm caught I won't be able to explain it.'

'If you're right, you'd be justified and he won't be able to say anything.'

'That's why I could do with you scouting it out for me.'

'Oh, for God's sake, Dermot.'

'Does that mean yes?' And Dermot smiled, genuinely delighted. He leaned forward and kissed her cheek about to say thank you, but the words were lost in the surprise of the sweet smell of her and the soft and gentle swish of her hair falling over him like delicate a silk scarf.

'What colour is it?'

'There's two. They're both small, the size of a large postcard, and one is thick with photos. They would fit in a pocket.'

'You can't expect me to go through his pockets.'

'I was only describing the size.'

'Well, I'm not promising anything. You do realise if I'm caught, I don't want the sack and Hennessy would never sack you. You're his blue-eyed boy.'

'If you see anything, and you tip me the wink, nobody's any the wiser, except us. There is one other thing.'

'You must be joking,' Jenny gave him a hearty shove and went back inside.

'You can't blame a man for trying,' Dermot followed her inside.

'Want a bet?'

In no time Dermot was relaxing into the drive, listening to the purr of the engine sweetly tuned by his own fair hand. He had never thought of himself as the blue-eyed boy. He knew Hennessy liked him though, why else had he given him the job and given in over the taxi? He had a lot to think about, and Jenny was wrong. He had already come a long way and just maybe had a long way still to go.

Ever since Pat married his sister life had begun to look up. For as long as he could remember there was just Louise and him. 'Just you and me kid,' she used to say, but he never fully believed that because there was Driscoll. Sadly, however much Dermot loved him, Driscoll was not good father material. Pat was a much better role model. This thought had only recently occurred to him but Dermot knew he owed Pat a lot.

Like the day Pat said, you want a car? You can have one. This was not a response to expect when you were in a cell for joy riding, alongside five other miscreants. When the guard had locked them all up, all five of them, each one in a separate cell, none of them had taken it seriously. The severity of the man had made them snicker, calling out to each other, egging each other on,

Honeymoon

even as they cooled their heels in the cells.

None of them had money, just long, hot Saturdays with nothing to do. After Micky'd had a scrap with Doolan, blood spurting from his nose and Doolan cursing and dragging himself off to the dunes and Dermot had tried to stop them and got a black eye for his pains, Micky said he had a plan. Five of them walked over the fields to the town fifteen miles off, hot and complaining, jogging and jostling through long switch grass grown knee-high, insects gnawing great holes in them till thirst was all there was left.

The car, brash and convertible was out of place outside the long terrace of houses all the same. They lusted after it, wanted to stroke it, stand by it, possess it. Dermot saw the keys in the gutter just by the front wheel and had the driver's door open and had slipped quietly into the driver's seat checking the mirrors for any signs of trouble, before any of them knew it. They went whooping and hollering, sitting up on the back and lurching the car, screeching the gears. Not one of them had the least idea how to drive. Not one of them had ever sat behind the wheel of a pedal car never mind a real one, an oversight that could be overlooked. How hard could it be? Jasus, even their mothers could do it. The tank was half full, they could go on for miles, so they all had a go once they'd worked out how to change gears and avoid the walls of quiet back lanes that provided enough protection to stop them being detected for hours.

Pat and Louise had come for him from the cell and he thought he was in for it for sure, a pasting, grounding, hours of community service. Pat vouched for him and said it would not happen again. He bargained that it was a first offence, which technically it was. He'd never been caught or found out, and certainly wasn't about to confess to anything. Pat had a way of looking at you that made you expect better of yourself. Dermot wished he could market that too.

He'd stood truculent and defensive with his friends, his fellow joyriders and their parents, angry fathers, simpering mothers. He was well out of that lot. At least with Louise you were one step removed. She cared, but not enough to belt you. Only one of the five was hangdog and that was because of the red weals discernible under the short sleeves of his shirt that certainly hadn't been there before his father arrived. Most fathers round here thought with their fists first. Dermot was lucky it wasn't his own father picking him up. But then Driscoll wouldn't have bothered coming at all. He had more important things to do with his time. If Dermot wanted to waste his own at the age of thirteen then that was up to him. The self-same argument Driscoll had used ever since Dermot was a small chap and could first remember. At least Driscoll knew how old he was. Every time he got into trouble, Driscoll kept abreast of his age, he could say that of him.

Pat was good as his word. The very next day a rust heap spluttered at the end their street. Louise never said a word. Dermot laughed out loud and thought Pat had played a trick on him but after a while, he'd not been able to resist. The smell of oil, and old leather, twisting the wheel, he'd loved everything about the car. He even loved the engine. Most of all he loved being beside Pat, the two of them quiet and easy under the bonnet or lying on oil-stained cardboard under the car and copying Pat wiping his hands with an oily rag. Dermot had always had big dreams and Pat always believed in him and the rest, as they say. The rest of them were on the dole.

~ * ~

At first, Rosie walked only where she could see the picnic basket marking the spot like a red full stop, to-ing and fro-ing in front of the house expecting Fergal to come out anytime soon. Gradually she was bolder and gave up her vigil. She headed for the thicket, striding out where there was still a path and clambering through undergrowth when there was not, almost enjoying herself, except she was on her own. Distant blooms and water shimmering through trees enticed her ever deeper into the wilderness of the garden, a prowling presence protecting the house. Rampant roses collapsed under their weight in a tangle of thorny limbs. Rhododendrons, grown to vast trees, competed on the climb to the sky. Crimson and deep purple blooms floated high above everything, early and unseasonable in the heat.

She had nothing with her; no pockets in her dress or the jersey round her shoulders. Even her shoes, though flat, were not practical. But the day was hot enough and the overhung garden was patched with bright sunshine where she could linger if she felt cool or gloomy. It never occurred to her that the grounds were so extensive that she could get lost. When she remembered to look at the time, she found she had forgotten her watch.

A dappled lake reached to a distant, tapering point. Trees dipped their trailing fronds. A family of ducks pottered near the bank, one lifting noisily, momentarily reflected in the water, rose into the sky then landed with a splash, only slowing once it hit the surface, making the water lap briskly against the stony banks. She kicked off her shoes and stepped out in the shallows. The water, though green, was crystal clear. The surface undulated as the sun caught it, with geometric patterns like Native American art and swirled about her, moving darkly away across the whole lake. Small fish darted, disappearing where the lakebed fell sharply. There was a growing stillness as if everywhere held its breath. No one and nothing moved. Perhaps Fergal swam here as a boy. She wanted to swim. Fergal would have to wait for her.

She folded her dress neatly on top of her shoes, a petticoat followed. She had intended to swim in her underwear but, entranced by the beauty and stillness of the place, removed that too, tucking it out of sight with her clothes under a bush. She launched herself into the water and a great silver arc pushed out ahead of her. She gasped at the sudden coldness of the deeper water away from the sun-warmed shallows and struggled breathlessly to find her footing. Then as her body chilled and she exerted herself, she found exquisite pleasure and basked like a water creature. Her body gleaming white under the green peaty surfaces seemed not to belong to her. To and fro she swam, emptying her mind, sometimes in the shadows of overhanging willows where the lake was deep and mysterious, sometimes on her back in more open water feeling the sun's rays warm her. Her fingers were quite puckered when she thought she should get out but then she heard someone coming. She lurked under the willows and hung on one of the lower branches treading water. She cursed her nakedness and waited. It would be just her luck if they had come for a whole day's fishing. She shrank close to the bank as Joe Kelly, near running, came towards her. His face grew out of proportion the nearer he came and the more dishevelled he looked, almost like a tramp.

When she felt it was safe, she clambered out and hurried into her clothes struggling as they stuck to her cold wet skin. She twisted her wet hair wringing water from it but still it dripped down her back and she shivered. She lunged along the path heading away from Joe Kelly, striding out to get warm and dry, but stopped after a while, realising it led deeper into the garden and retraced her steps. She made several abortive forays into the undergrowth with no confidence she was going in the right direction and always turned back to her start point leaving her disoriented. Time seemed to get away from her and she felt it must be quite late, everywhere so gloom-laden as if the day itself had waned. Fergal must be wondering about her.

Alone and chilled, she started at every noise and there were so many. She pictured wild boars in the shadows, eyes and faces on the bark of every tree. She was quite angry. If she'd had her phone, she would have rung Hugo, defender, dragon slayer. I'm lost, I've lost Fergal and it's my honeymoon. How he would have laughed. He would trot out the story at every family event and they would all have a jolly time at her expense. She laughed, come on old girl, you're making an absolute ass of yourself, the type of laugh attempting to feel sorry for herself produced in her family. She took a deep breath, looked at the sky and decided to go in the direction of the scudding clouds, remembering tracking games played with Hugo who'd delighted in terrifying her. Finally, she emerged wet and tousled from a thicket onto a broad path and came face to face with Joe Kelly, who looked as startled as she was.

'Oh,' she said, 'I'm just, well.'

He laughed and held out his hand, slightly mocking, 'Well I'm just Joe Kelly.' His hand was dry and fleshy, a hand like her father's, a hand with authority you would immediately trust. Only the eyes gave him away.

'I'm Rosie.' She hesitated before adding her new surname. 'Pierce.'

He attempted a joke, 'Don't tell me,' his voice reminded her of bees, 'a newlywed, just getting used to your name.' She did not want to simper, but she did; a silly girlish laugh as this older man made gentle fun of her. 'So, where's the lucky man, then?' Joe Kelly's eyes studied her, unashamed and penetrating, till she was uncomfortable.

'I left him by the house and now I'm not sure which way that is.'

Joe Kelly laughed and offered her his arm. 'So, he

lets you out of his sight, does he? I'd be delighted to escort you.'

She did not take his arm but felt Joe Kelly expected some response. 'We're staying in the village,' she said, 'I might have seen you.' They walked on in silence until they came to the front of the house, an air of melancholy in its faded beauty.

'Well, here we are. Sad to see the place like this, don't you think?' Joe Kelly said. She was non-committal, never having known it. They made their way towards the picnic basket, forlorn on the terrace. There was no sign of Fergal; she had pictured him waiting for her with a welcoming kiss.

'Thank you for...'

'Will you be...' She and Joe both stopped with a laugh. She insisted he go first and he shrugged. 'Well, it was nice to meet you, Rosie Pierce. Perhaps see you around.' Joe gave her arm a little squeeze. 'That man of yours should take better care of you.' There was a moment's hesitation when she wondered if he expected her to invite him to stay and perhaps share the picnic. Then he walked away. She watched the sprig of greying hair that bounced as he walked till he disappeared back the way he had come.

Embarrassed by Fergal's absence, as if it was a fault of hers that her husband of a week had abandoned her on their honeymoon, she did not call out, not wanting Joe Kelly or anyone else to hear her. She ambled round to the back of the house, thinking to look for Fergal. Brambles snagged her feet drawing pinpricks of blood and she cursed under her breath. On the point of going back to the cottage without him, Fergal burst urgently out of the house a yard or so in front of her, bent double to get through a low entrance. She did not have time to call out or reach and catch him before an old man emerged too. Both disappeared to the front of the house, Fergal full pelt with the old man following more slowly behind him. She went after them.

Fergal was still running, stopping only to sweep up the picnic basket, and kept running, without a backward glance, down the drive. The old man watched then hawked and spat on the ground. The gesture so revolted Rosie that when the old man turned and began to make his way back to the side of the house she melted into the shadows, hoping she had not been seen. She watched as he began to replace wooden slats that were leant against the wall, banging them in place with a curved fist. Wizened and wiry, her idea of a leprechaun, there was something about him Rosie wasn't sure of, perhaps too because Fergal had been hell-bent on getting away from him.

Finally, he disappeared to the front of the house and she crept forward brushing the slats with her hand. One fell loose. Had it not, she might simply have trudged back to the cottage, angry and dispirited. As it was, she prised loose another and another, exposing enough of the door to try the handle, catching her breath when the door opened easily. What had they been doing in the ruined house? And why was Fergal running away? She let herself in, in spite of misgivings. Perhaps there was something Fergal had missed in his desperation to get away that she could find. A large torch rested just inside and she smiled at the good fortune. Its beam gave her slight courage.

Rooms with and without ceilings, with and without floors, with and without furniture, some still with wallpaper falling in great arcs off the wall. Plaster crumpled to the floor startling her as it fell, as if the house was alert with memories, wanting her to notice. She stood on what remained of a kitchen floor. In places the quarry tiles had collapsed a good six inches as the floor beneath them had subsided.

A large dresser was built onto one wall, covered in dust and what looked like verdigris as if it had been under the sea for a thousand years. Made of shivered timbers washed ashore from one of many wrecks or ancient sessile oak, felled by axe and elbow grease, a labourer spitting on his hands to harden them or, fallen ripped from the ground after a night of high winds. It had a song to sing, a song of the ages, a song of the deep if only she could hear it. She rested both hands on it sensing life ingrained, willing truth from one of the house's oldest surviving inhabitants. It had been under stress, ravaged by time like some old hag who'd spent her life to excess and needed a makeover, new teeth, new hair, new skin. The wood was pockmarked, riddled with wormholes and nail holes and peep holes, splits and gnarls. It had lost all the blush and beauty of its youth, abused by the passing of years. Yet to her it was also beautiful, for its survival, its solid warm feel to the touch as if it remembered days of sunshine and roses. Her fingers lingered where the wood was whittled away as if by a cat sharpening its claws; a cat Fergal may have stroked. She opened the dresser doors, imagining bright china plates the family might have used but there was only a brick from the wall behind that had worked its way loose and lay in a pile of black soot.

She shone the torch deep inside the house. Its beam, casting worrying shadows, rested on an old stairway, a beautiful helix reaching up and up. She wondered what had happened to the furniture and all the stuff there must have been for a family with small boys. It occurred to her that the house had been stripped, pillaged and emptied over the years. Her scalp tingled uncomfortably. Something awful had taken place in this house, she could feel it. Keeping her back against the flaking wall as if afraid someone would come up behind her she made slow progress. Her heart pounded in her throat and she faltered. What was she hoping to find anyway? What if she was expecting a baby and the house collapsed around her? She retraced her steps fast down the long corridor and out into the daylight.

She hurried down the drive in the darkening afternoon and a sense of sadness weighed heavily. At least, she had seen inside. Once in the lane, she could see Fergal a little way ahead lolling against the wall, nudging the basket with alternate knees as if tapping out a tune.

'There you are at last,' he said as she drew close as if he had been waiting for her all day. She opened her mouth to reply, not knowing how to explain the enormity of her anger and disappointment at spending the day without him, and shut it as Dermot and his taxi cruised alongside almost as if he'd been expecting them.

Honeymoon

He wound down the window.

'I'm going back if you care for a lift?' Fergal refused. Rosie accepted.

'I've walked enough for one day. See you back there,' and she took the picnic basket from him, swinging it into his legs and climbed into the front seat beside Dermot.

'That hurt,' Fergal said, rubbing his shins.

'Good. It was meant to,' and she slammed the door. Then as if she hadn't said nearly enough she wound down the window and shouted, 'What the hell are you playing at, Fergal?'

Dermot raised his eyebrows and exhaled loudly, 'Ho, Missus.' He set off at a crawl till he was sure Fergal was not going to join them, glancing a few times in the mirror. Rosie told Dermot not to bother waiting and made a point of turning to look at the straggling Fergal.

'Lover's tiff?' Dermot said, 'go easy on him now.'

Rosie had a mind to be short with Dermot, but he made her laugh. Besides, she wasn't annoyed with him. She began to enjoy the taxi ride, grateful to be sitting down after the day's exertion. 'So, is this your holiday job?' Rosie assumed everyone's life was like her own. After school, there were part-time jobs you actually liked and college, not necessarily to work hard for a qualification, merely to please your parents and pass a couple of years or so until you were a proper grown up and had to start your career.

'No,' Dermot hesitated as if making up his mind whether or not to be insulted. 'I could tell you a load of shite that I run my own business with the taxi and everything and you'd probably believe me. I'm almost my own boss. As for college? It never came up. I'm from here and I work in the local bar. That's what I do. And the taxi, of course.'

Rosie thought perhaps she'd hit a raw nerve. 'I didn't mean anything by the question, just making conversation, that's all.'

'It's ok Missus. Don't give it a moment's thought. I wasn't any good at school so no one ever talked about college.'

Rosie was sorry she'd mentioned it. 'It's not all it's cracked up to be. It opens your eyes, I suppose, but working does that, or travelling.'

'I've never left these shores,' Dermot said.

Rosie stayed quiet glancing occasionally at Dermot's handsome profile and wondered about him. She pictured him being truculent at school and flunking exams. She'd had enough re-sits after all, and even Hugo. Perhaps with the same advantages as Hugo, Dermot'd be a high flyer too.

Dermot stopped the taxi at the pub, springing round to open the door for Rosie. 'Thank you,' she said, then remembered, 'I've no money on me, can we settle up later?'

'That's all right, Missus,' Dermot grinned broadly, 'I was coming anyway.'

She gave him a cheery wave. 'Call me Rosie.'

Rosie put the basket on the table, at a loss what to do now. She assumed Fergal would be back and would either be apologetic or angry. She tapped her fingers on the foil packets, remembering the intimate picnic the day before and realised she was hungry but did not want to eat. She went to the bedroom to look for her watch and flung herself on the bed, thinking she would read, but couldn't concentrate. Her phone had no signal so she couldn't send messages. She tried breathing deeply.

A list began to form in her head of practical things. She found her notebook and made columns each with a heading: facts, ideas, and to-do. All the lists were short, even the fragments of Fergal's past she already knew, names and dates of the deaths on the tombstones, the name of Fergal's orphanage, St. Dominic's or was it St. Francis? She would have to check that. She did not even know if Fergal had a birth certificate. Well, that would be easy to get a copy of even if the original was lost. She tapped her pencil against the page. Colonel and Lady Gopsill, she said aloud then wrote it down, sure it would lead somewhere. Then she wrote chemist under the to-do list. When she saw Fergal coming along the street, abandoned the list and rushed downstairs to greet him.

'That was a disaster of a day,' Fergal said looking at her from under his eyebrows like a dog in trouble.

'Oh, I don't know,' she said. Fergal asked her if she would like a cup of tea. 'Is that an apology?' She raised her eyebrows.

'No, I just wondered if you wanted tea?'

And somehow, they were amused and mollified. They willed each other to make up and understand. 'Why didn't you wait for me?' Rosie asked.

Fergal was contrite. 'You were so long I thought you must have gone already.'

'You big liar! You didn't give me a second thought. You were in the house all the time; I saw you fly out and the leprechaun who came after you. I was there, Fergal.'

Fergal hung his head. 'Don't tease me, Rosie, not about this.'

'Ok, but he was very old.' Fergal pulled her onto his lap and put his arms round her.

She told him of her swim. 'You should have come,' she said, 'it was wonderful.'

'I can't swim. It was my brother who loved it. It used to terrify me.'

'I thought you said you swam in the lake every day.'

'We weren't made to swim every day,' he paused for effect, 'only every other,' and Fergal laughed.

Rosie put her arms round his neck. 'Oh, you poor thing.'

'Pale, small and shivering in yellow seersucker bathers, dodging the great silver arc of water as my grandfather and my brother dived in. *Make a man of yourself.* He was always encouraging. I never learned to swim so I obviously never made a man of myself.'

Rosie ran her fingers through his hair and was tempted to flatter him. *You're man enough for me,* but she was still rather cross with him.

'I have this mental picture of my grandfather after a noisy, thrashing swim with my brother, striding out of the water growing taller with every stride till he stood way over me, then he would wash me considerately at the water's edge with carbolic soap and a rough cloth. He was always gentle. He never mocked, although my brother did.'

'Why don't you say his name?'

'Who?'

She smiled at him, 'Your brother. You keep saying, my brother.' It was as if she had broken a spell.

Fergal exhaled deeply, not quite a sigh, and then he stood up and tipped her off his lap, and said dismissively, 'Lorcan. Lorcan, then.'

She imagined it was the pain of the loss of his twin that still troubled him and that she would, over time, be able to help him, so she changed the subject and said brightly, 'You haven't told me what you did today.'

'Nothing much.' Fergal sounded even glummer and, although she was reluctant to admit it, as if he was wallowing.

'Why was it a disaster then?'

'Well, that's just a figure of speech.'

'Honestly, Fergal, I give up.' To Rosie, used to her open, uncomplicated brother, it just seemed Fergal wasn't trying. His long silences that might eventually have produced some clue to understanding his inner turmoil, some nugget of information, seemed like peevishness or sulking to her and she left him to it.

It was only Fergal who went to the pub that night. 'I'm sorry about before,' he said on his way out. 'I've a lot on my mind.'

'Isn't that when people talk to each other?' Rosie said.

'I can't explain this.'

'You could try.'

'I just can't talk about it, not yet.'

'Not ever, you mean,' she said, although she was not looking for an argument.

'Don't give up on me, Rosie'

There was a pleading tone in his voice that she did not like, or perhaps it was just the phrase that rankled. 'You'd better go if you're going.' She let exasperation sound in her voice, not even looking at him as he hesitated at the door and was glad when she heard him close it behind him. Then she was sorry that she hadn't been a tad more sympathetic. She knew his hopes rested on the house. Finding it in that state must have hurt.

In the bedroom, the peace of the white sheets and whitewashed walls was welcoming. She had no desire for anything but sleep. She thought of the enchanted princess who slept for a thousand years, and wondered if 'enchanted' was the chivalric term for 'up the duff'? A thousand years suddenly did not seem nearly enough to get rid of this heavy feeling. She lay on her back across the middle of the bed resting the flat of her left hand between protruding hipbones; there was nothing to say she was pregnant. She turned the warm gold wedding ring between her fingers and sighed. Somehow it had felt courageous to have stood out against her family and married Fergal. Except for Hugo, Hugo was Fergal's friend, backslapping, pints in their hands, boys together friend. Hugo was warmth and security. That was what love felt like, not this rollercoaster, never being quite sure, kaleidoscope of moods. Any slight twist and Fergal reassembled differently. It was all the same pieces; he just showed something totally different to her, a new facet. Perhaps she was emotionally stunted, one-sided, flat. She wondered if by simply getting on a plane and going back to London, even Hackney, running a bath, filling it with expensive bubbles and lying there in candlelight, if everything would simply go away. It was a technique she had mastered through several fleeting love affairs, all of which had petered out.

The memory of her great aunt's doom-laden voice disturbed her as she tried to drift off to sleep. *Marry in haste – you don't know him from Adam – barge pole and don't touch…if you want my advice.* Round and round till she was no longer sure if she was awake or dreaming, till she no longer had any idea of what love was. She could only find out by loving someone. Anyway, what gave them the right to make decisions for her over who she should love or shouldn't? And besides, it seemed after all, there was someone illustrious in the family; a colonel and a lady. She got up and stood under the shower for longer than was necessary, letting hot water wash everything away.

Swathed in towels she got under the covers then found her place in her book, sniffed the bookmark that she had drenched in her favourite perfume – the one Hugo wore – and felt reassured. Within minutes her eyes were heavy and she was aware the book slipped from her grasp and she was asleep with the light on, a dim, energy-saving light bulb that would glow incandescent after a few hours. It pierced her dreams and she was awake under the muslin canopy, and alone. She could tell by the cold echoing feel of the little house that it was empty but for her. She glanced at the clock at the bedside: it was two in the morning. Should she get up and wander the streets looking for him? Perhaps Fergal had been in a brawl or had fallen asleep in the pub. Most likely he was living it large with musicians and pretty Jenny in the bar.

She went to make a cup of tea and took it back to bed, a vast bed in a tiny room. Outside the street glistened wet under a street light but the pub was in darkness. She lay down and did not fancy the tea after all. She turned out the light. The skylight was black, the night cloudy. She thought of Fergal being walloped in the orphanage. She thought of two identical boys gazing at stars with their grandfather. She thought of Fergal shivering at the water's edge where she had swum. She thought of her unkindness, *you'd better go if you're going*.

~ * ~

Fergal's head swelled with freedom songs and laments, as music rose and died on successive waves of chatting and cigarette smoke. A woman next to him at the bar raised her lips to his ear, removing an ash-laden fag from her mouth. 'It's utterly illegal, of course, but the landlord's my brother, so there has to be peace in the house.' Fergal watched the ash droop and fall into a pool of beer beside the ashtray. 'You should put in a request,' the woman's lips were at his ear and her breasts were soft on his arm but he did not move away. He wondered if he should offer to buy her a drink. 'You're new here.' It felt almost an accusation.

'Taking a break, you know.'

'No one comes here by accident.'

'I'm looking up my family tree.' He adopted Rosie's

explanation, solid and respectable and it seemed to satisfy the woman.

'Driscoll's yer man for the history, he's old as the hills. He'll be lurking out there somewhere.'

He made to get up, he should tell this gem to Rosie, creep into the double bed beside her, feel the warmth of her and the cold sheets on his cheeks, but the woman had not finished with him yet. Her nicotined fingers manacled his arm as he tried to leave.

She pulled him closer and tapped the side of her nose, 'The landlord doesn't let him in. An old quarrel he never forgave, that's what he tells anyone who asks. Ask me and I'll give you the truth.'

He sensed tension in the air round him as if what she said was of interest to them all. It was only when he inadvertently spilled beer on her, trying to prise her off, that she released him. 'Look what ya did to me shoes, ya gobshite.'

He leaned against a wall, outside in the dark, sliding down to a squat, head pounding, his stomach hollowed out, feeling as he used to outside Mass with no breakfast inside him on bleak Sunday mornings. The cigarette smoke had given him a headache, blurring his focus till he was no longer sure he had a focus. He steadied himself after the encounter with the woman and wondered if it was a mistake to be here, a mistake to unleash the past. Perhaps it was too much to ask Rosie to understand. He thought of his fruitless search of the house, the neat pile of slatted wood propped against the side wall and cursed. Of course, there was someone in there. Of course, the house would already have been searched. What did he expect after all this time?

Someone spoke and breath, sharp enough to strip paint at a distance, seared his nostrils. The voice lilted incongruously, the sound of gentle wind through trees. Fergal could see the man's outline beside him, see the red dot of his cigarette and when the pub door opened with a whoosh of noise and light, he could see the glint of his teeth.

'It's Driscoll,' the man said. 'Let's go where they won't be watching.'

Fergal allowed himself to be led away, stumbling now and then on the uneven street, ignoring the coincidence that Driscoll even knew where to find him. 'We'll go to my place.'

The sound of the sea grew loud as if they were walking straight out into the incoming tide. The air was wet with spume. White waves dazzled when the moon rose and there was a cottage half camouflaged in the sand.

A lamp was lit and the splash of liquid into glass followed the sound of wooden chairs dragged over stone. Driscoll invited him to sit and handed him a glass, 'This'll sort you.' Driscoll did not sit down but began to sift the contents of a large wooden chest.

Fergal wondered at the mystery of this encounter, why the old man had not simply come into the pub till he remembered the old woman's secret. Then it occurred to him, 'Was that you up at the house today? You gave me a fright.'

'Scared the bejesus out of you, more like.' Driscoll

turned briefly to look at Fergal then continued scrabbling in the wooden chest, laughing long and low. He had one of those faces so gnarled by life, a body so wiry with overuse it would be hard to put an age to him. Perhaps he had lived here forever, an old man and the sea. Fergal looked furtively at his watch, it was late and Driscoll showed no sign of being ready soon. He thought of Rosie and hoped she was safely asleep and grew impatient to hear what the old man had to say. 'So, you know the old house then?'

'I did.' That was all. Then the glasses were being filled again from a flagon and finally the old man drew his chair near and sat down with him. 'I knew you'd needta see these one day.' He brandished a fistful of papers, newspaper cuttings and old photos that continued to rustle with the tremor of his hand.

'How do you know who I am?' Fergal said.

'The likeness is all over you,' Driscoll continued. 'Like your mother, God rest her.'

Fergal shook his head slowly, 'I don't have any memories or photos of her.'

'Well, no,' Driscoll placed a hand on his shoulder, 'no indeed.'

The gentle voice had slowed to a mere drip. Was this old man ever going to say anything straight out? Fergal wanted confirmation. He felt his whole life depended on facts. 'I just need the truth; I need to know who I am.'

'It's a woise man who knows that. And only a fool who'll try to tell it you.'

Fergal had to laugh. He repeated the word to

himself, woise, woise; a mixture of ways and wise; someone who knows the ways of the world. He felt the drink cut through him, knowing his ways and making its way straight to the heart of him. The voice lapped over him and he almost had the sense that who he was or had been no longer mattered.

THREE

Pretend: make it appear that something is the case when in fact it is not.
Of a child: an imaginative game.
Comes after
Pretence: an attempt to make something that is not the case, appear true.

Departed: dead deceased.
Comes after
Depart: leave, especially to start a journey; do something different from a usual course of action.

Despicable: deserving hatred and contempt.
Comes after
Desperation: a state of despair, especially resulting in extreme behaviour.

At the height of his desperation, 'despicable' became Granda's favourite word.

'It's despicable to leave a cat destitute, never mind an old man, the myrmidon. The house does not run at all. Dishes pile high in the kitchen and food is scarce.'

Force: strong pressure on someone to do something backed by the use or threat of violence.

Comes after
Forbidding: appearing threatening.
Foray: spirited attempt to become involved in a new activity.
Comes after
Forasmuch as: since.

The situation was forbidding forasmuch as it could not be forborne. That's egregious. Look that up, I dare you. It comes along with ego trip.

Leave me alone, why don't you?

With the usual forbearance and all the force he could muster, Granda sent Mystique on forays outdoors. Forasmuch as Mystique was not inclined to leave the house, in the normal run of things, he went, but his heart wasn't in it.

Neither Mystique nor Granda were the sort to leave the house.

If Mystique had not been so old he might have caught something for himself, instead, he licked the dishes in the kitchen and he and Granda became weedy.

That any better?

The heart's gone out of me.
I think I'm going to die.

Everyone's going to die. I'll look after you.
You always say that.
And isn't that what I always do?

I don't want to write for my living anymore, it's too painful.

Let's forage, there must be something left.
There's nothing left.

Granda searched the house, his voice echoing in empty rooms, 'In the name of all that's holy what could be keeping him so long?'
He prowled and scowled with the cat in his arms, hoping to find a source of food in one of the long forgotten rooms.

DAY THREE

Louise put the remains of the meal lovingly prepared for Dermot's visit in the fridge. Still, Pat had appreciated a mid-week roast dinner and the bottle of wine they hadn't quite managed to finish between the two of them.

She spoke to herself as she laid the table for breakfast, spooned out Pat's boiled egg and put an egg cosy over it. 'Well Dermot, we'll have to think of something else'. Perhaps she should go into the pub, walk the short way down the back lane and ask to speak to him in private. 'Dermot this is important and it won't wait'…face up to it as she'd had with Pat. She could even visit him in the tin can. That way she could find out about the burglary for herself. The missing album puzzled her. She had the family albums on her bookcase and none of them were missing. She'd checked.

She hardly noticed Pat come in. 'Aren't you having eggs this morning?' Pat registered his disappointment that Louise had not laid herself a place.

'It's such a fine day Pat, I think I'll walk over to Dermot's and check on him after his place was burgled.'

Pat hesitated, his teaspoon poised mid-air, 'I don't think it's fair to tell him just before he goes to work, if that was what you were thinking.' He put the spoon back on his plate and the yolk congealed as it cooled. 'A thing like that might need some getting used to.' Pat came to put his arms round her shoulder, his tone gentle and conciliatory. 'Do you want me to walk over there with you?'

Louise liked the way he included himself in the responsibility of telling Dermot. 'I wasn't going to mention anything. I only want to find out about the photos he's had stolen.' She released herself from his embrace, turning her back to wash a cup in the sink.

Pat sat down but did not eat his breakfast, 'You've done your best by him, you know.'

'I'll go anyway,' she sniffed. 'I thought about nothing else last night.' Her back turned resolutely towards him as she prepared to leave, prevented further comment.

Honeymoon

Louise had never visited Dermot in his container, never clambered the steep sand dunes to find the sheltered hollow where it had come to rest. Dermot had asked her many times, but she'd always found excuses, maintaining she disapproved of him living there and leaving it to Pat to help make it habitable except for a patchwork quilt she made him for his bed. Her real objection was the necessity of passing Driscoll's shack, something she hadn't done since the day she and her mother had walked out.

Close to, the crumbling shack, sheltered by its huge boulders, was a shock. Even more of a shock to realise that the old man bent over a trap to release a rabbit was Driscoll himself, his hair blown in white wisps on the early breeze. A long time had passed since they'd seen each other, let alone spoken. Their unwritten pact to keep out of the other's way for the sake of peace had been an art form in such a small village, reliant on Dermot to act as go-between. When she drew level with him, he looked up with an expression of utter surprise.

'You visiting me?'

'No,' she said, adding after a slight pause, seeing what she thought was a fleeting look of disappointment. 'Not that I'm not pleased to see you; I was going to visit Dermot.'

'He's at my place because of the break-in, waiting for locks so he feels safe at night. I'm letting him have a lie-in.'

'Oh.'

'He reckons it's Joe Kelly,' Driscoll said. Louise started. Driscoll clicked his tongue adding tersely, 'Done the burglary,' as if he hated to be misunderstood rather than reluctant to cause unnecessary pain. 'Dermot reckons it was Joe Kelly.' This accusation was almost worse.

'He's no proof who it was. What's he got to steal anyway? Where did this missing album come from? I thought I had all the albums at the house.'

'For a grown woman, you can be very naïve.'

'What's that supposed to mean?' she snapped, then relented. 'I've not come for a fight, or to rake up old history.'

'Old history has come to you though.' He spoke softly under his breath. 'No good ever comes of deceit.'

Tears threatened, of anger, of impotence. She bit her lip till it hurt, but still they came and she accused him, deciding attack was her best defence, 'Says you.' His quietness unnerved her.

'Your mother and I did what we thought best at the time for you and the baby.'

'You mean you discussed it?'

'Of course, we did. We were man and wife.'

Louise was conscious of herself standing beside Driscoll outside his shack and suddenly in danger of being engulfed by the unexpected reappearance of Joe Kelly and memories of all that went before. She did not want to think of those terrible days of losing Joe and finding she was pregnant.

'We loved each other in our way,' Driscoll continued, his voice no more than a murmur.

Honeymoon

'That's not how I remember it.' She tossed her head, a habit developed as a girl for keeping unruly hair out of her eyes.

'No?' His voice was so soft.

'You were a drunk.' Her sharp reply was like throwing acid in his face. She raised her hands as if she would take back the comment, but saw the pain she caused and wanted to inflict more, hating herself and Driscoll.

There was a pause as if both sides were gathering ammunition but Driscoll was not in fighting mood; mellowed with time and no longer drunk, Louise hardly knew him. 'This'll get us nowhere,' he said, and he pointed to the house with his chin. 'Do you want to be on your own and see your son?' Driscoll was very gentle, 'I've to walk to the water's edge with the rabbit, or I can do it later.'

Louise felt her nerve drain away and her limbs weaken. 'My son,' she repeated, 'my son,' savouring aloud the words denied her for twenty years. Driscoll put his hand out to steady her, laying it lightly on her shoulder. She had no memory of his touch. She looked at the steely arm connecting him to her and stared hard into his face, 'Have you told him?'

'No, Louise, I have not, nor would I but on the whole, I think we should have.'

She hung her head, 'All right.'

He mistook her meaning. 'Come in then. You might have to wake him. I'll make a cup of tea.' Driscoll did not immediately lead the way into the shack, but looked down at the dead rabbit and nudged it with his foot. 'There is something I should tell you first. God knows I meant to, but now with the guy back in town.' Air squeezed out of Louise and sounded like a groan, but Driscoll persisted. 'First, let me tell you I'm sorry.'

Louise couldn't imagine what her father was going to say. She was impatient with him, feeling his apology like a millstone. She did not want it; it had come too late. 'For God's sake,' a flash of anger made her face flare. 'Don't say another word.'

Driscoll looked surprised then folded his bottom lip over the top, sticking it out as if he really was buttoning it. Louise was fit to blow and instead of going to find Dermot she stomped off, grinding her heels into the sand, talking out loud and gesticulating into the wind. 'God deliver me, he would be one thing less. Between the pair of them my whole life is ruined. If I never saw him again it would be too soon.'

When she got to her part of the beach, her favourite place to think, she was too angry to sit down. Angry too that she hadn't listened to what Driscoll had to say, hadn't even asked after him, struck by how old and ill he looked: a changed man. Her gaze turned to the horizon where the new day flecked the sky fiery red. A warning, she thought. She turned away and walked back to the village.

She let herself into her shop pausing to inhale the sweet mix of perfumed soaps and chemicals. Her hands were shaking as she reached for her mobile to tell Pat of the latest development, but she put her phone away, squared her shoulders, made herself tea and toast and sat till she felt stronger. Reliving the past was not

Honeymoon

helpful, she knew. This was her life and until two days ago, she had been delighted with the way things were, even though she knew she had been living a lie.

She wiped her mouth for traces of crumbs with her fingers, straightened her skirt and put on her brightest smile. Fake it till you make it. Wasn't Dermot fond of telling her?

~ * ~

A sliver of sunshine fell across Fergal's eyes and he winced, drew himself up to sitting and looked for Rosie.

'You awake at last?' she said. 'Were you very late back? I didn't hear a thing.' She climbed back into bed, 'You look pretty rough.' Fergal rubbed a hand over his face but did not speak. 'Sorry I didn't come with you last night, I needed the sleep I think.' Rosie held out a cup to him, not pausing for breath. 'Look what the pub sent us. I was so hungry earlier but then I thought it would be a pity if we didn't enjoy it together, so I waited.' She settled herself with a basket of croissants, now cold but still sweet smelling and continued to ply Fergal with questions, undeterred when he didn't answer. 'What are all the cuttings and photos downstairs?'

As if suddenly come to life, Fergal banged his cup on the table beside him, spilling a little coffee, leaped from the bed and reached the bathroom in two strides.

'Oh, are you all right, Fergal?'

He groaned. 'Shut the door, can't you.'

It was difficult enough being a newlywed suddenly faced with the enormity of parenthood, without having to listen to the result of Fergal's excesses of the night before. Convinced he'd been knocking back the hard stuff with newfound mates she took herself and the breakfast back downstairs, settling at the table with a sigh. This was not quite what she'd had in mind for her whirlwind romance ending at the altar. Half-baked notions from love stories in women's magazines no way prepared her for what was going on in the bathroom and the intimacy of living so close to another person, which could only get worse if she was having a baby. She tried to imagine being mumsy, with beached-whale-breasts full of sweet-smelling milk, sour nappies, bottles of formula and shuddered. She dipped a chocolate croissant into her second cup of coffee and forgave herself the indulgence. This was not quite the cosy breakfast she had pictured either, but she might as well enjoy it.

She flicked through the pile of papers disorganised on the table and uncovered a stash of photographs amid the newspaper cuttings, some black and white, some sepia even. Small boys in identical gabardines with belts over round tummies, played on the lawn in front of a grand house while an adult in a long apron, a faithful retainer perhaps, leaned on a long-handled rake amid vast piles of fallen leaves. She peered at the small faces of the boys, wishing she had a magnifying glass to identify one as Fergal. There was no way of telling. It was definitely the house though.

Upstairs, Fergal groaned in the bathroom. Poor Fergal. Putting the photos aside in a neat pile, she started on the newspaper cuttings. Someone had taken the trouble to write the date on each one and highlight headlines. BODIES FOUND. How gruesome.

She sat up to give the account of Aidan Pierce's death her full attention. The loss of his wife in childbirth, seven years previously, was cited as a major factor. Suicide? It seemed his body had lain in the upstairs of the house while his children and his father, unaware and unable to cope, had slowly starved. How could a father do that in the full knowledge that his own children, his own father, would find him? It did not make sense to her. Yet in another clipping, the verdict was Aidan had died of a heart attack. Either way, his death caused such catastrophe for the young children waiting to be rescued with the decaying body in the house.

One child died as a consequence. She let the words sink in. No wonder Fergal had cried in the churchyard. No wonder his mind had tried to blank that. Enough trauma to disturb anyone or emotionally scar them for life. She thought of the flowers on the neat grave; this had not been forgotten, not by the person who tended the grave nor by whoever's collection these papers were, perhaps not by Fergal either, whatever he maintained.

A small cutting fell out as she was straightening all the papers. Fisherman drowns. Joseph Kelly's body was found washed up on the beach and a verdict of death by misadventure returned by the coroner. It seemed drink was Joseph's undoing. Bruises to his upper arms and those on his face and hands were not cause for suspicion, explained away by the action of the cruel sea. The date of the article had again been highlighted.

Joseph Kelly's body was discovered barely a week after Aidan Pierce's. Rosie felt cold. The coincidence was too great for the second Joe Kelly to be here by mere chance. She knew she didn't trust him. Deaths such as these, in so small a place, must have affected them all. Even twenty years after, there must be someone who remembered. There must be someone to ask.

The cottage was very quiet. She made her way upstairs, relieved Fergal was still in the bathroom. She ought to take a look at him but imagined hideous smells that she simply couldn't stomach, 'You all right Fergal?' she asked quietly, thankful he didn't answer. She pictured him, head in hands, fallen asleep on the lavatory and decided he would be best left alone. She dressed hurriedly, in need of a stiff walk to digest two breakfasts and all she had found out. She straightened the bed, discovered Fergal's jacket scrunched between the mattress and the wall and instead of hanging it on the back of the door she put it on, rolled the sleeves back and hugged it around her. She left a note. Gone for a walk, not even calling out again, not even letting him know where she was going. She didn't want to wait for him and she was sure, if he knew, he would want to come with her. Besides, there were things she could find out on her own.

The street was deserted and so quiet that the tap-tap of a woodpecker was the loudest noise. The bird's insistence seemed auspicious, alerting her or calling for her attention. What if Joe Kelly's father had been murdered? Or Fergal's? What if the whole village had covered up what had happened? She shuddered, imagining Hugo's disapproving raised eyebrow, *don't be so bloody melodramatic.* Her misgivings, as yet no stronger than the tap of a woodpecker's beak, were real enough.

The door to the chemists opened with such a loud and jovial jingle that Rosie jolted. No one came to serve her, however. She studied herself in the mirrored walls amid the gold letters that announced the pharmacy reflected several ways from the shop window. A woman's voice called from the back, 'Just a moment.'

Rosie waited, but still no one came. She looked into baskets of reduced items placed round the counter that gave the shop an old, fusty feel when really it was white and modern and smelled efficient. She stood by the glass counter, drawn to an assortment of soft toys piled high on top. The corner of a book, grubby and out of place, was just visible under a blue bear. She teased it forward to sneak a look, sensing the ingrained pattern in the stained leather cover under her fingers. She flicked the first few pages releasing a smell of earth and decay and her eye snagged on hand-written phrases. *I kissed her fingertips and put my rough fingers over them on her belly, not a belly yet, no sign of the lives growing there. Her flesh was warm to the touch: fertile: like land in sunshine.*

A door at the back opened, a woman inched backwards into the shop dragging a box behind her, giving Rosie time to thrust the book back where it had been under the toys, suffusing her with an uncomfortable heat, caught spying on intimate secrets, accused by her own reflection. She glanced anxiously over her shoulder to the street in case she had been observed, turning back, flustered, to the waiting eyes of the woman ready to serve her on the other side of the glass counter who smiled and held out her hand.

'I'm Louise McCann,' and she tilted her head at the lettering in the window. 'You were in the pub a night back with the young tenor.' Rosie took her hand, slightly puzzled, feeling almost like a celebrity, yet relieved her indiscretion with the book had not been noticed. 'We don't get many visitors and it's such a small place, so there's no hiding. They're trying to encourage tourists in rural communities. Although with the weather we have, not the last couple of days obviously. You've been lucky there. The weather can be wet and windy anytime on a small island in the Atlantic.'

'I think I read about that,' Rosie murmured, her face still locked in its initial smile. She remembered the woman too, how tenderly she had loosened the top button of her husband's shirt in the pub and thought she might be just the person to confide in and wondered where best to start.

'I expect it's in all the brochures. There's no point getting people's hopes up. The sky is always on the ground. Was there something you wanted?' Louise flashed Rosie a truly bright smile and finally, her hand was released.

'I'm Rosie Pierce and I'd like something for a hangover.'

'Pleased to meet you.' A box was produced from beneath the counter, in one practised move. 'You just add water and you can have up to six sachets a day, no alcohol of course. For your young man, is it?'

Rosie took a deep breath, 'Fergal. Yes. I think he. Fergal Pierce.' That did not come out as Rosie had planned. 'He used to live here when he was a boy.' The enormity of what she had already discovered about the Pierce family and the sudden change of expression on Louise's face overwhelmed her and she gave up, assuming from Louise's silence that Fergal's name meant nothing to her. 'There is one other thing,' Rosie said, relieved to see Louise's face soften. 'Do you have such things as pregnancy tests?'

Louise brightened, 'We do. In fact, we have the full Monty. A lot of the women don't want the palaver of taking the kit home so we have the facility to do it here, a nice private room at the back. Well, two rooms actually, if you count the bathroom, and there's no charge, it's just a service. Could I interest you in that?'

Rosie's reservations that she ought to be with Fergal dissipated as Louise, an obvious authority, lifted the end flap of the counter and ushered her to the small, clinically clean facility at the back of the shop.

Louise half drew the curtains over the window that looked out at the blank wall of a passageway, reached a box from a cupboard placed it on the small white painted table and patted it a couple of times. The doorbell jangled and Louise sighed in disappointment. 'Now who can that be when I wasn't expecting anybody?' She backed towards the door still talking. 'I could have made you tea only now there's someone. I'll lock the door for you but there's no need.' She gave a slight apologetic shrug of her shoulders, flicked the snick and closed the door behind her.

Rosie scowled at the box for quite some time as if it was an adversary, her mother even. Being pregnant would bring her inexorably back to her family, having finally successfully navigated away from them on the waters of life. She slid her arms out of Fergal's jacket, suddenly sweaty and slung it on the back of the wooden chair before seizing the box, tearing off the cellophane on the way to the bathroom and waiting stoically for the result.

She studied herself in the mirror, adjusting to the new order. 'You're pregnant,' she told herself sternly. She practised her brave smile, her enigmatic smile and imagined herself telling Hugo. *Hugo, ask me if I've any news.* And he would never guess. He'd say, *Go on then, what?* in his exasperated tone when he didn't really mean it. His mouth would turn down at the corners in mock horror. *You R? How will you ever cope?*

She felt a stab of conscience followed by a wave of guilt as if she was actually passing judgement. She ran cold water over her wrists. Her face was quite flushed and she splashed that too and dried it slowly on a paper towel. Fergal. She should rush back and tell him. She went back for Fergal's jacket and put it on. Tears pricked her eyes. She wiped them roughly on the cuffs and sat on the edge of the chair till she felt more composed.

Aware she had been a long time in the back room, she imagined Louise listening at the door wondering if she had let herself out through the window to the passage beyond. Maybe that wasn't such a bad idea. The shop was so quiet maybe Louise had let herself out, fed up with waiting. She unlocked the door as silently as she could and tiptoed back to the shop. Louise stood with her arms folded gazing through the shop window, 'Pushy bastard,' she said under her breath.

'Sorry?' Rosie said.

Louise spun round surprised to see her. 'Oh, not you.' She nodded to the street and the retreating figure whose greying hair bounced as he walked as if it had been combed the wrong way.

'He always was pushy, when I think, so it's no surprise.'

Rosie raised her eyebrows questioningly, 'Joe Kelly?'

'You know him?'

'No, not really. It's just everywhere I go we seem to bump into each other.'

'Oh?' Louise looked closely at her, 'Says he left something in my shop and could he take a look. For God's sake! He stepped in for all of two minutes a day ago and he wants to ransack the place.'

Rosie felt a fleeting disappointment that perhaps the grubby notebook under the pile of soft toys must belong to Joe Kelly.

'He's been away half a lifetime and he expects to pick up where he left off.' Louise opened the door for Rosie. 'Sure, you don't want all the domestic details, I'm sorry.'

They held each other's gaze, a moment of recognition for Rosie, gazing into the infinite blue depths of Louise's eyes, that here was a woman who might understand, who might know of Fergal's past.

'I don't suppose you know who tends the graves do you?' she faltered.

'What?' The limpid pools froze over and Rosie, losing her nerve somewhat began her garbled tale.

'We were at the churchyard yesterday to look for the grave. You see that's why we're here really, to find out about the past. There were fresh flowers there, so I wondered who put them there and if they could help fill in some of the details. Fergal was such a small boy when it happened, he can't quite remember.'

Louise had no idea, each to his own perhaps, but she was sure it was a custom here not to leave a child's grave untended. She supposed Rosie could find out if she asked around and suggested people at the pub might know.

Rosie smiled her thanks and still felt the need to explain. 'You see, we're not tourists in the ordinary sense and, although we are just married, it's not a honeymoon in the ordinary sense either.' And saying that, the crushing disappointment of her expectations of a honeymoon and the momentous discovery that she was expecting a baby caused her to dissolve into tears.

'Why don't you come back in and have that cup of tea? We'll put the sign up so we won't be disturbed. You can tell me all about it.'

Rosie allowed herself to be shepherded, mothered, humoured even. She imagined Louise was overjoyed to have someone new to talk to; she was certainly a good talker. For once, Rosie was quite unguarded, saying far more than she meant to. She bit back tears. 'It's really unfair. No one gets caught the first time. We were supposed to be waiting for the wedding,' Rosie smiled shyly at Louise, then wailed, 'I must be two months pregnant already.'

'Well, at least you have a husband to take care of you.' Louise patted her hand soothingly, noting the well-manicured, blood red nails. 'Drink your tea, you'll feel better. It is a shock, finding out.' Louise nodded so sympathetically Rosie felt she understood perfectly. She took a mouthful of tea and managed a brave smile.

'Do you have children?'

Louise sighed. 'In a manner of speaking.'

Rosie laughed. So, Louise told her a version of the truth omitting the part about underage sex, and being jilted by a lover all before she was fifteen.

That Louise had had sole charge of Dermot when he was barely three years old and she was still a teenager, having to work enormously hard to achieve what she had, deeply impressed Rosie. She was dimly aware that her life in London seemed brittle by comparison. She considered herself lucky, never having had to strive for anything. Not even for Fergal, if she stopped to think about it, who'd been presented to her by Hugo. Perhaps she was feckless, but then she had never been put to the test, so she couldn't be sure.

Despondent after what seemed like hours that she was no further forward in regard to Fergal's history, she made her excuses, thanked Louise for her kindness and promised to come back before they flew home.

~ * ~

Fergal's eyelashes brushed against cold white tiles of the

bathroom. His teeth had left painful bite marks in his knee. He must have been out cold for some time, bent double on the lavatory. His tongue felt too large for his mouth and tasted of sewers. A sewer rat, he thought. Everything was numb, except his brain. That throbbed, making him feel nauseous as if he'd been poisoned.

He did not want to be found like this. He struggled to lock the door just reachable from where he sat and climbed into the bath and ran the scalding shower. His brain thudded against his skull. He opened his mouth and let water stream away the taste of whatever Driscoll had given him, glass after wretched glass, hoping it would cleanse him of all he'd learned last night. The long-wanted facts were no consolation. He longed to exhale the truth, lurking and tingling his tongue, and let it escape through his tired jaw. He clenched his teeth as he'd done in the orphanage to keep secrets no one wanted to hear.

Once dressed, he felt almost human. What was left of the coffee was stone cold but he drank it anyway. Nothing was left of the basket of pastries except a few crumbs, which he stuck to a licked finger and ate, then wished he hadn't. He sat for a moment looking out of the window till the wave of nausea was gone.

He relived the day at the house, remembering his panic and Rosie coming down the lane towards him. Rosie, the sun in her hair, the beauty of her stepping out in the long grass, the swish of butterfly wings as she brushed past them, almost a ghost herself with the sun behind her; contemplating asking her help to search the house for his missing evidence but the clout to his legs with the picnic basket had brought him back with a painful bump, *What the hell are you playing at, Fergal?* A mistake to bring her here, he knew that now. He didn't blame Rosie for going out. In fact, he wouldn't blame her for leaving him, he half expected her to. But he had to find the notebook.

All the years he had cursed himself for leaving it behind, all the years he had promised himself the satisfaction of holding it in his hands. He had been so sure. How could he have got it wrong? A trick of the mind perhaps, it was so long ago now and there were, after all, several hiding places for two small boys in a rambling house with no one to supervise. When he'd known he was to be sent away, he'd run through the house as if wild horses were chasing him, but it was not escape he was after, it was retrieval. He'd been caught too soon and held kicking and biting and packed off like a wild animal in a cage. He needed the notebook to make sense of himself. It was all that was left to say who he really was.

Then it came to him; he could go back to the house now, calmly and search those other places. The house was key to his memories and he was desperate to get there and breathe in the old air, tear off the slats that kept out the light from his old home, see what he could find, what he could remember. He ran out into the street letting the door slam behind him running towards the path he knew so well.

A man sauntered in front of him and Fergal slowed his pace, not sure whether to catch up. There was something so familiar about him, the way he walked, the way he held himself, the way his hair bounced. Then he had it. His memory snapped back, like a secret compartment in a desk and revealed a secret. The boy who used to hurt them, the big boy who twisted their arms and gave sly pinches, leaving black bruises like police thumbprints, who always found them in whatever remote spot of the grounds they were playing. Or, when they'd be engrossed writing and the boy would materialise as if he'd been watching them and demand to see what they had written. It was only because there were two of them and could outwit him in spite of his size and ferocious fingers that he'd never ended up with their notebook.

Fergal lurked behind his former tormentor but twigs cracked under his feet and Joe Kelly turned round and waited for him, apparently not recognising him. He held out his hand, 'How's it going? I'm Joe Kelly.'

'I'm Fergal, pleased to meet you.' There was no flicker of memory from Joe Kelly. Why would he recognise him, a child he'd bullied?

'You're the guy on honeymoon always detached from the lovely bride.' And as Joe Kelly laughed, Fergal lowered his eyelashes like a portcullis to guard against further attack. Their father had once whispered to them both, 'I don't like him either,' as if he knew without having to be told. They had never breathed a word of their torment or their fear and only a few times had to suffer him as he stood in the kitchen, as lugubrious Father Malachi extolled his virtues to their grandfather. So here he was, almost avuncular in his sharp suit, a fine actor, or else his own memory a clean slate. His hair, always a distinguishing feature, had given him away.

When they got near the house Fergal stopped, anxious to prevent Joe Kelly deciding to come with him. 'Perhaps see you in the bar tonight,' he said and held out his hand.

'Righto.' Joe Kelly stood, elbows wide, both hands in the pockets of his trousers. He pulled them out almost as if he would produce something, then took Fergal's hand in both his and held it, looking Fergal earnestly in the eyes, till Fergal suspected that after all, he would have a full-blown apology out here in the wild garden.

'Why don't I call by the cottage and have a drink?'

Fergal almost laughed at the offer he couldn't refuse, 'Yes, why don't you? That'll be grand.' He retrieved his hand, put it in his trouser pocket, wiped it surreptitiously and waited for Joe Kelly to walk off.

When Fergal neared the house he still felt Joe's eyes watching him, but not for anything would he turn round and look. He set about tearing off slats from several of the lower windows, breaking into a breathless sweat to keep his mind off Joe Kelly. The slats covering the door were stacked against the wall as they had been the day before; entry was easy.

There was a torch inside the door that he had not noticed the day before. The beam dulled as he stopped at the doorway to each room, lingering, feasting his eyes or closing them, willing memories to come. Drawn into the kitchen, he breathed in the earthy dank of the once warm and welcoming room. He flung open the doors of the vast dresser built into the fabric of one wall. It struck him that the dresser had been systematically stripped of its riches. How enticing the gold painted china had looked, even to a small boy, in the glow of the range. There had been a row of teapots along the top. Now there was nothing to glitter, just dust and droppings.

His knees clicked as he squatted to delve into the dresser and into the past. An image of his smaller self came to him, fingers damp with black cobwebs, nails scuffed, using both hands to rock a loose brick in the back from side to side till he had enough purchase to pull it free to reveal their secret hiding place and grasp the prized notebook. The brick lay loose on the floor of the dresser; it fitted easily in the fingers of one hand. The hole in the wall was empty; the notebook had already been removed. Someone else must have it now. He shut his eyes against the disappointment.

He had hoped to lay a ghost from a close written world locked in the pages of a notebook he'd dreamed of since childhood with the turbulent other language, muted but clear in the labyrinth of his mind. Words were the clue to his unravelling, escaping in the fluidity of his life. Only facts could free him. He reeled from the kitchen, deeper into the house, cobwebs and memories thick about him.

He opened the door to the bedroom he used to share with his twin. Light from the torch did little to dispel the gloom but he pictured exactly the neat division of their possessions, the rows of shoes and folded clothes all lined up either side of the room as if each had marked their own territory. In the middle of the room had been the large double bed. He thought of the iron frame and the shadows it cast on the wall like bars and their game of pretending they were in a prison cell. Then he thought of the loose floorboard underneath it and edged forward gingerly where he hardly dared put his weight in case the floor would not hold him. On his hands and knees, he felt for the knot he knew was there that fitted a small finger and made it possible to lift the long plank. He flailed his hand inside finding nothing and was again momentarily a small boy feverishly hiding scribbled notes.

Once, they had found their grandfather on his knees prodding under their bed with his stick and they had crept up and knelt down beside him giving him such a start that he raised his stick at them as they fell about laughing. They had assumed he'd been fishing for the cat, Mystique.

Their grandfather had had his rooms on the same floor, a large airy bedroom with an interconnecting door to a heavily draped sitting room with its own fireplace. It was to here they had retreated when Aidan disappeared, those endless days of that other lifetime. Perhaps it was for warmth that they stayed in these upstairs rooms. Perhaps their grandfather was afraid. Fergal supposed no preparation would have been made for the sudden disappearance of his father and their grandfather had been incapable of running the house with two small boys, incapable even of looking after himself.

Aidan had had the top floor to himself, one room rolling into another, into another. It had seemed a vast and wonderful place, festooned with books and posters, and flamboyant scarves that must have been his mother's. They were allowed the run of it, when they weren't outside, as long as they were quiet. That was all Aidan asked of them. They had gorged on books to the backdrop of the fast tap-tap of their father's typewriter. In his memory, his father was hardly ever away from it and when he was, he had a pen and notebook in his hand. Fergal hesitated on the threshold, half expecting to see Aidan's ghost look up with an absent-minded smile, aware too that there had been someone else here the day before, perhaps even Driscoll, someone who had taken all there was to take. He flung back the door and light flooded across the floor from the row of long windows.

It felt a minor victory, to have been in this house, to have reclaimed it. It made him want to laugh out loud and cry at the same time. The house, though not as he remembered, was at least still there. It belonged to him, though its contents, some of which he still hungered for, had gone.

He found a sheltered spot in the garden wilderness and lay back with his head in his hands nursing his triumph and disappointment. He gazed up through the intricate patterning of leaves and branches from overhanging trees and emptied his mind into the gaps. He was neither asleep nor fully awake and when he came to himself after perhaps half an hour or even longer, he knew for sure what he would do.

He ran with long, easy strides, his feet slapping the sand, feeling the stretch in his lungs and his thighs. His shoes in his hands felt like oars speeding him forward.

On and on he ran as he used to with his brother. It felt good to run as he hadn't run for years. Then, as his breath laboured and his lungs were fit to burst he slowed to a dogged pace, breathless and sweating by the time he reached Driscoll's shack. He found Driscoll sitting outside on an old easy chair sheltered by the wall.

'I was wondering how long it would take you to come back,' Driscoll said. Fergal leaned forward, hands on knees to get his breath, before wiping the soles of his feet on his jeans and replacing his shoes.

'I've been to the house.'

'Thought you might,' Driscoll said. 'That's why I've stayed away. Didn't want to frighten you any more than necessary.'

Fergal ignored his laugh, squared his shoulders and inhaled deeply. 'I expect you could tell me why the house is empty?'

Driscoll's lower lip jutted out, coming to rest over his top lip, with alarming elasticity. 'You better come inside,' he said.

Fergal took in the room. In daylight it looked disconsolate, like the old house, as if no one owned it. Apart from a couple of upright chairs and the chest that had held the papers, there was nothing, no pictures on the walls, no personal effects, as if Driscoll was moving out. Fergal thought to ask but was too anxious to find his own possessions.

Driscoll sat on one of his upright chairs and invited Fergal to do the same with a slight nod of his chin. His fingers picked at the hem of his shirt and he began to make little sucking noises as if he lubricated his gums.

Fergal assumed he was preparing an answer. Driscoll took off his shirt discarding it on the floor. He wore a clean singlet exposing a pigeon chest and a few sparse grey hairs. 'Hot,' Driscoll offered in explanation. He rested his hands on his knees, his arms stretched like rope, sinuous and strong, without an ounce of spare flesh.

He was, Fergal thought, no bigger than a child, or perhaps a leprechaun. His jeans, gathered at the waist with orange bailer twine, had been cut short and fringed as if they had been meant for someone much bigger. Driscoll tucked his feet behind him, crossing his ankles so the ancient sandals he wore slipped to the floor with a slight slap. The unpleasant smell that clung to Driscoll the night before, that Fergal couldn't help but notice, was thankfully much fainter.

Driscoll stared defiantly, 'What did you have in mind?'

Fergal held his gaze. 'What about the personal things…clothes, books, you know?'

'I can't vouch for all of it but I expect much is still in the village.' Driscoll cleared his throat emptying the content into his well-used handkerchief and began to talk as if he'd rehearsed it. 'For a couple of years, everyone kept their distance from the house. Then when it looked like no one was going to turn up and claim it, a few of us helped ourselves and took furniture to sell. It was Hennessy at the pub put a stop to it. He saw to the emptying of the house, sold off larger items that would anyway have gone to ruin as the house began to crumble and banked the proceeds. Some of which was used for repairs and kept the roof up for a while. As far as I know, some money may still be in the bank.'

Fergal had to restrain the impulse to interrupt, waiting for him to finish with a rising sense of hopelessness, 'There's a notebook I want. It's important to me. I don't really care about the rest.'

Driscoll fumbled in his pockets for the stiff handkerchief and wiped his nose very thoroughly and the little sucking noises began again. His head nodded up and down and from side to side like one of those toy animals people have in their cars. 'Like, I said much of it may still be in the village.' There was a long pause. Fergal assessed this information and did not suspect Driscoll of being evasive.

'Do you have any more questions?' Driscoll said at last. When Fergal said no, Driscoll insisted, 'I'd like to tell you though, now you've had a chance to see the reports. I thought the story would be buried with me after all these years and not a word.' Driscoll touched Fergal's hand with his fingers as if he asked his permission.

'No one knew Aidan was dead and no one even knew he was missing except for the old man and the two small boys. Even at the height of his desperation, it would never have occurred to the old man to send for help.' Driscoll looked intently at Fergal. 'If the priest hadn't paid a call, because Aidan had missed Mass, you might not be here either. Probably just after his money, although he was in the habit of calling in for a little chat with the old man in Irish. The day Father Malachi finally came, there was no sweet smell of peat on the fire to mask the terrible damp and make up for the buckets and leaks and the lukewarm tea kept going on a great range for days on end. There wasn't a hint of the niceties he was used to either, no farls or cakes, nothing of that nature.

'Malachi went running from the house calling for the Gardaí. He sent for whomever he could think: the man from the social, the woman from the orphanage, the local judge, the medic, me. If you hadn't been sent for, you were no one. He called on everyone in the Holy Family to bless them and save them: The Lord, the Sweet Mother of God, Jesus, Mary and Joseph, all the Angels and Saints in Heaven, but by then it was too late. No one answered his prayers. He trembled. He had never seen the like and that was not from want of looking or from a sheltered past. This event was truly unsurpassed. Come Holy Spirit. The whole world came too late to the rescue.

'There was a great furore in the village because of the boy who died, the whole village felt responsible for that. They did what they thought best. They obfuscated, let grief disintegrate amid lies and whispers and denied what they had seen, denied that by omission they had a part in it. There were recriminations and rumours but by then the trail had gone cold, birds had flown. No one ever knew what had happened, except your father and those who'd fled.'

Suddenly Fergal burst out, 'Don't you see? Don't you? I must have killed my brother, eaten all the food there was in order to survive.'

'No, Fergal, no.' Driscoll put a steadying hand on his

shoulder, 'There's no evidence of that, nothing like that anywhere. You were just a child.'

Fergal's head sank on his arms.

'Never put that on yourself. Good Lord above.' Driscoll's voice was thick and low as if his throat pained him. 'Is that what they taught you in England, a godless, cruel country.' Driscoll rocked him gently, slowly, forward and back, patting his back perhaps to drum sense into him. 'You were always the stronger of the two. You were a little devil and Lorcan was born small. You mothered him yourself. If anything, you will have given him your food.' Fergal stayed with Driscoll's arms around him, his cheek grazed against the sparse hairs on Driscoll's chest, unable to speak, unable for the moment to lift his head as if lost in his own world.

'There now, Driscoll said, releasing his hold. He offered Fergal a drink of the beastly stuff of that first night. When Fergal refused he poured himself one, raising the glass before downing the contents, although not in celebration.

~ * ~

Rosie was undecided which to do first. Tell her news – their news, she corrected herself, hand Fergal the fluid replacement weighing down her pocket, or take herself off to the beach. In a moment's hesitation under the blank bedroom window, so brief it was all but imperceptible, she decided to tell the news. She hugged herself with her arms, suddenly chilly. The cottage had the empty, echoing feel of the night before. Rosie placed her small packet of fluid replacement on the table for Fergal. She climbed the stairs to the peaceful bedroom. The cuttings lay exposed on the bed like a game of patience as Fergal must have left them. A coincidence she decided, rather than a symbolic or deeply meaningful display. She hovered, picking up papers and scanning them half-heartedly. She was in no mood to study them again. Too restless to wait for Fergal she needed air and headed back to the beach.

Sand stretched way out to the distant sea, its surface shifting with the wind whipped her face, sticking to her eyes, wet with wind tears. She left her shoes by the log and strode to the sea's edge, feeling the sand blasting her shins, its soft graze between her toes, and the surge of cold water, gulls calling on the wind. Rosie cast the facts on the water to roll like stones along the seabed with the creatures of the deep, burrowing into the good earth whence they came. Maybe no one would ever know what had taken place in the house but she would do her best to find out all she could. Establishing the facts might be of some consolation to Fergal and surely the worst had already happened? She loved Fergal. His past was irrelevant to them really, but even she would rather know. The rhythm of the sea lulled and fortified her, firmed her resolve. Now was her chance. She had often wondered, if she were ever called upon to do something, anything heroic, how she would respond. Her life of hoops to be jumped through before beginning for real, waiting on the margins, endless days being stuck inside while the sun was shining, having to sit when she wanted to run, had been to please others. She prepared herself to turn her back on the endless disappointment of her old life starting with something immensely practical and supportive.

She went back purposefully to where she'd left her shoes, stuffing in her feet, sand and all, impatient at the prospect of telling Fergal and about to set off when Joe Kelly appeared beside her, crept up in the blast of the wind and made her jump. 'God, you startled me,' she said, annoyed he should choose to pester her when he had the whole expanse to wander in.

'So I see,' he said, laughing, but did not apologise. 'Mind if I?' and he sat beside her not waiting to find out if she did mind or not.

The wind had made her eyes stream, and her nose run. She sniffed and fished in the pockets of Fergal's jacket for a tissue but there wasn't one. Joe Kelly pressed his handkerchief on her, a folded square of white linen, putting both his hands on hers, 'You're far too pretty to cry.'

You're far too old to flirt with me. She managed a dry laugh that she felt was lost on him. She used his handkerchief, blowing into it loud and hard. 'It's just the wind, anyway,' she said, as she handed it back. Joe Kelly waved it away.

There was a pause. He leaned forward with his elbows on his knees and stared openly. 'Still on your own, then?' his high-pitched, girlish laugh surprised her. She did not want to betray Fergal. Oh yes. He was vomiting into the lavatory after a heavy night and I wasn't with him then either and now I've no idea where he is. She was angry but it was not Joe Kelly's fault. 'He's having a lie in,' she said finally.

'Is that so?' Joe smiled wolfishly and she thought she could tell what he was thinking and it made her blush. She gazed out to the distant sea until she was calmer, feeling his eyes on her still. It was not, as he was hinting, a maidenly blush after a night of passion that would necessitate a lover having a lie in. Nor yet was it the regret that this unconventional honeymoon had involved no such exertion. It was because she was beside this stranger who made semi-lewd suggestions and she had let it pass. Today was not a day for battles after all.

'I saw a newspaper cutting about your father,' she said, 'at least I guess Joseph Kelly was your father.' Joe blinked eyes of steel, mechanical and slow as if he photographed her yet revealed nothing of his inner workings. Rosie explained, 'It's his anniversary, isn't it? He died about this time, I think?' Joe nodded. 'Is that why you're here?'

'Sorry?' Joe said.

'I didn't mean to pry. It seemed a coincidence that we keep meeting and I was curious. I'm sorry,' Rosie said.

'Oh, you needn't be. He's not the reason I'm here.'

'The report said he was a fisherman,' Rosie persisted even though she sensed Joe's discomfort.

'Let's just say he wasn't one of the good guys. He made his living best he could. He did all sorts, including fishing. I'd like to see the cutting if you've still got it.'

'Well, Fergal had it but I'm not sure who gave it to him or if they want it back.'

Joe Kelly smiled, 'It's ok. I think I can guess where it came from. What else did this cutting say? Anything interesting?'

'Not much, it was only short. He drowned, so they recorded death by misadventure.'

'That would sum him up, a life and death of misadventure,' and Joe Kelly laughed mirthlessly.

'I'm sorry,' Rosie said again, beginning to suspect Joe Kelly might need sympathy.

'Like I said, you needn't be.'

'I meant everyone should love their father.'

'In an ideal world, sure.' Joe smiled at her. 'So, you're here for an anniversary too?'

'Honeymoon,' Rosie corrected him.

'Ah yes. You should watch that man of yours, keep him up to the mark or he'll lose you.' Rosie sighed. 'Was that totally predictable?' Joe Kelly said.

'A bit.' She turned to give him a smile. Behind him, at the far end of the beach, a ribbon of smoke curled up. 'Someone's having a bonfire,' she said.

'No,' he said turning to look, 'there's a house if you can call it that. It's more of a shack.'

She looked at the desolate spot way down on the beach, 'And someone lives there?'

He smiled at her. 'Yes, he's like the old man of the sea. He's lived there as long as I can remember.'

Now she was interested, an old man might have memories. She thought of the wizened man she had seen coming out of the house after Fergal. 'A friend of yours?'

'Driscoll? You could say we're old friends getting reacquainted. I've been away twenty years and I've just blown back.'

'Like Fergal.' Again, he gave her a cold stare and she felt she had revealed more than she should have. She stood up to go and Joe Kelly stood up too.

'I'll walk you back,' he said, 'I'm going that way.'

'No, no.' The idea appalled her. 'I'm not ready to leave the beach yet,' she lied and hoped he would take the hint.

'Tell me,' he said, putting his hand on her arm and she wondered what on earth was coming, 'You've been in the chemist's this morning. I wonder did you see a small notebook anywhere?' Rosie could not have been more surprised if he'd hit her.

'Are you watching me or something?'

Joe Kelly was quick to deny it, 'No, no. It's just…'

Rosie interrupted him, 'Well good,' and stomped towards the sea, not looking back or saying goodbye. Angry that Joe Kelly had caught her out, angry at the thought she had been observed without her knowing and as she walked away from him to the sea, angrier still that she had on her best shoes that might be spoilt by the salt water. When she did look back, there was no sign of Joe Kelly but that didn't necessarily mean he wasn't there.

~ * ~

It was not often anyone asked Louise for a pregnancy test and Rosie, a genuine newlywed with sweet childish eyes, was, in fact, one of the few customers to use the

Honeymoon

back rooms that Louise and Pat had thoughtfully refurbished. A hangover cure, that old chestnut! She smiled at Rosie's initial pretence. She prided herself that she was a good judge of character. Louise sold enough of those to the young lads too bashful to ask for condoms. Not Dermot, of course. He never bought either. Perhaps girls had not yet registered with Dermot. God knows she dropped enough hints. Louise used to take the test all the time when she first got married as if merely taking the test would make all the difference. She didn't bother now of course, but she didn't remember it ever taking as long as it took Rosie, but then, her test had never been positive. She had been tempted to tap on the door and ask if everything was ok; an older, wiser woman lending her full support and the wealth of her experience. She understood the enormity of it and an oasis far from the eyes of the world was her way of ensuring as best she could that no one suffered as bleak an experience as she had on first finding out she was expecting. Louise scanned her shop catching sight of herself reflected repeatedly and forgave herself the lapse of professionalism that she had actually put her ear to the door of the back room. There had been no sound at all as if Rosie Pierce had fallen asleep or legged it through the back door without paying.

She thought of Joe Kelly with mild annoyance. He'd got no further than the counter the other day. If he'd put something down, it would be there. A small book stuck out over the edge of the counter. She wondered how she'd missed it. It was so dirty she held it at arm's-length then tentatively put it to her nose. Had Joe Kelly dug it up? She wrapped it in a plastic bag and dropped it in the bin. 'I'm not doing Joe Kelly's dirty work for him,' she told herself and went back to the soft toys, lifting them one by one to dust underneath. Then, deciding they did not look good after all, went to the back of the shop for an empty box and piled in all the toys. All bar two, a pink and a blue elephant, which she left as if in conversation one with the other. Dust collectors! She could just hear her mother saying it.

She wrote on the box in big black letters, SOFT TOYS, then returned the box to the back of the shop.

Louise usually closed for lunch, especially when it was quiet like today, giving herself time to walk to the beach if it was fine or go home and fit in a few chores. Sometimes Dermot joined her so it was no surprise when he let himself in at the back of the shop. His unsmiling, almost sullen face was so unusual Louise was worried. 'Driscoll said you came to find me,' he said.

'I'm going home for a cup of tea and maybe a bite to eat, if you fancy,' she said brightly and linked her arm through his and propelled him along to the house. 'What's it with you?' she asked. 'You're awful glum, now I come to look at you.'

'Jenny thinks I'm a loser and she won't take me seriously.'

'Is that all?' Dermot flashed her a look. She knew that warning sign and softened her tone, 'I mean, why do you want to be taken seriously? You're not even twenty.' True, but he still had feelings.

'And she's not even eighteen, but she's got ambition and she says I haven't.'

Louise clicked her tongue, 'Take no notice what she says. She's just a slip of a girl with ideas.'

'Maybe I should go to college, go travelling, take a gap year,' Dermot said as if thinking aloud. Then he set off grumbling, 'And there's the break-in. You're not in the least bothered. You've not even poked your head around the door the once, so you've no idea. Imagine someone rummaging all your things without your permission.'

The thought of Dermot living rough in the container doing his ablutions in the sea like a backwoodsman or a homeless person, still made Louise uncomfortable. She gave his arm a squeeze 'Well, I would have come today to your old container but you weren't in. And that reminds me, that photo album you said was taken, you haven't got any, I've got them.'

Dermot sighed. They had reached the kitchen and he flopped on a chair and said reluctantly, 'If you must know, I got it from the old house. I've been saving things from ruination.'

Louise gasped, turning back from filling the kettle, 'There's plenty of people would call that stealing, me included.'

Dermot smiled sheepishly. 'Driscoll says the house is a wreck and everything in it is salvage.'

'And he's the world authority on what's legal and what isn't?'

'He knows what he's talking about.'

Louise felt like slapping him. 'Only when it suits him! I suppose his crazy home is full of stolen booty too.'

'That's the funny thing. It used to be Aladdin's cave

but I was in there last night and it's practically empty.'

'Have you two been pillaging the house between you?'

'I've got a few old books, Louise, off the top floor.' Dermot waved his hand dismissively, 'They'd be in a terrible state by now if I hadn't put them somewhere dry.'

'One of the visitors who's here now has come to look at the house. It could even be his house, for all I know. So, get ready to account for yourself.' She looked at him fiercely, leaning the small of her back against the rim of the worktop and folding her arms and he laughed. He got to his feet and hung an arm on her shoulder.

'And one of those visitors, Joe Kelly, broke into my home and took my stuff. So, is that what you came to talk about so early in the morning?'

'You've no proof it was him,' and suddenly exasperated, added, 'this is ridiculous.'

Dermot raised his eyebrows, 'What is?' She inhaled deeply. How much longer could she delay telling him? How many more ways could she imagine it? The words buzzed in her head and, as she let go her breath, she was hardly aware she said them out loud. 'Driscoll isn't your father, he's your grandfather.'

Dermot looked at her strangely. 'That's good. I never knew my grandfather.' There was a pause. Louise cast around for the table or a chair back to hang on to, finding it hard to stand and unable to believe she'd spoken aloud. Dermot's face was ashen as if he'd received a body blow. Any moment he was going to work the rest out for himself. She took a step towards him and with a hand on each of his shoulders, looked intently at him.

'Dermot, I'm trying to tell you. I'm your mother.' He threw his head back and laughed. Her hands slid helplessly to her sides and she waited for him to stop laughing. He looked at her strangely again,

'You're not old enough, for one thing.'

'Just.'

'Oh my God, you're not joking.'

She put her hands up to touch him again, hesitantly, as if he was some delicate creature she might frighten away, 'I'm sorry, Dermot, for not telling you sooner.'

Dermot turned away from her so he almost had his back to her. 'Ho. And I was worrying about a little thing like a break-in.'

Louise pulled his arm, wanting him to turn so she could see his face. Dermot shook her off. She thought he was going to walk away but he didn't. He just groaned as if he was in pain, one curled fist either side his head. Louise stood behind him hardly daring to breathe, aching to reach out and touch him. Dermot groaned again then suddenly spun around, 'Why have you told me now?' He searched her face as if the answer was written there.

'Dermot. I'm so sorry. I didn't love you any less because I pretended to be your sister.' Even to her ears, the words sounded hollow.

'Yeah right.'

'You've every right to be angry.'

Dermot threw his hands up. 'D'you know, Louise,

I'd rather be on my own just now, I don't want to say something we'll both regret.'

Louise could have cried. What did she expect? What else do you get from a lie but heartache? 'Those times were so different, Dermot. Ireland's barely stopped incarcerating unmarried mothers. I don't expect you to understand the shame of illegitimate babies.'

'That's just great, now I'm illegitimate.' He picked up one of the chairs and slammed it back under the table. 'And only an hour ago I had prospects.'

'Oh, Dermot.'

He retreated to the back kitchen and flopped at the table, his head in his hands and Louise followed, collapsing opposite him. The room grew so still she could almost hear silver flecks of dust dropping. The hard seat dug into her legs. Whoever designed it wanted shooting. Whoever bought it deserved the same. She let her eyes follow the swirls of flock wallpaper. Why on earth hadn't they ripped it off when they'd got married? She always meant to do things and never got round to them, let things slide. She had meant to tell Dermot, but silence had come more easily. Dermot sat so still she wondered if he had fallen asleep. She would have to move. She could not sit still any longer. Her legs were dead. As she eased herself forward on the upright chair, trying not to make it creak, Dermot raised his head and looked at her as if he hadn't sat in a stupor, as if today was any other day.

'You putting the kettle on at all, Louise? I think I'll still call you Louise, if you don't mind.'

Louise opened her arms wide and he allowed himself to be hugged. He laid his head on her shoulder, letting it rest there for a while. She wrapped him in her arms until she felt his muscles stiffen and knew he had had enough. She sniffed away tears. Dermot was eerily calm. She had not known what to expect. Not this, she supposed, not this barrier. It was like looking at him through a windowpane and not being able to reach him. He would not allow it.

They waited for the kettle and she offered him cake. How fortunate was that? She had felt like baking the other day, it was soothing, so the tins were still full as Pat hadn't had a chance to find it all. Dermot rummaged in the cake tins, as he always used to.

'There's some of your favourite there, millionaires' shortbread. I made it instead of doing the lotto. It gives about the same odds.' She'd made him laugh, that was good. 'I'll have a piece with you, blow it.'

They moved with their tea and their cake to the table in the kitchen and sat as they had when he was a little boy and she was studying. 'Do you remember that, Dermot? We both always had our heads in a book. And you were such a gorgeous boy.' Louise spoke of everyday things as if to make her news more easily absorbed. 'All the mothers thought you were the bee's' knees. They all wanted one like you. And there was Ma pretending you were hers and all along we knew the truth. We ended up living the lie, I suppose.'

'Did you know that Driscoll always said he doubted I was his?'

'God, no!' she was incensed, 'troublemaker.'

'He said that was why she'd left him in such a hurry.'

'It never would occur to him that she left because he beat her when he had the drink inside him. He knew you were my baby.'

'I don't think she would have left him but for me,' Dermot said slowly.

'Well, that is something we'll never know.' She hesitated then said, 'I love you, Dermot. You were the best thing and leaving Driscoll was the second-best thing in my life. Living with the olds was good. Well, for ages it was. Till granddad started with the you know what.'

'No, what?'

'Dementia. He didn't last long, thank goodness for the rest of us.'

'That's heartless, Louise. I never would have suspected it of you. Not till now, anyway.'

'It's the truth, Dermot. He had a good life and lingering along like that only upsets everyone else.'

'I'll remember that when it's your turn, and I'll shove you in a home.'

'All right, Dermot.'

'And don't say that crap about it's only natural I'm angry.'

The flash of anger like a lightning bolt was a relief, Louise thought, but it usually meant a storm was coming. She bit her cake, letting the chocolate melt in her mouth. Dermot did the same. 'These are good,' he said, 'better than usual.' Their breathing was laboured listening to the sound of each other trying not to make eating noises in the silence. Dermot looked only at his cake. Louise looked only at him. 'Perhaps it's best if I go away,' Dermot spoke quietly.

'Oh, Dermot, don't say that.'

'I was thinking about it anyway.'

'Ah, you were not. You were thinking about your taxi and making a go of it.'

'Well, things change. Besides the taxi's a crap idea. It'll never work in this edge of the world, whatever Hennessy thinks. I feel as if I've been living on the edge for a while. This has pushed me over.'

'Please don't go. Please leave it a good long while before you do.' Dermot had finished his cake and his tea and was about to push away his chair. 'Have another.' She sounded desperate, she knew.

He took another cake. 'This doesn't change anything.'

'What do you mean?' She hoped he meant it didn't change anything between them but she knew that was not what he meant. The way his shoulders slumped and the way he wouldn't look at her, told her all.

'Just because I'm eating cake with you doesn't mean I forgive you.' He stopped and looked directly at her. 'Let me get this straight, somewhere here is a man who doesn't know he's my father?' Louise felt clammy as if she might faint and the words sounded distant in her ears. The cake felt like lard in her mouth and was difficult to swallow. She was unable to stop herself crying, unable to speak for the tears. If only Pat had been there. But then, this was something she had to face on her own.

Dermot was already on his feet, shoving his chair

back underneath the table and looking down at her. 'You do know who my father is, I take it?' Dermot sounded so cruel, so unlike himself, that Louise was shocked and caught her breath as if she'd been winded. Recovering quickly, she was livid. The plate bounced as she threw her cake down; her chair scraped as she jumped to her feet.

'Stop right there! I'm not taking that from my son or my younger brother. You needn't think that just because you're angry and I'm sorry that I'm going to let you start insulting me. You have no right to sit in judgement. No man does.' Louise's temper got the better of her.

'Let's just say, I'll be in touch, hey?' Dermot slammed the door on his way out.

'And that won't solve anything.' She shouted after him although she knew she shouldn't have. She had lost patience with holding her tongue, holding everything in, squashing her life out of shape till she could not breathe, could not be herself as if she'd been corseted in stays. Motherhood had been denied her as surely as if she'd been sterilised; that one tumble in the sand on a moonless night with the waves thrashing in their ears and the fear of God in her.

She had relived it, every last detail over the months, the years, that followed but could never explain why Joe had been in that state that night when normally he was so respectful, so careful of her. What had prompted the desire, the passion? Had he raped her? No. She hesitated. There had been no way of saying no, that was true and it had all happened rather hurriedly, rather fast. She remembered the feeling that her lips were bruised by his and the stubble on his chin as the weight of him dug her into the wet sand grazing her shoulders. She remembered the shock of her white flesh against his brown arms and thighs. She had given in to him, to the fire of his desire, but it had not been her idea. He had not been gentle. They had been courting, that was true. He had kissed her that was true. She had wanted him. What fourteen-year-old girl would not be flattered by the attention of the handsome, older, wiser boy?

Her mother had warned her, 'Those five years Louise, make the difference between a man and a boy. And Joe is a man now. You should just be careful.' She had smiled into her mother's serious face, so careworn and white it looked embroidered and, not understanding what her mother meant, had assured her that everything was fine. She knew the facts of life and no way had they ever done anything like that. They'd only been holding hands up till then.

Sometimes she could still hear the flick of stones against her window waking her. She had been so deep asleep. At first, the sound had been part of her dream. Her mind had incorporated the stones and turned them into animal footsteps and then heavy rain and only then had she realised they were pebbles and she should get up and see. She had slipped out into the night with nothing more than her nightclothes. Had there been a moon she would have glowed like a spirit dancing across the sand in her bare feet. Had her father caught her on the way out; there had been so many what-ifs. Joe had taken her breath away and had run with her, pulling her after him to a quiet place. Not that anywhere is quiet with the tide up, but to a deserted place. Certainly deserted. Stars had made a silver canopy over them. She had shivered but it was not freezing; she remembered that. Then Joe had gone. He did not even walk her back to the house. There was no romantic post-coital hand holding, standing under the stars and promising each other the earth. Perhaps they had slept. She remembered the rush of cold when he had stood up away from her, fumbling with his clothes and hastily putting them back on as if ashamed and wanting to be rid of her as quickly as possible.

Only now did it seem it might not have been anything to do with her. She had assumed that she had done something wrong, something to displease him, as only a young girl can, brought up to please and be subservient and to feel that what people thought of you was the most important. Look where that had got her: without the love of her son. She was sick of going over it now, sick of the years of feverish worry. She had done what her mother thought best at the time. Perhaps parents only act in their own best interest.

She followed Dermot along the alleyway and let herself quietly in at the back of her shop. Perhaps she was the one who should leave, be a mature student somewhere else, sell up, start over. Her head swam at the thought of it so she stopped. Ever practical, she took a duster and rubbed hard at marks that were not there, till the place shone and looking defiantly at her reflection amid the overly grand, gold lettering of her name, she mouthed, 'They can all go boil their heads.'

Slowly a simple plan formed. She would ask Joe

Kelly to leave. He owed her one favour. She retrieved the notebook from the bin and stuffed it into her handbag thinking at least to remove all trace of him.

~ * ~

Jenny collared Dermot at the rear entrance of the pub. 'Oh no you don't, burglary or no burglary. If you play any more stunts like that, disappearing to your sister's when it's my turn for a break.' She barred his path with her arms akimbo.

'Not just now, Jenny.' He turned sideways to get past.

'Don't you 'not just now me' after I did that errand for you.' She stood her ground.

'Oh that,' he said.

'And he was in his room so I had to pretend I'd come about room service.'

Dermot registered her anger and how pretty she looked, but could not muster any expression of thanks, merely stuffed his hands in his pockets. His voice lacked its usual bounce. 'To be honest it wasn't really my stuff, I was just minding it.'

Jenny put a hand on his arm, her white brow puckered. 'Are you ok, Dermot? You look like you've had bad news or something.' Dermot shook his head but did not volunteer any information. 'You look awful actually. I'll leave you in peace and quarrel with you another time about taking advantage.'

Dermot wanted to remain the focus of Jenny's bright eyes for just a little longer. 'It's Driscoll,' he said, wanting also to unburden himself and not knowing where to begin.

'Oh my God, has something happened?'

'You might say so, in a manner of speaking.' Dermot concentrated on moving the toe of his shoe over an imagined blemish on the floor. 'Louise has just told me that Driscoll isn't my father.'

'No way!' She put her head to one side and her curls bobbed, wrinkled her brow, trying to work it out.

'Turns out, he's my grandfather,' Dermot shrugged.

'That's ok then,' Jenny sounded relieved at first as if the transition from father to grandfather was no big deal, until she made the next logical step. 'So, Louise isn't your sister either.'

Dermot shook his head. He studied her face waiting for her to work it out and for the light in her eyes to change. Maybe she would hate him for being illegitimate. She stood very close to him. He sensed the slenderness of her waist under the soft folds of her blouse and he wanted to hold her, kiss her and bury his face in her hair.

'She's your mother, right?' Her voice was soft and sweet and rather than move away she moved closer, both hands on his shoulders, her eyes on him full beam. 'Oh my God, Dermot. Why has it been a secret all these years? You poor man.'

The relief of her concern brought tears to his eyes. She held him in her arms and he knew he would be forever grateful to her for understanding the enormity of this revelation almost even before he knew it himself. His heart broke. Hours before Jenny had destroyed him with her thoughtless comments and now this. Behind him, a door quietly closed. He did not want to look round or stir from the delicious lightness of her arms. 'That was Hennessy,' she whispered. 'He saw us and backed away.'

Dermot raised his head and sniffed, 'The gentle giant.'

Jenny let him go, sliding her hand down his arm and touching her fingers on his. 'I guess you'll get used to it,' she said. Again, her head tilted to one side as if considering him and his plight. 'I've no experience of it, I'm afraid, but it doesn't change who you are, you know, in yourself. Not for me, at any rate.'

Dermot smiled a watery smile. It was as if the ground beneath his feet had opened up so that now he knew he walked along the edge. 'It's hard to know what I feel,' he murmured. 'I've no balance at all.'

'Why don't you tell Hennessy you've had bad news and you need some time to yourself? Clear your head. Walk by the sea a little.'

Dermot's shoulders hunched and he drew in a deep breath and considered this possibility. 'No,' he said at last, 'I'm better here.'

'A few jobs to get through, take your mind off, hey?' Jenny suggested.

She was again very close to him and Dermot inhaled deeply, calmed by her perfume, on the point of closing his eyes and kissing her. The door behind them swung open with a whoosh. Dermot opened his eyes glumly. Hennessy filled the doorway.

'Ah, there you are, the pair of you.' He smiled his

lopsided smile. 'I've been looking for you,' and he coughed politely. Dermot raised his eyebrows to Jenny by way of apology as if he had got them into trouble. Hennessy had just the knack of making it obvious when the mark had been overstepped without ever raising his voice. 'I wonder will you check the schedule for me, Jenny? Joe Kelly's wanting a lift to the airport at the earliest opportunity.' He looked over his glasses at Dermot, till Dermot wondered what it was he was about to say. 'The fellow's in the bar waiting to be served when you've the time.'

Joe Kelly was leaning over the bar, hauling himself up to take a look behind and see if anyone was coming, his finger poised over the polished bronze bell. Dermot came up behind, glad to make him jump and laughed as he straightened up. He thought he would get in his retaliation before Joe Kelly settled with a drink.

'Actually, Mr Kelly, Joe, I'd like a word with you. In private. Perhaps we could step into your room?'

'Sure.' Joe Kelly looked at his watch. The innocent action so infuriated Dermot that he did not wait for the privacy of Joe's room.

'Some property's gone missing from my home.' He cleared his throat. 'I know it was you, Mr Kelly, so if you wouldn't mind, I'd like it returned before you go jetting back to England.'

Joe Kelly smiled. 'Ah, the shipping container on the beach, right? I'm sorry I broke in. I apologise unreservedly. I know I shouldn't have.'

Dermot had expected denial, a tussle, even. He couldn't believe it was going to be this simple. He

Honeymoon

trudged behind Joe Kelly on the way upstairs. 'Round here it's still a crime. I don't know how it is where you live.' He waited impatiently as Joe Kelly calmly unlocked his room, pushing the door repeatedly because something had fallen behind it. Ripped envelopes and sheets of paper, some screwed into balls, were strewn everywhere. When he saw the state of the bedroom Dermot was unnerved but pressed on. 'There were the two things I'd like back; the photographs and the book.'

Joe Kelly scratched his head. 'That's just it. Someone seems to have beaten you to it, I'm afraid.'

'They did this to your room?' Dermot surveyed the mess, far worse than Joe Kelly had left in his container. Joe Kelly laughed seeing the look on Dermot's face.

'No, no, I did this. I was looking for something. What I mean is, I no longer have the book. I still have the album, you can have that back, but not the notebook, it's gone.' Joe Kelly did not look suitably abashed.

'You're awful free with someone else's property.' Dermot was more annoyed with himself over the loss of the book than with Joe Kelly. He had not even read it, having only recently rediscovered it, hidden amid the other books that lined his container, Driscoll's contribution to help make it a suitable home, from his stash of plunder. Dermot looked about for the photograph album but every surface, even the floor, was scattered with papers and envelopes, screwed up or torn or stacked in little piles.

Joe invited Dermot to sit on the bed, half-heartedly sweeping away the mess to make space and uncovered the album. 'We could go through these together if you like.'

Dermot raised an eyebrow, 'Bit late for that, isn't it?' He wasn't particularly interested in the album. The only faces he knew were Driscoll's and Hennessy's, but it was the principle. 'Well I suppose I could,' Dermot said, collapsing onto the bed, feeling almost sorry for Joe Kelly. He picked up the album, open beside him and the small passport photo of Louise winged to the floor. He bent forward to retrieve it. Fresh-faced and with her eyes closed as if she was about to burst out laughing, it hinted at a different Louise to the one he knew. So much had changed since Joe had first shown it. He felt like a different person. He almost laughed. He was a different person and so was she.

'She was pretty, wasn't she?' Joe said, leaning forward eagerly.

'So, what are you doing with a picture of my sister?' Dermot said, studying him. 'Was she your girlfriend or something?' And before Joe could answer he added, 'Actually she's not my sister.' Dermot handed Joe the photo. 'She's just this minute told me she's my mother and I'm illegitimate.'

Dermot did not stop once he had started and ceased to look at Joe Kelly. 'My whole world's upside down and to be honest I thought I'd pick a fight with you for breaking into my home but you're being so reasonable, I haven't the heart.' Joe Kelly lurched as if he was drunk, steadying himself on the table and sank back in the chair. 'You all right Mr Kelly?'

'It's Joe, just call me Joe,' he half gasped.

Honeymoon

'You're awful pale, Mr Kelly. You're not having a heart attack on me, are you?'

'How old are you, Dermot?' Joe Kelly did not need confirmation. The proof was sitting a few feet from him.

'Twenty next birthday,' Dermot said proudly, then admitted, 'Ok, I just turned nineteen.' Joe Kelly groaned. 'You're really pale,' Dermot said with concern. 'Maybe you should have the drink after all.' Dermot leapt up to open the minibar. 'There's not a great choice left, I'm afraid.' He took a small can of Coke for himself and waved a mini bottle of gin at Joe Kelly, still ashen, forehead beaded with sweat.

'Just tonic,' Joe managed, his voice feeble, 'Did Louise say who your father is?'

'We've not had time for the finer details yet,' Dermot replied and made them both laugh. Joe Kelly's mouth pulled out of shape as if buckling under emotion, unable to decide between laughter or tears.

'I think it might be me.'

'Don't tell me!' At first, Dermot assumed Joe Kelly was pulling his leg, but soon realised. 'Bloody great. My father's a burglar from England. I mean, that's just what you want to hear. No wonder no one ever said.'

'No one ever told me either. It's come as a bit of a shock.'

'You're telling me.'

'Dermot, I swear this is the first I knew of it.' Joe Kelly was very pale and stared into nothing and Dermot wondered if he should just go, walk downstairs and carry on as if nothing had happened. Well, nothing had happened, except nothing would ever be the same again.

Dermot studied Joe Kelly who continued to stare at nothing and wondered why he hadn't known immediately. The likeness was obvious; even his hands, even the perfect lozenges of his fingernails that he tapped absently on his chair. Dermot stuffed his hands under his legs and tried not to make the comparison. He considered the effect of having three fathers. This guy who was the real McCoy and certainly better looking than Driscoll; he would give him that. Pat, who should have all the credit and Driscoll who had just taken his final bow, so to speak. It was like a lid lifting on a different world that he would rather keep shut. His mouth twitched involuntarily as if he would cry again or laugh out loud or words he didn't really mean would begin to escape.

Joe Kelly gasped as if there wasn't enough air in the whole world to satisfy him then lapsed back to his former torpor and continued to stare at his hands. Dermot shifted uneasily, half afraid Joe Kelly might collapse and need the kiss of life. He stood up, began to edge towards the door, wanting to creep away unnoticed, but Joe, suddenly awake, focused on him with missionary zeal.

'This changes everything.' He loomed ever closer as if preparing for the kill or worse, about to smother him in some fatherly embrace. Dermot groped for the door handle behind him, desperate for an exit. 'I've only ever had myself and the past to consider up till now,' Joe Kelly said. 'I could be part of your life, well with your permission, and you could be part of mine.'

Dermot stopped himself laughing out loud at the earnest look on Joe Kelly's face and the ridiculous situation forced on him. 'Hold on there, Mr Kelly, Joe, I can't even say what difference this'll make to my life, never mind yours. Besides, I don't know you from Adam.'

At this Joe Kelly seemed to shrink in on himself. He retreated, collapsing back on the chair. 'No, of course not, of course, and there's Louise to consider.'

Dermot harrumphed.

'Don't be angry with her, Dermot. She can't have had it easy.' Joe Kelly was suddenly authoritative. 'Having a baby like that, especially then. Times were so different, you wouldn't believe.'

'So I've been told,' Dermot said.

Joe Kelly's colour had not improved. Dermot wasn't sure he could leave him alone just yet and stepped away from the door. There was nothing much left to say but he was still curious. 'So tell me, without the details, obviously.'

Joe nodded as if the request for information was Dermot's due and his duty. 'I went to England. I wrote to Louise for years asking her to join me, only it never happened. The letters went astray.' Joe waved his hand round the bedroom at all the papers scattered there and when Dermot looked more closely he could see that indeed they were handwritten letters.

'What, all of them? All of these are letters to Louise that went astray? Was it grand passion and Driscoll forced you to go?'

'No,' Joe fixed his eyes on Dermot, 'but he was the one who made the letters disappear. He gave them back to me only the day before yesterday.'

'That's criminal. Why did he do that? Were you a really bad guy?'

'Maybe, not bad, just young, that's all. I was just twenty.'

'I was bad at one time.' Dermot confided. 'It was Pat, you know Louise's Pat, put me straight.' He stopped as if considering the alternative. 'Maybe I'd have had to run away but for him.'

'I used to think Driscoll looked out for me but now I'm not so sure,' Joe said.

'He's not a great one for looking after people,' Dermot agreed. 'I mean when I thought he was my father. Louise never speaks to him. Do you know that?'

'No, I didn't know. But like I said, she can't have had it easy.' He shook his head at the thought of it. 'By the way, she doesn't know I wrote to her, and I'd be grateful if you didn't tell her.'

Dermot thought of making a sign to zip his mouth but instead just finished his can with a gulp and began crushing it, flattening the cylinder with a few deft twists and continuing to twirl it between his fingers for effect. Crushing cans had been his speciality in the heady days of his misspent youth, now an art form that mesmerised onlookers and a mindless tic when he was nervous. Joe Kelly watched intently as the sound of buckling metal and Dermot's rapidly moving hands became the focus in the room.

'I was wondering,' Dermot went to place the can on the table and flopped back on the bed. 'Did you come back after all this time to claim Louise?'

'Not exactly.'

'No? Then why are you back now, if you don't mind me asking?'

'No, I don't mind, Dermot.' There was a long pause. 'I hoped to find out about Louise, of course, that's why I brought her photo, but,' Joe shifted in the chair, crossing his legs then uncrossing them and leaning forward. 'It's complicated. There was a lot going on back then. You could just say it was time to sort it out.'

'And was it a coincidence you broke into my home?'

'I'm sorry, truly. It was stupid. I was just being nosey. I'd been to see Driscoll, I was upset about the letters and,' Joe looked at Dermot as if begging him to be lenient. 'You must admit it's odd finding a container there. You've made a good job of it though, all those books.'

Dermot was not aggressive by nature and knew he would forgive Joe. 'Pat helped a lot with the big stuff and made it so I could live in it. Driscoll helped with the books,' Dermot laughed. 'He called it poaching. He used to take me to the big house at night and we'd roam around and help ourselves to stuff.' He stopped smiling and looked earnestly at Joe. 'I'd be grateful if you didn't tell Louise that.' It had been a huge adventure, delving into the house with Driscoll. He had felt like a buccaneer. Now he supposed Louise might be right and he had got that all wrong too.

Their conspiracy to keep Louise out of the loop

made a tenuous bond and a moment of understanding between them. Dermot was the one to look away. 'Anyway. It was nice talking to you, Joe, but I've work to do. If you could just tell me who's got the notebook.' Dermot opened the door and stood in the doorway.

Again, Joe Kelly looked defeated. 'I left it in the Pharmacy. Louise denied all knowledge so I believe it's with the other visitors. I believe she must have it.'

Dermot held the door, 'I suppose it's just a coincidence that other guy is here? You didn't arrange to meet and you're in this together, or something complicated like that?'

'No, I'd no idea he was coming.' Joe shook his head. 'Never met her before and not seen him since he was a child. I do know who he is though, obviously.'

Dermot began backing away even as Joe Kelly was still talking.

'Well, so long, Dermot,' Joe raised his hand in a final farewell. He sounded so disappointed that Dermot was on the point of making rash promises. 'The taxi to the airport,' Joe said, almost a last ditch to make a claim on Dermot.

'Tomorrow, right,' Dermot said firmly and walked down the main stairs aware that Joe Kelly stood in the doorway but did not look back. Hennessy himself was waiting at the bottom, looking up as if expecting him. 'Everything ok, Dermot?'

'Yes, Mr Hennessy.'

'You're sure now?'

'Yes, Mr Hennessy.'

Hennessy rested a hand on Dermot's shoulder. A

gesture so avuncular and so invasive, Dermot was anxious. 'There's a nice pot of tea and a plate of beef sandwiches waiting for you in the snug. Fill your boots ready for tonight, eh?'

'Yes, Mr Hennessy.'

Dermot escaped to the snug to find Jenny there too. She put her cup down and rushed to meet him, wrapping her arms around him. 'You ok? You were so long I thought something must have happened.'

'Is that why Hennessy was at the bottom of the stairs?' Dermot unclasped her hands from around his neck so he could look at her.

'I had to explain where you were. D'you know what he did? Laid on this tea and told me to wait for you.'

Dermot planted a kiss on the tip of her nose. Then he kissed her on the lips, for real. 'I've wanted to do that for ages,' he said.

'I know,' Jenny smiled.

'Really?' Dermot took her in his arms and kissed her again. She returned his kiss. When he broke away, slowly opening his eyes and coming to land he took hold of her hand and pulled her towards a seat and into his lap. 'Are we an item now?'

She shrugged.

'Let's eat,' he said, 'I could eat for Ireland.'

~ * ~

Rosie lingered by boulders big as giants where the sea had scoured hollows and formed a series of pools. Tiny crabs scuttled, miniature starfish clung for dear life to under-hanging rock. She squatted, absorbed in observing but conscious of the shack with its wild roof inexorably drawing closer. Gulls swooped on white spume looking for fish. The sky, white as cotton wool, had absorbed the little curl of smoke from Driscoll's home as if soaking up liquid. She told herself that just because she was near the shack she didn't have to call in, and at the same time, knew for certain that she would speak with the oldest man in the village, if the opportunity arose.

The shack was further than it had seemed. Occasionally a strong gust whipped sea spray causing her to dodge out of the way with a mix of pleasure and shock as the enticing cold slapped her. By the time she neared the shack, a hint of sun brightened the horizon, lighting the white sky with a spool of silver.

Driscoll appeared in his doorway as if he'd been expecting her. 'You look about right,' he said, stepping aside to invite her in. She raised her eyebrows. 'I mean you look a good choice for him.' He paused, 'You must be Rosie.'

'That's a compliment, I think,' she laughed. She recognised the man she had seen coming out of the house after Fergal and held out her hand. 'Well, I'm pleased to meet you, at last, Mr Driscoll.'

Driscoll nodded. 'Life is all luck and coincidence, don't you think?'

'I hadn't really thought about it.' Rosie was nonplussed and had not expected philosophy.

'You better come in. Himself is here.'

'Who? Fergal?' She had almost forgotten the man himself in her quest to find out more about him.

When he heard Rosie's voice, Fergal leapt up to meet her, about to hug her but at the last moment he folded his arms over his hollow belly and hugged himself. He was sheepish, 'Hello Rosie.'

'Hello yourself.' They stood apart like relative strangers.

'How did you know I was here?'

'I didn't. Believe it or not, Fergal, I came to see Driscoll.'

'How did you get here, then?'

'Same as you, I suppose, I walked.'

'Yes, but I knew where to come.'

'I found out for myself. It is possible you know. Stuff happens even when you're not around.'

They were enjoying bickering and had almost forgotten Driscoll who, sensing as much, melted discreetly back into the shack. 'I'll be inside, when you're ready,' without waiting for a response. Fergal seemed to relax.

'You look sexy in my jacket,' he said, slipping his hand around Rosie's waist. 'I wondered where it was.' She smiled, giving herself to him.

'Seriously, how did you know to come here?'

'I've been hearing about Driscoll and I thought he'd be worth talking to.'

Fergal studied her questioningly. Rosie was business-like, almost fierce. 'You do want to find out about yourself, I take it?' She glared at him, heavy with the knowledge of the pregnancy test, then softened. 'Driscoll's lived here all his life so he should remember.'

Fergal acknowledged the truth of that. 'This is

where I came last night after the pub. Turns out Driscoll was in the house that first day and frightened me half to death.'

'I saw him come out after you.'

'You never said.'

'Yes, I did. We've some catching up to do, I think.' Rosie felt she needed to take charge of the situation. Fergal pulled her close.

'I'm sorry,' he said softly, nuzzling her with his chin, 'we shouldn't have come here, it wasn't fair to ask you.'

She put her fingers to his mouth to stop him speaking. 'Shh,' gently like a mother soothing a baby. 'This is important,' and remembering the newspaper report and how awful it must have been to read all the details, added, 'Harrowing perhaps, but still important.' She pulled away to look at him. 'Driscoll thinks I'm a good choice for you.'

'That confirms it then.' He kissed her briefly but tenderly on the lips and they stood in each other's arms. 'What have you been up to today?'

'Nothing much,' she lied, 'you?'

'About the same.' She knew he was lying too and she laughed.

Driscoll emerged from his shack carrying a tray and placed it on the ground between them. Three delicate china cups and a matching pot and a plate with a circle of plain biscuits sat like an oasis of beauty. 'If Mohammed won't come to the mountain,' he said. Rosie offered to pour and Driscoll led the way back inside and Fergal carried the tray.

'I expect you've some questions,' Driscoll said. He

offered Rosie a biscuit then seated himself on the wooden chest leaving the chairs for Rosie and Fergal.

'There is one thing, Mr Driscoll,' Rosie said, glancing to Fergal for approval, 'I don't understand why the newspaper reports vary so dramatically.'

Driscoll shook his head as if going over some comment, some revelation, then fixed his eyes on her. 'Times were very different then. What hope would anyone have of finding the truth with all the suppression of facts and reports that went on? Police informers and MI5 spies ran amok amongst us, even here in the South. Innocent, unarmed people gunned down. There was talk, plenty of it, but no proof and every reason to suspect. Old scores were easily hidden amongst other atrocities and there were many deaths and everyone disinclined to believe the facts. People were abducted from their own homes and never seen again or murdered in their own beds. Families pitted against each other.'

Fergal and Driscoll were lost in their own worlds, one speaking, the other listening almost as if a spell had been cast and they were both in a trance. Perhaps Driscoll's story had already passed to the realm of myth. She had that niggling doubt felt earlier that morning that everything was not straightforward, as if this was a story Driscoll had gone over and over. If she could keep silent about being pregnant, perhaps they knew more than they were telling. She was glad of the tea and, helping herself to another biscuit, found she was quite hungry, not having eaten since breakfast.

'Some accused Aidan Pierce of treachery and

assumed he'd committed suicide. No way would that be true. Whatever, the result was a tragedy. He did not deserve that end.'

Rosie kept her eyes on Fergal too, as the old man spoke. His face was a mask. Perhaps that was a technique he'd practised in the orphanage. If you gave no clue as to what you were thinking, no one need ever get to know you, no one would wallop you. She was riveted and listened intently, trying to untangle the truth from this version Driscoll was telling.

'The old man was sent to an institution and Fergal was sent away. The old man never saw you again. He refused to speak to anyone, not even to Father Malachi, not even in Irish. They thought he was raving mad but it was just the grief of burying a son and a grandson together.' Driscoll clicked his tongue and shook his head slowly side to side. 'One boy starved to death and the other poor lonely boy packed off to England with a pack of lies. 'Fresh start', Malachi said. 'He'll forget all the sooner if he thinks he never had a brother'.'

Driscoll stopped speaking. The stark facts distilled and settled in the silence, each one a fresh body blow. Rosie began to dissect the story. Exile to a foreign country must have felt like banishment to a small boy. Secrecy must have felt his only protection. Again she wondered about the grandparents, the Gopsill's, and would have asked Driscoll but the conversation took a different turn.

'Here,' Driscoll said almost brightly and reached a stone flagon from beside the wooden chest. 'There never was more need for a drop.' He began to pour generous amounts into the teacups, smiling at Rosie when she put her hand over her own cup.

'Here's to you and the baby,' Driscoll raised his china cup. Fergal's head shot up as if the word baby had electrified him. He looked straight at Rosie and his mouth stuck in a perfect round O. 'If I'm not mistaken,' Driscoll said. 'I've seen girls with the bloom of new loife on them in my time. I didn't mean to put my foot in it, sorry.'

Rosie reassured him. 'Fergal knew before I did, or guessed, at least.' She turned to Fergal and explained gently, 'While you were out of it earlier, I went to the chemist and did the test there. It's only a matter of timing; I just found out for sure this morning.'

Fergal had tears in his eyes. He pulled Rosie to him and hugged her. Tears dripped wet on her scalp. They stood like that for ages till Rosie grew quite hot, stifled and wanted to break free.

Fergal spoke to Driscoll, not letting go of Rosie. 'Perhaps you'd like to help us celebrate?' Finally, he loosened his grip. She stood apart, smoothing down her clothes. 'Yes, why don't you come and eat with us in the pub?'

Driscoll smiled indulgently at them both. 'That's kind of you to ask, but no. I don't want to be a gooseberry. Besides, I don't go out much now.'

'You'd be more than welcome.' Fergal wiped one eye and then the other on his sleeve, smiling apologetically. 'These few days...it's rather a rollercoaster.'

'From where I'm standing too,' Driscoll said. He looked forlorn, Rosie thought, seeing for a moment just how old he was. She was relieved the story was over. The mention of the baby, the hope of a new generation, had cleared the air.

'Oh, wait now,' Driscoll said, suddenly animated. 'I have something for you, Rosie.' He went to the wooden chest, produced a small box and handed it to her. 'Open it. I'd like you to have it.'

Inside the box was a circular brooch of pearls and rubies that lit Rosie's face with delight. 'It's beautiful, but...'

'No buts. I gave one to my wife who's no longer with us and this one was to be for my daughter but she disowned me, so I can't think of a better home for it to go to.'

'Oh, I'm sorry to hear that, about your wife I mean and about your daughter. Wouldn't you like to keep it in case you are reconciled?' Rosie looked to Fergal for support but he just shrugged. 'It must be an heirloom, you can't just give it away.'

'I'm not just giving it away, I'm giving it to you,' and Driscoll made special emphasis on the word you.

'I don't know what to say.'

'Think of it as a wedding gift or a christening present.'

She leant forward and kissed him, 'Thank you.' Driscoll's eyes looked particularly rheumy.

'I think he likes you,' Fergal whispered as he pinned the brooch on Rosie's top.

Driscoll smiled at them, 'Suits you. You look a picture.' Rosie thanked him, then, as if reminding them to go he said, 'So you'll be back across the water tomorrow, then?'

'Yes, the end of our honeymoon,' Rosie said.

'Congratulations to the both of you.' Driscoll raised his cup. 'It's been a pleasure to meet you.' He put the drink down without tasting it. Then he took Fergal's arm and dropping his voice, spoke with quite a different tone. 'Don't go bragging about who you are or where you've been to them all in the pub.'

Fergal stared at him as if he'd been hit.

'It's not a threat. I'm just letting you know for your own good.' Fergal still looked horrified. 'It's just woiser not to broadcast news – that's all – it'll be all over the place soon, anyway. Look,' Driscoll was still trying to explain to Fergal, 'it's convenient to have short memories here, then all of a sudden, old scores are dragged up. Besides,' Driscoll prodded Fergal's shoulder marking a slow rhythm as he enunciated each last word, 'it pays to keep your cards close.'

By the time they left the house in the sand, the beautiful sweep of the bay was bathed in the evening sun. 'That's a nice memory to take home,' Rosie said, fingering the brooch. Fergal hugged her and gave her a little squeeze. 'I'm so sorry,' Rosie added.

'What about?' Fergal asked.

'All you've had to shoulder on your own.' Fergal gave her another squeeze but said nothing. 'What do you think he meant at the end?' she asked.

'We'll probably find out in the pub.' Fergal stopped walking and turned to face her, 'Will you give up work before the baby's born?'

Rosie's mouth fell open in surprise. 'Give us a chance, Fergal, it's only been five minutes.' She was snappish with this sudden change of conversation and had it in mind to say there were other topics more pressing.

'Well, will you?'

They were feeling for boundaries, testing each other in a loving rather than a quarrelsome way. Rosie breathed deeply to quell a wave of nausea, elated that the new life was making its presence felt. 'God, I don't know. We've never discussed having a family.'

'Is there anything to discuss?'

'Fergal, honestly! This isn't the third world or the middle ages, not quite. Besides, I'm just starting out in my career.'

'Marketing or motherhood? It's a tough one.'

'Shut up, Fergal. There's the expense to consider and what if you're made redundant? Even solicitors lose their jobs.' Fergal did not answer and Rosie began a list as if thinking out loud. 'We might have to move to a good catchment area. Otherwise Daddy will insist we put the baby's name down at a public school as soon as it's born.'

'What's wrong with the local primary?'

'Fergal, we live in Hackney. What sort of a start will that be for a child?'

'Sounds very middle class.'

'Meaning what, exactly?'

'Well, babies are just born and then their parents look after them. One of them stays at home.' This from a man with the most dysfunctional start she could think of. She looked to see if he believed what he was saying. 'This is going to be a major argument.' Fergal was almost gleeful. To Rosie, still burdened by Driscoll's story, it seemed Fergal talked about the baby to avoid discussing his past.

~ * ~

Louise headed purposefully and quietly up the stairs of the pub to Joe's bedroom and did not think anyone had seen her. She ignored the 'do not disturb' sign, tapped on the door, and took a deep, calming breath. She could hear rustling and then Joe called out, 'Just a tick.'

Louise stood for longer than a tick expecting any moment to have to account for her presence. 'I can call back if it's not convenient,' she said half apologetically to the closed door.

'Louise?' The door opened immediately.

Louise was not smiling. 'I've come to ask you a favour.' Joe Kelly opened the door wider and let her in. She crossed the room and stood with her back to the window wondering now at the wisdom of her mission. Joe sat on the bed, inviting her to sit on the upright chair as he did so. She remained standing, 'I think you should go home tonight,' she said. Joe opened his mouth to reply but Louise added, 'It would be the one thing you could do for me.'

Joe stared at his hands and did not reply. Louise took in the room, the unmade bed and the mess. Envelopes were everywhere, on every available surface, some laid in rows on the floor. Letters were stuck half in and out as if Joe was preparing mailshots. She glanced at an envelope on the table beside her. 'This is addressed to me,' and she looked at him mystified. Then she pulled out the letter.

'Don't,' Joe almost shouted, too late to stop her. 'Please don't.'

One after another Louise picked up envelopes, laying each one back where it had been like a patchwork, but still could not grasp it. Each one was clearly franked with a postmark twenty years old and each one was addressed to her. 'Where have these been all this time? Why didn't I see them?' Joe did not answer. His hands moved as if grasping for words. 'You wrote to me,' she felt defeated. 'All the time you wrote to me and I never knew.'

A bubble of anger welled up so painfully Louise thought she was having a heart attack or, at the very least, angina. She crumpled onto the chair. She opened her mouth several times to speak but closed it without saying anything, and that did not happen often. She felt lightheaded and leaden; laughter welled up with tears. The day shattered into a thousand tiny pieces, reassembled again and again like a kaleidoscope with different permutations, different possibilities.

'I wanted you to come to England,' Joe said. 'I thought you must hate me for that last night and that's why you never answered.'

'There's a lot of letters.' Louise whistled and gently brushed those on the table with her fingertips.

'Every week for two years. Then I gave up.' He shrugged.

Louise sensed the desperation that would drive a boy

to write solidly for so long with not a single reply. 'So why have you got them?' She looked at him searchingly for some logical explanation. 'Did they get lost in the post?'

Again, Joe just shrugged. Fleetingly, she remembered how he would evade her questions when it was something he didn't want to answer and she was exasperated. 'It's time for answers, isn't it? There's been too much untruthful silence.'

Joe raised his eyebrows and breathed in deeply. 'Does that include you?'

She also remembered his slightly mocking tone when he teased her and wondered if she was being teased now. 'The fact that you wrote has changed things. I can guess who kept them. Driscoll? Am I right?' And a vision of Driscoll snowed under with a hundred or so letters made her smile.

'I think he thought it for the best,' Joe said. Louise harrumphed and Joe smiled at her. He sat forward on the bed and taking hold of her hands looked at her earnestly. Louise wondered what was coming but did not move her hands away. 'You may as well know now, so we're straight. Dermot has told me. He guessed, which is more than I did.'

Louise could feel her heart and hear its beat full in her ears. Something was expected of her but for the life of her, she could not think what. 'I see,' she said, but she did not see. She sat immobile for some time trying to make sense of her feelings. 'I suppose he'll be off with you back to England?'

'No,' Joe said gently, stroking her hands with his

thumbs. 'We talked man to man, if not father to son and got a few things ironed out. It's come as a shock, you know, to both of us.'

'I've had years to get over it, I suppose.' She spoke without irony and Joe nodded. She would have liked him to take her in his arms like he did on that first day, but somehow, they were further apart than ever and she was relieved.

'I'd like him to come, of course, but I don't think he's ready. He needs to sort things out in his own mind first.'

'I'd like some answers too. You owe me that, I think,' Louise said, but before Joe could say anything, she added briskly, 'By the way, was it you broke into his container on the beach?' Joe Kelly had no answer ready. 'Well Dermot was right then,' Louise said. 'I hope you're not thinking of taking the stuff away with you?'

Joe was unrepentant. 'He has his album back and I have already apologised profusely. It was an aberration.'

'No, it was theft,' Louise said, then she paused, shaking her head sadly. 'That's not it really. I want to know why were you running away that night? Since everything is coming out, and why oh, why you've come back?'

Joe sighed. 'I'm sorry, Louise.' For a moment it seemed he was going to cry, but he steeled himself and continued. 'The night I left. What a legacy. If I'd had any inkling about Dermot.'

'Yeah, right,' Louise scoffed and Joe looked hurt. He cleared his throat but she did not relent and looked at him expectantly.

'So,' he said, shifting his position on the bed, 'I came back for selfish reasons. Partly because I wanted to see you and see the old place again.' He shook his head and looked down. 'Obviously wasn't meant to be.'

'Do you believe that shite?' Louise asked and he laughed, taken aback by her irreverence, 'because I don't. We never got together because my father and perhaps my mother too took it upon themselves to keep the truth from us.'

'Maybe,' Joe shrugged, 'but it amounts to the same thing.'

'Why did you come to me that night?' She felt if she had all the facts then maybe it would be easier to cope.

'Because you were the best thing that ever happened in my life.' Joe was in earnest but Louise was in no mood for sentiment.

'Well, you certainly destroyed that.' She saw that she had wounded him and momentarily was glad.

'I'm sorry, Louise.'

'There's no point now, it's too long ago.'

'It's never too late.' He raised his eyebrows.

'That's shite too and you know it.' He laughed again at her liberal use of the word. She laughed too. 'You've still not answered my question. Why were you running away.'

Almost grudgingly he said, 'I left because of the trouble at the big house. I was there when the man died.' Louise drew in breath so sharply it whistled.

'What I mean is, I ran away when they started to beat him.' Louise opened her eyes wide but didn't say anything, just looked at him. 'It was a long time ago and things have changed,' he said, 'don't you think? Now there's Dermot.' Louise felt her temperature rise, a searing heat, a searing anger, a searing violence.

'Don't fecking talk to me about Dermot,' and she burst into tears, hot, angry, copious tears that nothing could stem. She rushed for the door, stopping on the threshold. 'I almost forgot.' She fumbled to pull the notebook he'd left in her shop out of her bag. She thrust it at him, still in its plastic bag, tossing it on the bed when he did not take it as if she couldn't bear to keep anything of his. She was through the door and halfway down the stairs before Joe even came to the door and called after her. She wished now she hadn't pressed him to explain as slowly it dawned on her the problems that had beset her for so long amounted to nothing.

~*~

The cup of tea Pat had made for Louise, expecting her any moment, was stone cold on the table. He could have christened the meal but he was unsure what to cook and didn't want to prepare the wrong thing. He had looked at his watch and the kitchen clock a thousand times hoping something ordinary had detained her but was plagued with doubts. Suppose Louise had run away with Joe Kelly? Suppose she had not been at work at all and had ridden off with him? The longer he delayed checking, the longer he could pretend. The quiet emptiness of the house reminded him of the time when Dermot first moved out and he'd felt again Louise's disappointment that the longed-for children of their own did not fill the house with laughter.

When at last he was ready to face the world, the front door opened. Louise's obvious distress wounded as surely as a knife twisting as she began to tell him of Joe Kelly and the love letters she never received, and the cruel deception on Driscoll's part. He still expected her to announce that she was leaving him, but it turned out to be Dermot who was threatening to leave, now that he had guessed Joe Kelly was his father.

Pat had his arms around Louise's to steady himself as well as comfort her. 'Why have you shouldered this by yourself?' he asked even though he suspected that he already knew. 'I'm ashamed you did not feel you could trust me.'

Louise did not say anything but laid her head on Pat's shoulder and let him hold her. Pat listened to her heart, her breathing, hoping to give her strength from his encircling arms. 'You know, when you agreed to marry me, I thought I was the luckiest man alive. I hardly dared ask you.'

She raised her head to look at him. 'Pat, you asked me three times. You couldn't stop asking me.'

'Well, I just couldn't understand why there wasn't anyone else in your life.'

'Everyone moved away, the girls at school, there didn't seem to be any young people left.'

'Thanks very much.'

They laughed. 'You know what I mean, Pat. You'd left school by the time I started. Anyway, you weren't from round here.'

'True. Ten miles on foot is a distance, especially if you have to go there and back. Didn't make courting easy,' he added as if the memory was still vivid.

'Why expect things to be easy?'

'No, you're right, and I don't, not really.'

'Sure you don't, Pat. There's nothing lazy about you.'

'Nor you neither.'

'We sound like some poor old pair from the home.'

Pat let out a deep sigh. 'I have been thinking, Louise. I know how much you would have liked children. I'm ashamed I didn't speak out about it till now.'

'Pat, will you stop being ashamed all the time.'

'It never occurred to me to talk about it. You just accept what comes and that's foolish. Very foolish. Especially these days when they can fix it all.' Pat was shaking his head. 'I'm sorry we've not had children, Louise. I guess that must be my fault. It's not too late for us, you know. We can do the tests and see why not.'

When Louise did not say anything he added, 'I just want to explain to you how it is. I thought you would be leaving with Joe Kelly, and it feels we've been given this chance to be honest with each other. Not everyone gets that or takes it.'

Louise kissed him gently. 'Honestly, Pat.' They stood with their arms circling each other like branches of two entwined trees. 'Maybe we're too old and we should be grateful with just the one.'

Pat smiled and shrugged, 'We'll see.'

Then Louise remembered something Joe had said that had troubled her. 'Joe Kelly's just told me he was involved in that business up at the house. I thought the man died of a heart attack. Joe Kelly said they beat him.'

'It was a long time ago, Louise.'

'Maybe so. But that young couple are something to do with the house. Do you think there'll be trouble?'

'Like I said, it was a long time ago.'

She kissed him again and disentangled herself. 'Actually, you know, there is something I'd like.'

Pat looked startled for a moment and then smiled. 'Ok, Louise, fire away.'

'I want to go out on the town more. I don't want us to keep ourselves to ourselves anymore. There's nothing to keep secret and all their tongues can't hurt us now.'

He laughed. 'Is that all?'

'Your turn,' she said. 'Ask whatever you want.'

'What about Driscoll?' She looked at him in surprise.

'What about him? Don't bring him into it. He doesn't deserve it.'

Pat stopped her. 'Don't speak like that about your father, Louise.'

'I'd rather not speak about him at all,' she bristled.

'Ok, truce. No one's asking you to have him live with you or look after him in his old age. I'm just saying, now is the time for forgiving. I'll take you for a drink, so long as I don't have to wear a collar and tie.'

'Dermot will be there. Do you think he'll mind?'

'I think he'll get used to it. Maybe, on second thoughts, we should leave it a day or two.'

~ * ~

Rosie wore her tightest black trousers, relieved at the ease with which they still did up, expecting to have ballooned immediately. She chose a black halter neck top that would set off the brooch and smiled at her reflection, turning herself first one way and then the other, satisfied that she would do. Fergal hugged her. 'You look good enough to eat and I'm starving.'

'You're always starving,' and she leaned in to the mirror to put on her mascara.

The pub was so quiet that their cutlery sounded out against their plates. Rosie and Fergal felt the need to whisper and finally gave up talking altogether. Fergal had no trouble demolishing what was on his plate and the food was delicious. They had both chosen fish, the flesh so pale and delicate it could have been porcelain. The tension made Rosie's head throb, and she was rather miserable. She knew they should talk about the newspaper cuttings and looked for opportunities in the silence to say something.

There was no sign how the news had affected Fergal, or if he was affected at all. She wondered if she ever would understand him. She wanted to ask about his grandparents but the chance for that didn't come up either. For one brief moment, Rosie saw her married life laid out before her. She wondered at the folly of marrying at all and saw for the first time that her life would never again be her own, as her mother had tried to warn her. How powerless she felt under the weight of her vows in the face of this great institution.

Gradually the bar filled up and the strumming of instruments and gentle, harmonious humming softened her mood. Fergal was ready to go home. 'Let's get the bill, I can think of better things to do on the last night of our honeymoon.' He raised his eyebrows suggestively.

Rosie didn't even laugh. 'I still fancy a pudding, actually. This is supposed to be a celebration and I am eating for two.'

Fergal smiled glumly. 'Ok. I can wait.' He summoned Dermot to see what was on offer. Dermot began to rattle off the list then he petered out as his eyes focused on the brooch at Rosie's throat, drawn to it as if magnetised. Rosie resisted the temptation to touch the brooch under his gaze.

The wine and the tension made her want to giggle, but the sound that erupted was more of a belch, 'Oh, excuse me,' and she giggled helplessly anyway, hoping Dermot would not think she was laughing at him.

'Do you mind me asking where you got the brooch?' Dermot said, and Rosie sobered instantly.

'Not at all.' She was her most charming, 'It was a gift.'

'My, that is my, that is,' Dermot stuttered, rapping his head twice with the palm of his hand before finally deciding. 'Someone in my family has got the exact same brooch as that.'

'Perhaps there's more than one of them,' Fergal said helpfully.

'Must be.' Dermot did not seem satisfied.

Rosie saw no point in keeping it a secret, even though she was sure Fergal kneed her under the table. 'It was from the old man, Mr Driscoll. We went to visit him earlier.'

'Well that does explain a lot, he is my family.'

'So, you're related to Mr Driscoll?' Rosie said brightly.

'It's complicated,' Dermot said, turning his mouth down and went back to listing puddings as if he'd simply been switched back to waiter mode. 'Let me guess,' he said to Rosie, 'the Magnificent Chocolate Jesus, is it?'

'That's the one,' Rosie smiled sweetly to make up for Fergal's scowl.

As Dermot left, Fergal leaned in close to Rosie and almost snarled. 'We were supposed to be keeping our cards close to the chest, remember?'

Before Rosie could ask Fergal not to be so surly he was nodding and smiling at Joe Kelly fast approaching, pint glass in hand. Rosie's heart sank, her turn to be surly, but either Fergal did not hear her groan or else he ignored it. He stood up, all charm and nervous energy, to shake hands with Joe. Joe turned his attention to Rosie, taking hold of her hand that she had not offered, and not letting go, asked, 'You enjoyed your stay here, finally?'

Fergal answered for her. 'Yes, thanks it's a lovely village, and we've had a great time.'

Joe Kelly did not turn his gaze away from Rosie. 'Do you know, I've never seen you two together.' It could have been criticism or mere observation.

'Have you not?' Fergal said.

They could see Dermot at the bar putting finishing touches to a vast pudding and all focused their attention on him. 'That for you?' Joe Kelly asked, pointing his chin towards the pudding and still ignoring Fergal. He laughed aloud when Rosie said it was. 'Best of luck! Hope you enjoy it.' Still laughing, giving Fergal the briefest of nods, he made his way back to the bar as Dermot was about to light a sparkler he'd inserted in the ridiculously mountainous pudding. Joe sat the other side of the bar and something about their exchange disconcerted Rosie. She couldn't hear them, of course but she noticed Dermot's look of utter disgust.

Within moments Dermot placed the pudding on the table with a flourish. Rosie nearly died laughing, all misgivings forgotten. 'Fergal, look at it, there really is a statue of Jesus made of chocolate.' Fergal smiled at Rosie's absolute delight.

Dermot produced two spoons with a knowing wink. 'It's grand isn't it?' Then he looked earnestly from one to the other, willing them to say something. Finally, Dermot nodded in the direction of the musicians and said, 'Will you be singing again do you think, Mr Pierce?'

Fergal shook his head. 'No, not tonight, I doubt it.' Already, he was focused on the chocolate Jesus, and began wolfing it down without any pretence at sharing.

'Hey,' Rosie said, 'I thought I ordered that.'

The two of them battled with the pudding, and as they put down their spoons, quiet applause went around the room. 'No one ever finishes those monsters, well done!'

The band took up a tune and someone sang, *Gotta be a chocolate Jesus, makes you feel good inside.* Laughter erupted in a little trill with a tinkling of spoons on glass.

'So, I was right about a pudding,' Rosie smiled. 'Now we'll have the bill, please.'

She leaned into Fergal on the short walk back to the house. Fergal had his shoulders hunched and his hands in his pockets. 'That was odd, wasn't it?'

'I felt like punching him,' Fergal said.

'Not Joe Kelly, Dermot, the fuss he made about the brooch.'

'Maybe you're getting paranoid,' Fergal said.

'Thanks a bunch.'

As soon as Fergal had pushed the door of the cottage closed he pulled Rosie to him, kissing her mouth hard. She was surprised because he had seemed so cross with her through the meal but was beginning to relax and enjoy the moment when someone began thumping the door. Either they'd been followed home or someone had been waiting for them. It made them both jump. Fergal cursed as he banged his head on a thick whitewash buttress. They hesitated, still with their arms around each other. Streetlights glowed through the glass above the door.

'Just leave it,' Rosie whispered, 'they might go away.'

'I know you're in there.' It sounded like Dermot.

Fergal kissed her cheek and whispered, 'You go on up, I'll deal with it.'

'Don't be long.' Rosie kept hold of his hand till she

was at the foot of the stairs. Dermot was starting to shout again as Fergal opened the door and stepped out into the street. Rosie retreated to the bedroom and watched from the window leaning against the windowpane, one hand twisting at her brooch.

They stood a little way off silhouetted by a street lamp, like paper cut-outs in a magic lantern show, their movements exaggerated with male posturing as if they were squaring for a fight, summing up the opponent before battle. She felt uneasy, excited almost; it made her want to shout out, join in. This was something new. All battles between Hugo and her father had been verbal, vitriolic tongue-lashing. This was a locking of horns. She would put her money on Dermot any day; half a head taller than Fergal and more muscled. She tried to think what it could possibly be. Hadn't Mr Driscoll mentioned old scores? What was the comment Dermot made to Joe Kelly? Perhaps there was more to be uncovered about Fergal's past. Death and cover-ups filled her head.

When she saw Dermot reach for his inside pocket, like a gangster going for a gun, she felt a surge of adrenaline. In a flowing move, she was down the stairs and through the open door and had leapt on Dermot, his neck in an armlock and his hair firmly in her grasp. If Hugo had taught her one thing, it was how to fight and mean it. As she and Dermot fell heavily to the ground she thought how proud of her Fergal must be for saving him. Dermot shouted loud and long, making such a commotion on the quiet street that lights went on in nearby houses. A few doors opened, even a few onlookers from the pub started to make their way towards them and wondered should they call out the Gardaí.

Fergal was prising her off, bending her fingers back painfully, till eventually she let go and Fergal yanked her to her feet, 'Rosie, for God's sake what's got into you?' Dermot was rubbing his hairline with alternate hands. Rosie twisted her fingers together and felt foolish.

'I thought you'd come to murder Fergal or rob us. I don't know what I thought,' Rosie said.

Dermot made light of it, 'Do you read a lot of crime fiction? This may be the back of beyond, but we're quite civilised really.'

Fergal apologised again and again and, glaring at Rosie, invited Dermot into the house, saying it was the least they could do, ushering him in first and leaving Rosie still outside in the street. She was rather shaken and her knees still trembled. For once, she did not mind being relegated to the kitchen when Fergal asked her to make tea and Dermot said he'd prefer coffee. She stood with her back to them and waited while the kettle boiled, listening to their banter. It seemed as if her life that had been perfectly controlled was in free fall. It was thrilling in a way but the loss of control meant she could not be sure whether she would laugh or cry at any given moment.

When she delivered the drinks, Dermot said she should 'lighten up', and Fergal nodded, pulling her to sit beside him on the couch and kissing her on the cheek. He said he was proud of the way she had leapt to his defence and he and Dermot laughed with their heads thrown back till they both had to clutch their sides. She did not find it so uproarious. Perhaps on retelling, to Hugo or the girls in the office, it would take on the proportions of a tall tale and they would laugh and she would laugh with them. It wasn't that she had no sense of humour; she knew how to laugh.

A sweet memory came to mind of when she and Hugo were children. Their mother had been talking on the phone in the kitchen for what seemed a very long time. Hugo had sneaked in to take an orange for each of them from the fruit bowl before their meal, thinking their mother would not be able to stop him. From where she perched on a stool she could just nudge Hugo with her foot on the seat of his pants and, in doing so, his prized oranges sprang from his grasp and rolled along the floor. He re-enacted the move: picking up the oranges, hitting himself on the bottom and throwing the oranges to roll on the floor, over and over repeating the action like a demented automaton. He had been helpless with giggling so infectious that she'd had to clutch her sides from the pain of laughing and her mother had become incoherent on the phone, just managing to say she would ring back. It brought tears to her eyes.

She did know she had made a fool of herself, was still making a fool of herself, she just couldn't help it. They simply did not understand. She began to cry, silently at first but then it was obvious. It was just that Hugo never made her feel a girl in his company or when he was with his other friends and was always careful not to exclude her. That was the point, surely? No one should be made to feel a third party, not in the group. Dermot apologised. 'I didn't mean to startle you.' Fergal told Dermot it wasn't anything to do with that, and to clarify added, 'Rosie's just pregnant,' blurting their secret out to the first stranger.

'Congratulations,' Dermot said.

Fergal's casual betrayal brought more tears. She had imagined they would break the news together after their return. Hugo or her mother would guess there was something different about her because they loved her and they would be sworn to secrecy for the next few weeks till everything was on the safe side so as not to disappoint her father and her aunt. Fergal had managed to broadcast it as if it wasn't special at all. She felt utterly alone.

Then she was livid. She knew when it was appropriate to laugh, and laughing at her because she was a woman and pregnant at that, was not one of those times. She wanted Dermot to go. She put her cup back in the cold puddle in the saucer, her hands still a little shaky. 'I expect we'll see you tomorrow then,' she said without smiling. Fergal did not take her hint and looked like he was settled in for the night.

Dermot shifted uncomfortably, 'Actually, before I go, there is something you can help me with.'

Fergal smiled obligingly, 'Fire away, Dermot. Can't promise, mind you.'

'Well,' Dermot began and continued so seriously that even Rosie found it endearing. 'Someone broke into my home and made off with some of my property. Now that seems to have changed hands along the way and I wondered,' he looked directly at Rosie, 'If you could shed any light on the matter.'

'I don't think so, sorry.' Rosie knew nothing of a burglary.

Dermot tried again. 'I don't quite know how the one item in particular got passed on but the burglar tells me he no longer has it and, with you all about to leave the country, I thought I'd better locate it.'

'Perhaps you should tell us what it is,' Fergal said patiently.

Dermot looked at Rosie, 'Joe Kelly thinks that you have it.'

'Me?' she said. There was another knock at the door and Rosie jumped.

'Speak of the devil,' Fergal said, 'That'll probably be Joe Kelly.'

'How do you know?' Rosie and Dermot asked together.

'He's coming round for a drink.'

'What, now? It's almost eleven o'clock. You might have asked first,' Rosie said.

'He rather invited himself. I forgot about it till now, and I assumed he'd forgotten too.'

Joe Kelly had already stuck his head round the door. 'Hello. Ah, Dermot, I'm glad you're here,' Joe said without enthusiasm.

'How's it going?' Dermot sounded lacklustre too and the subject of the missing property was quietly dropped.

In his hand, Joe held a bunch of wildflowers beginning to wilt, which he held out to Rosie. 'I picked these for you.'

'Thanks,' she said, indicating that Joe should put them on the table rather than take them from him. 'It's a shame we're going in the morning.' She began to open and close cupboard doors noisily, making a show of looking for a vase. In the end, she stuck the flowers messily in a mug and put them back on the table.

'You've not heard, I take it?' Joe Kelly seemed pleased to be the bearer of news, 'There'll be none of us flying out tomorrow. Not you, not me. There's been a volcano erupted that's blowing its dust all over and they've decided to cancel the flights. Either we stay or come to some arrangement with Dermot,' he smiled encouragingly at Dermot. 'Well, Dermot, how much would you charge to take us to the ferry?'

'I'm torn between charging double for the trouble or nothing just to be rid of you,' Dermot said, but no one laughed.

'How long does it take for volcanic ash to blow over?' Fergal looked at Rosie for approval. 'We could stay on a day at least. There's still things we could do.' Fergal immediately got out glasses and opened the whisky he was going to take home to Hugo.

'Don't pour me any.' Rosie moved her glass away.

'We can always get some more,' Fergal said defensively, as he handed the drinks.

'Not for me either, thanks,' Dermot said, so Fergal shared the extra whisky with Joe Kelly.

Rosie inhaled disapprovingly. 'I'm going to get some air,' she said and thought Fergal looked relieved.

'I'll go too,' Dermot said, springing up. When they were a safe distance from the house, he said, 'I'm sorry I told you to lighten up. I didn't mean to upset you.'

'It wasn't you who upset me,' she said. 'Thanks, anyway.'

'About that property, a notebook?' Dermot said.

'Ah.' Rosie thought she knew. She turned to him, looking him in the eye, 'It's awkward, isn't it? I don't think it was yours in the first place.'

Dermot looked uncomfortable, 'How d'you work that out?'

'It doesn't take a genius. It's obvious that someone or some people have been taking everything they can lay their hands on out of the house.' She shot him a look and he smiled sheepishly, 'That small and rather dirty notebook, that is what we're talking about I take it? I bet my bottom dollar that notebook came from the house.'

Dermot gave his explanation that he was only saving books from ruination since the house was falling to bits. Rosie laughed at the opportunism. When she told Dermot as far as she knew it was still in the pharmacy, he tutted. 'I'll never see it if Louise has it still.'

Rosie shrugged. 'What's Joe Kelly's connection? Why do you think he was interested?'

'I've wondered that myself,' Dermot said, 'Things have got complicated to say the least since he's been here.'

'You needn't worry. I won't give you away. Just out of interest who else has stuff from the house?'

'My father, that's to say, oh for God's sake.' Dermot knocked on his forehead. 'Driscoll, you know the old man.'

'Oh yes, I didn't realise he's your father?'

'He was until today. They've all been pretending since the day I was born. Turns out he's not.

'Oh, Dermot. I'm so sorry.' Rosie placed her hand on his arm so that they stopped and she smiled at him encouragingly. 'It must be awful to find out like that. At least Fergal has always known who his parents were, even if he never knew them. If that makes sense.'

Dermot shrugged, 'Not really. Nothing makes any sense today. I'm hoping for a better day tomorrow.' And they both laughed. 'Louise brought me up anyway and turns out to be my mother after all.'

Rosie reached up and gave him a kiss on the cheek. 'You're a credit to her. She's done a lovely job.'

'Thanks.' Dermot touched his cheek where the kiss had landed, 'I can't let her take all the credit. There's Pat too, her husband.' He looked at her and smiled. 'About the stuff from the house.'

'It's a long time ago now,' Rosie interrupted. 'It happened before you were born probably. I wouldn't worry. Let's hope it turns up. Did you read it?'

'No, I started to, then Joe Kelly came along and stole it. I don't think he had time to read it either.'

'Good.' Rosie was emphatic. 'I don't think Fergal would want everyone to see it.' They walked in amicable silence for a while then Rosie said, 'I'm sorry I pulled your hair. I honestly thought you were going to attack Fergal for the brooch. I know, ludicrous.' They both laughed, then were pensive for a while till Rosie said, 'I wonder why Driscoll gave it to me? Unless it came from the house.'

'We didn't actually steal anything valuable. It wasn't some vast salvage operation. The big stuff had already gone well before we came on the scene. Well, before I did at any rate. Besides, Louise had her brooch from her mother. She told me that much.'

'I love the brooch but if it's one of a pair, maybe I should give it to Louise.'

Dermot shrugged. 'I can't help you there, I'm afraid. Anyway, I'm off home. Let me know if you need a lift in the taxi. Can't say I relish a long drive with Joe Kelly on my own.'

'Don't you like him either?' Rosie was conspiratorial. Dermot's laugh sounded hollow. 'I've just discovered he's my father.'

'Oh dear,' Rosie said, dismayed she always said the wrong thing.

They had wandered as far as the beach and stood looking out at the silvering sea in the darkness, a stiff breeze played over them. Rosie's mobile rang and she scrabbled to retrieve it from her pocket. 'I'm sorry, Dermot,'

'I'm off, anyway,' Dermot nodded a farewell to her.

She watched his retreating figure, raising one hand to wave as she put the phone to her ear. 'Hugo!' The relief of hearing Hugo was immense and she burst into tears. Glad that she was alone out on the quiet stretch of beach.

Hugo was not concerned. 'Is that new husband beating you?'

'Oh Hugo,' she wailed, knowing he would tease her forever after but it was good to hear him. 'We can't even come home,' she wailed. 'All flights are cancelled because of that volcano and Fergal wants to sit tight.'

'Oh, and is that why you're crying?'

'No, not exactly.' She sniffed. 'You wouldn't believe what's been going on, that's all.'

'Intriguing!' Hugo always sounded slightly mocking. She remembered childhood tears of frustration as Hugo had teased the life out of her. 'Listen,' Hugo said, 'is Fergal there? I wanted to ask him something, and he's not answering his phone.'

'He's having a drinking sesh with some bloke. Reception's rubbish in the house, anyway.' Rosie's tears dried with a bit of effort and one almighty sniff. 'Hugo, I want you to do something for me.'

'Anything, you know that, though technically you are no longer my responsibility. Kidding, kidding, don't start crying again. Hang on.' His voice muffled as if Hugo had put his hand over the receiver and said something.

'Hugo, are you alone?' she should have known he would have a girl with him.

'Just reaching for a pen. Fire away.'

'I want you to look for Fergal's other family. I've got a name and it's quite intriguing.'

'I take it Fergal hasn't asked you to do this?'

'Well, it might be a nice surprise for him, if he's got family.'

'Ok, fire away.'

'It was on the grave. His mother. Beloved daughter of Colonel and Lady Gopsill.'

Hugo whistled.

'He never told you that, I suppose?' Rosie said with some satisfaction.

'No, he didn't.' Rosie could hear his pen scratching. 'Ok, leave it with me. Don't bother asking Fergal tonight. It's late. I'll try tomorrow and see if I can get through. Chin up, eh?'

She laughed, glad to hear a voice from home. She had an ally and felt she needed one.

~*~

Joe Kelly and Fergal had their heads together, hale and hearty, like men with too much hard drink inside them. She had seen her father like that many times and her mother always hated it. Joe accosted her almost immediately she walked in, 'I was just telling your man here that I'm writing a book about the place and it's good to meet someone from the big house, even though he left at a tender age.'

'I thought you said you were a solicitor,' Rosie said.

Joe shook his head, 'Nope, not me. You must be thinking of some other guy who's returned from over the water.' He laughed and Rosie disliked him more and more. 'I've always been a writer. Well, tried to be. I've turned my hand to most things over the years. I've done a lot of building. A writer has to be diverse like an actor till he can give up the day job.' She didn't believe a word he said and was about to ask him if he was in print but Joe turned to Fergal returning to their conversation and excluding her as if he had just had a bright idea. 'I think I must have left here before you were sent away. I'd have known about it otherwise.'

She felt near tears, so unlike herself, that she made the excuse she was too tired to be sociable and made her way to bed. She heard Joe Kelly say he ought to go and Fergal say it was fine, Rosie wouldn't mind. She wanted to scream, 'Yes I bloody well do mind'.

She lay in the big white bed listening to their voices, picturing Fergal giving Joe Kelly his undivided attention. She would have liked to be a fly on the wall and half-heartedly considered sitting at the top of the stairs to spy on them as she and Hugo had done as children when their parents had dinner parties. Somehow, they always gave themselves away and their mother would shoo them back to bed, sometimes with threats but mostly with promises.

She heard the refilling of glasses, the slosh of liquid and an unmistakeable chink as presumably they toasted each other and the whir of an electrical gadget, maybe the fridge. If she concentrated, she could hear what they said and drifted in and out of their conversation. Fergal cleared his throat. 'So will you be going tomorrow, Joe?'

'Yes, I've done what I needed to. I'll be back of course, though I've no family to speak of left here, just memories, some good and some not so.'

You dirty great liar, she thought. If only it had been Joe Kelly she'd pounced on. She would have pulled his hair right out. She felt very sorry for Dermot, dismissed like that and yet perhaps there was nothing between them, father and son. You can't suddenly feel love, she supposed.

Joe seemed intent on cross-examining Fergal, his age, the date he left, why he'd come back. Rosie wanted to hear from Fergal, in his quiet measured tones and wondered why she hadn't simply asked him outright herself. She lay perfectly still on her back, straining to hear.

'There's nothing to tell, I'm afraid,' Fergal said. 'I was one of the first people from the care system to want to go to university. Perhaps because I was an oddity I was allowed to stay on at school. I don't know where the idea to study law came from, but they encouraged me all the way. I'm not saying it was easy, but I hardly knew anything different.'

'Have you specialised?' Joe Kelly asked.

'Property law,' Fergal said, 'seemed a safe bet.'

Rosie shivered. An image of quicksilver, jiggling in the petri dish at school, came to mind. That fluid silver ball, too poisonous to touch, that they had passed from one to another, that could sliver into tens of quivering ball bearings or reassemble to one blob at any time, had left them wondering how it could be so toxic, so viscous and so fascinating all at the same time.

This honeymoon gave Fergal a perfect smokescreen to gather information. Had she not felt so tired she might have lain in wait to confront Fergal with this truth. Try as she might to stay awake she drifted off to sleep, unable even to account for her own dreams.

'Would you excuse me a moment?' Fergal took the stairs two at a time, raised his head above the stairwell, waited a moment or two then crept back down.

Joe Kelly raised his eyebrows, 'Asleep?'

Fergal nodded and sat on the settee facing Joe. 'Why did you invite yourself round?' Fergal asked. Joe Kelly blinked. 'Come on,' Fergal goaded, 'it wasn't for the pleasure of my company. I'm curious to know why you're here.'

Joe Kelly smiled and fiddled with his cuffs, stalling before he answered. He had felt so sure of himself earlier, so full of hope with the discovery of the beautiful boy, an achievement even if the part he had played had been minimal. Tonight, of course, he knew the boy was a stranger and he was out of his depth. He was again the runt, the motherless boy shunned by almost the whole community. He almost hadn't turned up; he definitely wished he hadn't now. He just knew his soul cried out to come home. He wanted Fergal to understand. He wanted to unburden himself, to be forgiven, to atone. He took a deep breath and looked Fergal straight in the eye. 'I came to see my old home, my old sweetheart. Turns out I should never have gone away. The son I knew nothing of is nearly twenty years old. I missed it all.'

'That's harsh,' Fergal shrugged, 'must be difficult to pick up those reins.'

'Maybe in time, you know.' Joe looked helplessly at Fergal. 'Dermot's grand, truly. Grand.'

'I see,' Fergal said but showed no surprise. 'So, where do I fit in?' Fergal opened his hands as if the answer would fall neatly into them.

'Ah, yes,' Joe Kelly sighed. 'I came to lay a ghost, finally face what happened.'

Fergal's eyelids lowered a fraction and Joe soldiered on. 'My father beat a man senseless with his bare hands and continued to beat him. I saw him: he saw me. To my shame, I did nothing to intervene. I ran away. Being witness to violence wasn't rare, hiding under some hedge, in some ditch, caught out on the way home from somewhere and too frightened to do anything. I was a teenager sick to my stomach with fear. It's taken most of my life – therapy, drink – to find the courage to come back. It is not easy to admit being a coward and that your own father's a bad lot. Sure, he was encouraged by the politics of the time and by those wanting a thug like him to do their dirty work.'

'I suspect something like this happened to my father,' Fergal nodded. 'Unless.' He sprang to his feet with a surge of energy. He thrust one arm on the back of the sofa behind Joe, pinning him down, hissing, 'You were there, weren't you?' Fergal's face was so close, Joe was sure Fergal would hit him. Joe's shirt stuck to him with sweat. He had seen that glint before, felt that tension in the closeness of another body. He closed his eyes, Fergal's breath in his face smelled of chocolate and alcohol. 'I want names.' Fergal paused between each word so it sounded more a plea than a threat and Joe knew the moment had passed.

With a wave of enormous pity for them both, Joe had an urge to reach out and hug Fergal, wrap him in his arms, hold on to him and beg his forgiveness. He shifted sideways and Fergal immediately backed off as if the movement brought him back to himself. They didn't speak for a while, but neither of them looked away.

'I'm sorry,' Fergal said at last and flopped back on the chair opposite Joe.

'I'm sorry too,' Joe said, and nervously ran a hand round his collar as if it choked him. 'I'm sorry you were caught up in it. I'm sorry I was.'

'Caught up in it?' Fergal snarled, 'It's not something you forget, even aged seven, the sudden disappearance of your father and the total disintegration of your world and a posse of men thundering past full pelt.'

Joe wanted to console him. He had a few whiskies inside him and the edges were blurred as well as his words.

'We were starving. Did you know that? They killed my brother.' Fergal's voice was so flat it was disturbing.

'You should let it drop, Fergal. Let it go. That's my advice. It's too long ago.'

Fergal let out a whelp like an animal in pain. 'I can't, it goes too deep,' and his head sank in his hands.

'And that's why you want names?' Joe said, 'To what end? Revenge?'

'Maybe.'

'You've got your wife to think of. You owe it to her and to yourself. Live in the moment and look to the future. Career, family; it's all before you and all for the taking. All the things I don't have and wish I did.' Joe watched Fergal's face and saw he listened intently. He hoped he was coming round. 'I've spent my life atoning for my father's guilt. At last, I've managed to let it go.'

'I've tried to make it just about the property.' Fergal's voice became more business-like. 'I've established it's mine and I intend to have it.' He paused for a moment's breath, adding very quietly, 'But I owe my brother more than that.'

'Why? You survived and he didn't, you mean?'

'It's complicated,' Fergal shrugged.

'Tell me,' Joe said, 'Why have you brought Rosie here? And on honeymoon, too? I can understand why you came. We're two sides of the same coin, but it's a lot to ask a young girl like that.'

'I can't explain it myself. Perhaps I wanted someone to remind me what's normal and decent.'

Joe Kelly shook his head, 'It's none of my business, but have you thought of getting professional help?'

Fergal laughed, 'There was more than enough of that in care. They didn't know what to do with me!'

'Well, you've done all right, haven't you? Almost establishment, a property lawyer. What's the point now? It's so long ago, most are dead and Driscoll's a changed man.' Joe gasped as he realized his mistake. Again, Fergal was on his feet.

'You telling me it was Driscoll?' He began to pace like a caged animal, one hand balled into a fist punching the other. Joe Kelly was appalled. What had he unleashed? He'd come to make amends and he'd made matters worse. He tried to restore control, the older man cautioning calm.

'Driscoll was there, as I was, but I told you, it was my father.' Joe's throat tightened, he felt tears on his face. 'It went too far. Out of hand – beyond all – I don't know.' He put his head in his hands and couldn't stop the tears. He searched his pockets for a handkerchief but not finding one used the cuff of his jacket to wipe his face. 'I'm sorry,' Joe said.

Fergal stopped pacing, perhaps moved by the sight

of him, and came to sit beside him on the couch. He put his hand on his arm. 'Sometimes, I wish I could cry,' Fergal said.

Joe was unnerved. He let Fergal's hand rest for a moment before easing himself free.

'I should go,' he said. 'Tomorrow's another day, work calls and I've a journey ahead of me.'

They stepped out of the cottage together. 'I'm sorry,' Joe said again.

'I know,' Fergal replied, quite calm and rational and held out his hand. 'Here's to the book,' he said as if they'd merely been discussing the weather.

Joe Kelly kept hold of Fergal's hand and searched his face. He wondered should he extract a promise from Fergal not to do anything stupid, anything he'd regret. He said, 'Think of Rosie and remember why you married her.'

'Oh, I know I'm a lucky man,' Fergal said. He looked up at the starry sky. 'No moon, tonight.'

Joe looked up too, 'Makes you feel very small, doesn't it.'

Dermot still slumped on the beach, in danger of falling asleep in the sand only to wake cold and stiff before dawn as he'd done many times in the early days, too tired yet to walk back to the container. He thought of the notebook and wished again that he had read more of it. His head reeled with all that had been uncovered in such a short space of time. A Pandora's box, with all the secrets better kept locked up. Why had no one ever told him? Surely his presence wasn't such a disgrace? Dermot sighed. Was he left with hope? It was too early to tell, too much for him to cope with. Maybe he should go to Driscoll now and ask him outright. Driscoll was full of surprises and full of secrets. *It's never too late to say you're sorry, Dermot,* was one of his gems. Perhaps Driscoll had always been preparing him for the truth about his real parents.

Dermot was about to shift when he heard someone coming towards him. He held his breath. Joe Kelly passed right by unaware he was there, stomping along the sand, away from the cottage and the pub. Dermot waited for him to pass. The last thing he wanted was an all-night vigil with Joe Kelly. Almost drunk with tiredness, Dermot rolled to his feet as another figure loomed out of the night, lithe as a cat on velvet paws, and followed Joe Kelly like a shadow. The place did not feel his own with so many strangers in town. He arrived home exhausted, barricaded the door from the inside, still waiting for the locks Pat would help him fit, latched the window Pat had thoughtfully fitted and fell gratefully onto his mattress.

~*~

Rosie woke, surfacing slowly from a deep sleep, but she had not been dreaming. It was still pitch black and the bed was cold beside her. An old fear claimed her. Irrational as most fears but indelible as the letters in rock. She flailed for the bedside light, forgetting where she was in her panic and knocked it to the floor. She lunged across to the other side of the bed, feeling more carefully for the light and succeeded in switching it on. Her fear receded, back into the dark night. It troubled her rarely now, but it was always a sure sign that all was not well. It was her barometer. Others had premonitions or asthma attacks; she had this terror of the dark.

One night when their parents were at a party, Hugo had been left in charge. She can't have been more than nine years old, so he would have been thirteen or fourteen; old enough to know what he was doing. They were alone in the house and he was her guardian. When it was her bedtime he'd frogmarched her to her bedroom at the end of a rather long corridor. Trees had cast moving shadows all along it, through the open windows. As he'd put out her light and prepared to close her door he'd told her he'd seen a face outside. He'd run back down the corridor to safety leaving her pleading with him to come back and rescue her. She'd screamed till she was exhausted but he never came. Why this tease had frightened her so, or why she hadn't simply gone to find Hugo, she'd never understood. The following day, too ill to move, the doctor was called and she was packed off to hospital with suspected scarlet fever. Hugo looked suitably contrite when he'd come to visit, but neither of them told their parents what had gone on.

Four o'clock. The house felt empty but she called out for Fergal, just in case. Now where was he? The certainty that Fergal was not being totally truthful stuck like a painful lump in her throat. She lay with her light on hoping to fall back to sleep and fretted the facts she knew and those she didn't. She wondered exactly where she fitted into Fergal's long-term plan. Even allowing for memory being unreliable and volatile, like versions of the truth, it seemed the house had been on Fergal's mind for years. She was still convinced this was not all he was after.

FOUR

The house started to give off a stink through the night, through the day, seeping through the contents of drawers and clinging to the clothes on our backs. It escaped under unopened doors and could not be ignored. Even Mystique took to moping, desperate too it seemed, and spending time outdoors, in spite of the incessant rain. Grandad explained the stink: stench, decay, death.

'Something's got trapped inside the damn roof and not been able to escape, some poor thing has died,' spluttering in English to communicate since there was no one left to hear. 'Lord save us; the whole house has turned against us.' He gathered Mystique in his thin arms and travelled. For want of money, he took only the one favourite grandson with him and kept his journey to the house, starting at the top floor, the coldest and dampest part of the house needing the most buckets in the rainy season. The rainy season in Ireland was the longest season of the year, a disrespecter of boundaries or limits, always intent on breaking records.

The roof caved in to the final indignity of the stink and could be heard crashing intermittently. Rain fell like a silver veil outside and in, covering the truth as best it could. When Granda opened the door of the final room, Mystique sprang from his arms with fright towards the open window, had rather fly out through the air, spread-eagled and falling to earth, with Granda calling after him, than be in that room.

Is that where he went?
Who, Granda?

No, you son of a myrmidon, who d'you think?
All I know is it sent them ill, raging and rampaging.
Who? Who is it that you mean?

The situation was decaying.
Can situations decay?
Everything else has, so why not?

Gardaí: the state police force in the Irish Republic.
Comes after
Garble: reproduce in a confused way.

Investigate: carry out a systematic inquiry into an incident to establish the truth.
What has that to do with anything?

I thought it might shed light on the
Incident: a violent event such as an attack. Unlawful: not conforming to or permitted by law or rules.
You think it's something despicable then?
Don't you?

Stethoscope: medical instrument for listening to the action of someone's heart
Comes after

I'll tell you what it comes after. It comes after a dirty great shock to the system the like of which you never recover from. You did not see the thing.

What thing?
The stink

If you're not going to tell me you shouldn't have mentioned it.

Shroud: length of cloth in which a dead person is wrapped for burial, a thing that surrounds or hides someone or something.

What does it matter now?

Forget: fail to, or deliberately cease to, think of someone or something.

I'll never forget.

Granda saw to it that all the flowers were picked, with Mystique leading the way down the garden, twitching his tail. There would be no more sleeping in the sun, no nice warm patch in the daisies. Armfuls were carried into the house.

The body was laid out on the dresser. The sweet smell of the mound of flowers gave off the hint of must as the damp destroyed them.

Honeymoon

Malachi looked at the dead child's face, a white china plate surrounded with flowers, the exact same face as the child who stood before him.

'Which one is this?'

'Lorcan.'

'No,' Granda roared, over and again, mad with grief, and no wonder, son and grandson to be laid in the cold earth together. 'Fergal's dead.'

Time split and through the chink was life through another's eyes; a chance to be the favourite, the good, the why can't you be more like your brother? brother.

Shut up.
Shut out, get shut of.

Comes after
Shunt: to move from pillar to post in a despicable manner,

Orphanage: a residential institution where orphans are cared for.
Comes after
Orotund: pompous.

With Mystique gone, Granda had no options left. He could not envisage a lonely life without him. An orotund old so and so took charge of the situation, shunted him off and broke the bond forged between brothers to suit his own ends.

Amen: so be it.

DAY FOUR

The first crack snapped in Dermot's dream like a face slap. Jenny, the girl of his dreams was wrapped tightly in his arms and he was about to kiss her. With the second loud crack the dream receded. Dermot fumbled to open up and stumbled outside, needing to empty his bladder now that he was awake. His shoulders hunched as he waited for the relief of the flow before he realised there was something wrong.

The sound of shattering glass burst again and again as if raucous guests were showing appreciation after a decent party. Light flickered off the metal of the container and he spun around at once excited and frightened. Fire creates a distinct light unlike any other. It could only be Driscoll's shanty. Dermot ran, alert now, along the top of the dunes, before taking the steep sides in huge strides, slithering down to the back of the old house. One end was already alight, shooting flames into the dawning sky. Smoke crawled under the eaves, thick and knotted like a living, heaving vine. More glass shattered, blowing out at him as an arm of flame punched through, aiming for his face. He dodged the searing heat, folded an arm over his face and hesitated. He was very afraid, not of the fire, but of losing the old man.

He shoved the door feeling the paint begin to bubble

under his hands in the heat of the wood. Smoke and heat scorched his throat and made his eyes stream, half blinding him. He groped grimly, searching for the bed, groaning every time his fingers burned. Already the bedding was smouldering. He did not know if Driscoll was still alive as he hauled him up and folded him across his shoulder like an overcoat. He thought only of escape, aware how merciless the fire had become.

He staggered clear, gasping as if his throat had closed over. Sand impeded every step, closing over his ankles, till exhaustion and Driscoll's dead weight forced him to his knees. He laid Driscoll gently in the sand, dragging him further up the steep slope nearer his container, finally collapsing on his back beside him. The fight to gain control of every breath blotted out all else. When finally he opened his eyes, charred embers glowed above him like fireflies floating gently down to earth. Driscoll moaned and Dermot turned towards him. 'Are you hurt?' Dermot's first concern.

'I'm alive. You?' They lay together listening to the sounds of the fire and the sea some distance below.

'Lucky for you I was staying here. Lucky for you I woke up.' Dermot said.

Driscoll rasped, 'Sure I'm very lucky. My whole house just burned away. You should have left me.'

With his remaining strength, Dermot hauled Driscoll to the container, laid him to rest on the mattress and covered him with the sheet. Driscoll held his arm feebly, 'Thanks, Dermot,' and almost immediately was asleep as if drugged and lay as still as death. Dermot lay beside him, exhausted and stifled by the stench of fire in his lungs, his hair, his skin, but it was something else that kept him awake. He pieced together the events of the night, the explosions of glass and the heat. He must have been inside the shack but he did not remember that. He remembered the pain in his lungs as he tried lifting Driscoll and the weight of him gradually becoming unbearable. He remembered Joe Kelly and his shadow prowling in the night, Joe Kelly wanting to be part of his life, and felt the burden of that too.

He had fresh water in an old rain butt he'd rescued and lugged home from the shore and longed to stand under the deluge of cold, clear water to let it take away the smell, take away the pain, let it clear his head. As he tried to take off his clothes he saw that his hands were bloody and at the sight of them, realised they were the source of pain. His face smarted with the cold water where the searing heat of the night had roasted his skin. The stench of burning flesh made him retch. He managed to pull on an old tracksuit before the pain of his hands was too much. He could not bear to look at them. He had two new pairs of underpants that Louise had given him, having ordered the wrong size for Pat, new and clean and he wanted to wrap his poor damaged hands in their soft cotton. Even that was tricky. His body trembled and his fingers had seized up and refused to work individually. He draped the pants, one over each hand and folded his hands under his armpits, crying out with the pain that was suddenly worse.

Dermot nudged Driscoll gently on the shoulder but Driscoll made no response at all, lying like a corpse draped in his sheet. Alarmed, Dermot put his head on

Driscoll's chest and listened to the faint lub-dub, unsure at first if the sound was only in his ears. He put his face close to Driscoll's mouth and felt breath on his cheek, but Driscoll did not wake up.

'Don't die on me now.' Dermot felt panicky. He needed help. He tucked his hands protectively under his arms and stumbled headlong through the overgrown path, the shortest way he knew. Louise would help him; he could trust Louise, he knew, and Pat. They were his first, his last, his only thought.

Dermot moved along the main street like a shadow clinging to the walls till he came to the house. A light shone through from the back. Thank God. He uncrossed his arms ready to tackle the door, sending shooting pains right through him and he tried not to cry out. All the effort it had taken to get here and he could not get in. He leaned his forehead on the door cursing under his breath and the door sprang lightly open.

Louise was standing in the kitchen with her back to him. When he called her, his voice husky and unlike himself, she turned. 'Dermot! You nearly gave me a heart attack.' Her face lit with delight and she strode towards him wiping her hands on the apron tied over her dressing gown. He held his hands up in their unusual bandages to stop her crashing painfully into him. She laughed, 'Glad to see you've found a use for the underpants,' but Dermot could barely stand and collapsed onto the lintel for support. 'What is it, Dermot? My God you reek of fire.'

'I couldn't wash the smell away.'

She cradled his hands, touching them lightly before

he had time to draw them away and back into himself to absorb the pain. 'Come on,' Louise pushed him gently into the back room and sat him on the couch, lifting his feet for him and put a blanket over him as he began to shiver. 'Deep breaths now, Dermot.' She sat beside him with a calming hand on his shoulder till the shivering subsided, then peeled back the underpants. She stared for some moments at the wounds and then at Dermot who was white with shock. 'These burns are deep. I'm going to cover them and they might be less painful. I think I've got something till we get proper help. What was it? Your breakfast?' She shook her head half suspecting he had returned to his former wild ways and could not help voicing her misgivings. 'Dermot, Dermot, Dermot, what have you done?'

'You don't understand.' In the shock, Dermot was barely coherent.

Louise called quietly from the bottom of the stairs up to Pat, already stirring and waiting for a cup of tea, 'Come down right now, Pat.' She tried to minimise the panic in her voice but even her whisper was hoarse with emotion. 'It's Dermot. His hands are awful burnt.'

Pat was beside her in no time, kissed her gently, instantly lessening her worry. Dermot's eyelids flicked open in alarm at the sound of Pat's gravelly whisper, till he recognised him. 'Hello Pat.'

'What's all this?' he said, pointing to Dermot's hands, also suspecting some failed prank rather than heroics. Dermot was in tears and Pat did his level best to comfort him. 'I'm sure we can help, Dermot.'

Honeymoon

'Thank God,' and 'good man' was repeated several times as facts were established that Driscoll had survived the fire thanks to Dermot and was now lying in the container. Pat took charge, already dialling for the emergency services. Dermot should be put to bed properly and the doctor summoned. Louise would stay to look after him till the doctor arrived. He himself would meet with the Gardaí and show them the way to Dermot's container and they would decide from there the next best step.

Louise laid cling film over the damage, padded his hands with cotton wadding and wound clean bandages gently over and over. She apologised every time he winced but Dermot, exhausted by the night and the pain, could not keep his eyes open. He was very pale. She watched the rise and fall of his chest. His hands rested stiffly upturned on his lap as if they were very painful.

It was fully light when Dermot woke in the stillness of his old bedroom. Sounds from the rest of the house came to him, comfortingly familiar, the drone of Pat's voice from the kitchen, a deep bass rumble that he had often fallen asleep to as a boy, a blast of music from the radio, and the volume swiftly turned down before he could recognise the tune, Louise's no-nonsense heels on the tiles of the kitchen floor. The throb of his fingers, curled stiffly, palms uppermost on top of the covers, momentarily forgotten, the stench in his mouth and nose, momentarily relieved. He imagined he could smell bacon cooking or maybe it was something sweet. Dermot heard the sirens wail and pictured Driscoll speeding along the lanes to hospital. He closed his eyes satisfied he had done all he could.

Louise and two men were beside him. 'You've to go to the hospital. The ambulance is here. They sent the chopper for Driscoll.'

Dermot tried to sit up and failed.

'Stay there Dermot,' one of the men in his green serge was reassuring, 'we've a stretcher for you.' As they prepared to lower him onto it, struggling in the narrow bedroom. Louise took charge.

'Wouldn't it be easier if you had one of those chairs? The stairs are too narrow. He could always walk down.'

One of the ambulance men, already breathing hard with sweat beading his brow, appeared relieved, 'If you think he can.' They helped Dermot to his feet, 'Take your time Dermot,' and almost carried him downstairs, and from there they stretchered him to the waiting ambulance. Pat came with him. Occasionally Dermot would open his eyes and see Pat still looking at him. The journey seemed to take forever.

~ * ~

Rosie's morning was blighted by nausea and a sense of glumness that they would not soon be packing to go home. There was no plan, no definite way forward as if time were suspended. The suspicion that she had been misled nagged at her like a misery. Fergal lay like a log except for the snoring, and the reek of booze. Perhaps that was why she was nauseated. She washed and dressed noisily but still did not disturb him. She thought of leaving a note then huffily changed her mind. All she could write would be 'Out' and he would know that by her absence – if he woke up at all. She longed to sit undisturbed, slowly turn the pages of a newspaper and eat hot buttered toast. She thought wistfully of mornings at home with her parents that had seemed so stiff and distant but now so welcome.

Smoke hung in the air, blown in from a thick black coil somewhere at the far end of the beach. A small knot of people stood outlined starkly against the sky as if they'd been painted on. She thought immediately of Driscoll, seeing in an instant, charred remains, the old man in his chair fallen asleep with a cigarette in hand and hoped he had stayed asleep and hadn't woken to the struggle, the horror of it. She rushed upstairs and shook Fergal awake, 'Get up Fergal. There's something wrong. Something's happened. It could be Driscoll.'

Fergal was mercifully alert. He pulled on yesterday's crumpled clothes, grabbed her hand and together they ran towards the beach. Rosie grew short of breath as Fergal quickened the pace. She began to lag behind, her heart thudding. Pebbles sucked at her feet almost defeating her altogether. 'You go on; I'll catch up.' She could see he was torn, his dream already fading in his eyes. 'Go on, Fergal, I'll be behind you.' She watched the fine muscles of his calves, still white from city life, working like those of an athlete as he moved away. Something else she did not know about him, perhaps he was a runner.

There was nothing left of the house they had been in the night before. Occasionally a row of flames would ignite from the red-hot embers and dance briefly along the ground. The small knot of people she had seen earlier had unravelled to a respectful semicircle. Fergal stood beside Joe Kelly. She joined them, putting her arm round Fergal, leaning into him. He was shaking. Voices were kept to a murmur, a soft low hum. No one could quite believe what they saw and yet they all knew that it had been waiting to happen; the old man, the drink, the old cottage.

'If it had been daytime, we might have seen it.'

'The old bugger had a good long life.'

'He died like a Viking.'

Gradually people began to disperse, drifting away in twos and threes to walk slowly away, turning once or twice to view the desolation behind them. 'Sad business.' Joe shook his head and sighed, 'I used to love Driscoll; he was like a father. I thought I was in love with his daughter.'

There was something so sad in his voice that Rosie felt she had misjudged him. He was here searching for his past and the loss of Driscoll affected him too. 'I used to love that house. Much of my youth was spent there,' Joe continued. 'It's all so long ago.'

Everyone assumed Driscoll was dead. Standing here with the heat and the ruins of the fire, she was not so sure. 'You don't know he's dead,' she said. 'Driscoll might not even have been at home when the fire started and I sincerely hope that he wasn't.'

Fergal looked at her with a long slow stare as if returning from a place a long way off, a look that Rosie had come to recognise.

'We should think of going, Fergal.' She took his

elbow trying to turn his gaze away.

'I'll walk back with you if you don't mind,' Joe said, and he gave Fergal a hearty slap on the back. 'We did get through quite some whisky last night.'

Fergal began to whimper like an animal in distress, his face folded in on itself and tears rolled down his cheeks. Rosie was bewildered as if this was happening to someone else and she tried to hug him, soothe him by patting his back, embarrassed this frailty was witnessed by Joe Kelly. Fergal rested the weight of his head on her shoulder as if laying down a burden however briefly as almost immediately he stood up and wiped his eyes on the hem of his shirt.

They walked on in silence, Fergal between Rosie and Joe Kelly. Every so often she was sure Fergal was still weeping. At one point Joe Kelly handed him his handkerchief, another beautifully ironed and folded linen square. All the care that had gone into the laundering made Rosie think of her mother. Someone must love Joe Kelly very much to look after him so well. She could not help being curious, 'Are you married, Joe?'

'Why do you ask?' He was defensive as if she had disturbed some reverie.

'That hankie is so carefully ironed, that's all.'

'I do my own ironing.'

She understood then that he must be lonely, and she saw him pining away in England away from the country where his heart was and wondered if it was in some way the same for Fergal.

They came to the cottage door and to her relief Joe

Kelly did not expect to come in, intent only on returning to England. 'I'll see if Dermot can take me to the ferry,' he said.

'Hardly! Driscoll's house has just burned to the ground, maybe with him in it.' The words were out of Rosie's mouth before she could think to soften them.

'You're right,' Joe said, 'what was I thinking? But there must be more than one taxi, even a bus or a train from somewhere. I'll come to say goodbye before I go if there's time. It's been good to meet you, Mr and Mrs Pierce.'

He held out his hand and Rosie shook it. There was nothing calculated in his look, no attempt to guess what she thought, or even to hide what he was thinking, just something vulnerable as if he was deeply unhappy and she felt sorry. 'I hope,' and for the life of her, she couldn't think what she could hope for him. 'I hope you have a good journey,' she said at last. Joe Kelly walked away and she thought it might be the last time they saw him.

'We should stay and sit it out, don't you think?' Fergal said, as soon as the cottage door was closed. 'Find out what's happened. Besides, it's quite something that a volcanic eruption kept us on honeymoon. Shame we already made the baby, because that would be even more auspicious. How long does volcanic ash take to clear? Should only be for a day or two at the most.'

Rosie said nothing. She leaned her hands on the back of a chair, firming her resolve to go home with or without him.

'You know, we could call your brother.' Fergal

seemed remarkably cheerful. 'Maybe Hugo would like to come and get us, stay a few days.'

She was desperate to be home but had not thought to ask Hugo for a lift. 'Actually, he rang me last night.'

'You never said.'

'We've spent the last few days never saying anything to each other, for one reason or another.'

'Come here,' he took her in his arms, 'has it been so awful?'

'Well yes, if you must know.'

'I'm so sorry, really I am. I'll make it up to you.' Fergal showered her with little kisses. 'Breakfast? Perhaps we'll get some news in the pub. Give me five minutes while I get washed.' When she heard Fergal bolt the bathroom door, Rosie considered packing her things and running away, going home to her old life but before she could even open her suitcase Fergal came out of the bathroom, sweet smelling and towelling his hair. 'You were quick,' she said.

'I didn't want to keep you waiting for me too long,' he smiled.

She watched Fergal getting dressed, surprised that she should still feel desire. 'I'm sorry about the fire,' Rosie said. 'Driscoll must have meant a lot to you, a link with your past.'

'That's the funny thing,' Fergal combed his hair with his hands, 'I don't remember Driscoll. Even the photograph he gave me and told me was of him, I'm still convinced that's my grandfather. He went out of his way to be helpful, though.'

'It's odd, don't you think, that the fire should happen

now, while we're here?' She did not wait for an answer. 'Where were you last night, by the way?'

Fergal stopped smoothing his hair and turned to face her. 'I was here with you.' His eyelids lowered just a fraction.

'Except for the time you weren't. I was awake ages in the night and you definitely were not here.' Rosie challenged him, sticking her chin out defiantly. 'I was really scared.'

'Poor you,' Fergal said, kissing her forehead, 'I'm sorry. I stood out for some air when Joe Kelly left.' The explanation came easily and she accepted it.

'I remember him, though, Joe Kelly.' Fergal looked at her expectantly. Rosie did not grasp what he meant.

'From the past, do you mean?'

'He was just this big boy who used to torment us.'

Rosie was horrified. 'But that's awful. Why did you invite him in? Why did you get drunk with him?'

'Actually, he invited himself and I didn't get drunk with him. I kept an eye on what we both had. He might be able to drink half a bottle of whisky with no consequences, I know I can't.'

'But you stank this morning. It made me feel sick.'

Fergal breathed in deeply, 'I'm sorry.' He wanted to hug her but she didn't want to be hugged and stood immobile out of his way.

'I could almost feel sorry for him. Poor bastard!' Fergal said, 'From what Joe told me last night, he had a rough deal.'

'You've probably had as rough a time as he did, Fergal. And there's still hope for you,' she said.

He laughed, 'At least I had a happy start and now I've got you and Hugo, a proper family.'

'You poor little things, all of you.' She had a vision of the boys in the photograph having their life spoilt by Joe Kelly, who in turn had his life spoilt. 'What did he want?'

'To talk about the past, I think.'

'Was it helpful? I suppose it has come back to you being here.'

Fergal let his shoulders rise and fall as if mustering what to say. 'Not helpful exactly. The past has always been patchy. And it does come back in flashes, little episodes, you know while I'm asleep or out walking, just going about life.'

'I was wondering why you chose our honeymoon to come back.'

Fergal stared at her. 'Perhaps I wanted you to be with me. Perhaps I thought you wouldn't marry me if the truth was too awful. Is that what you want me to say?' Fergal moved away and she thought she had lost him. With his back towards her, he said, 'It's the anniversary of my brother's death. That's why it's now. Homage if you like, because I survived and he didn't.'

Rosie was stunned silent under the weight of sorrow Fergal had borne all these years. She rested her head on his back, feeling his tight muscles relax. 'I'll try to understand,' she said. After a few moments, she remembered the notebook. 'Oh, I almost forgot. You know that property Dermot said had been stolen? I've seen it.'

'What?' Fergal sounded angry and spun round to look at her.

'Just wait, I'll explain. You should be thankful, not cross.'

'I'm not cross.'

'Fine,' she said. 'A grubby notebook, handwritten and smelling of underground passages was in the pharmacy that day I went.' Animated, Fergal demanded to know the colour of the cover. When she said she thought it was brown, his face fell and he turned aside. 'Aren't you even going to look for it, aren't you at least curious?'

'It's not the book I'm looking for.'

For the first time, Rosie felt they were getting somewhere. 'You came to find something, actually something?' She tried to keep calm, keep her voice completely without the anger and frustration she really felt. Fergal fidgeted, then took both her hands in his and began talking.

'I know for sure that I left a notebook hidden in the dresser in the kitchen. I see myself putting it there, I see my brother putting it there and I want it. I want its store of memories. I want to feel again that sense of communing with my brother. Its pages have echoed in my head since I was a boy. I'd never have left it behind only I didn't have time to get it before they came for me.'

'Oh Fergal.' She felt on the verge of tears. 'Why didn't you tell me?' Rosie was used to everything upfront and open. Fergal didn't answer. She was getting used to that. Then he surprised her.

'We were allowed to run wild and free. The old biddies at church said we were feral, like beasts in the field. Aidan maintained we were just free range.'

Rosie laughed in spite of it all.

'Aidan wrote little stories for us, fun things, almost daily, almost a diary. Usually, when we woke in the morning there would be another instalment, another message as if he'd been up for hours already. He gave us his old typewriter to keep us occupied I think so that he could work. My brother always wanted to make a dictionary and I wanted to write, or maybe the other way round. It's all in there anyway. We kept it together, thinking each other's thoughts. Writing is how we communicated, and Aidan, we lived in a silent house most of the time. Grandfather would only speak Irish and, when we were around, Aidan would answer in English for our benefit but we only got to hear half the conversation. That was part of the trouble; we only ever knew the half of it. I don't know it all now; we were too young and I don't remember although I've tried.'

'Why did you want to keep the book hidden?'

'It was Aidan's idea, I think. We had secret places all over the house where we hid little messages. That's why I needed to get inside. That's why it was such a shock to see it all boarded up.' Fergal laughed. 'Aidan maintained the house was full of spies. He didn't even want us to show it to Granda. There were only the four of us in the house, but I suppose we did have one regular visitor. Perhaps that was it.' There was a slight pause and Fergal didn't elaborate.

Rosie said thoughtfully, 'It's possible someone has your things.'

'That's what I'm afraid has happened. I went all through the house and found nothing.' Fergal's head hung low. He sounded so dejected.

'You know that Driscoll went into the house and took stuff with Dermot?'

'Probably with the best of intentions, the house is in a pretty desperate state.' Fergal stroked her hand, putting it to his lips to kiss her fingers.

'That was Dermot's explanation too.'

He smiled, 'Do you think they had another motive?'

She shook her head. She hardly trusted anyone here; they all seemed self-serving and involved in one cover-up or another. Eventually after years of living with an untruth perhaps you get to believe it, perhaps in a strange way, it becomes the truth. It must be infectious too.

'That little book just turned up,' she said, 'perhaps your one will too.'

He kissed her affectionately on the cheek. 'Thank you. You might be right. I think it must be meant.' He smiled fleetingly.

'What do you mean?' Rosie shrugged. It seemed to Rosie that every time Fergal told her something he also held something back. 'Have you told Hugo any of this?'

'No, why?'

'He was the one who told me you were an orphan. You didn't even tell me that much.'

'I told him because I wanted him to tell you.'

She looked at him thoughtfully. 'Why did you do it that way round?'

He shrugged. 'Perhaps I was sounding you out, wondering if you would mind that I don't know my past. Some people are funny about that.'

'Who, for instance?' She did not understand this reasoning but she knew of her parents' doubts.

'I just know it affects some people,' he said then hesitated. 'Anyway, I was concentrating on the house.'

'I gathered that much.' She stared at him. 'I'm just wondering why you didn't tell me.'

'Well, I wanted to see it first. See what was left and what was possible.'

'And is something possible?'

'I don't know yet. It depends.'

'On?'

'Well on you and on lots of things.'

'For goodness sake!' suddenly Rosie was angry. 'Like what?'

Fergal looked surprised at her exasperation and hunched his shoulders instead of speaking. Rosie kept asking. 'Like what? I'm mighty tired of this game, Fergal. Why don't you just tell me.'

Fergal took a deep breath, 'Actually, there is something.' He was so grave Rosie was worried. 'I don't want to upset you, but there is more.'

She stifled a groan, on the verge of telling him that in spite of what she'd just said she couldn't take any more. What more could have happened? She retreated to the bed, suddenly nauseous with it all and lay staring up at the ceiling, her hands resting on the flat of her belly.

He lay down beside her, propped on his elbow, turned towards her, 'Something that has bothered me for most of my life. It's been a great source of shame.' She could not suppress a sigh, but he did not stop. 'We were left with nothing when Aidan disappeared and it slowly became apparent that something had died in the house. Grandfather and my brother went searching and they found Aidan's body. I never saw it.' Rosie blinked at him, shocked by the vivid recall of what he said was patchy. 'By the time relief came, it was too late for my brother. He gave up the will to live I suppose. I think he died from shock as much as hunger. We laid him out with flowers on the dresser in the kitchen.' His voice dropped to no more than a whisper, tears dripped off his nose.

'That day, when we were finally found, the priest, Malachi, came to the house shouting and panicking, like some great bird of prey in his black cassock.' He snatched at his face to stem the tears. 'I told Malachi that it was me who was dead. I swapped names with my brother. I was always jealous. He was always the favourite so I told the priest that Lorcan had died. I am Lorcan. I am both of us.' His eyes were lowered like a supplicant pleading with her to understand and be lenient.

A surge of panic silenced Rosie. She rejected his revelations as if they had nothing to do with her and deliberately withheld the words she knew would console him: *we could call the baby Lorcan if you like, even if it's a girl.* Fergal had duped her. He knew so much more than he had told her. Her mind zinged; she tried to stay calm, breathing deeply, to ready herself to say something, anything. She tried not to think of the little boys going hungry, of the horror of the discovery of their father. She did not want to think at all and would rather be on her own to make lists so the facts were in some coherent order. She closed her eyes and tears squeezed from the corners and ran silently to the pillow. Perhaps Fergal would suggest they do up the house and live in it and she would die in childbirth too.

Fergal kissed her eyes as if to stem the tears, stroking her forehead and comforting her. 'It will all be fine, Rosie, you'll see. I'm so sorry. Don't cry.'

'You better tell me why. Why was your father attacked and killed?'

'I don't know,' Fergal said.

'Haven't you tried to find out?'

'It was a violent time. I think he got mixed up with undesirables.'

'Well, why? How?'

'I have tried to find out. Seriously. It's like a wall of silence. All trails lead to nothing. Money was a motivator, I think.'

'Come on. What do you mean, undesirables?'

Fergal took a deep breath to ready himself and rolled onto his back staring at the ceiling. 'It seems it may have been political. I think he may have uncovered some IRA operation that he felt compelled to tell the British government, or MI-whatever number they called themselves. The North was an occupied country and there was no shortage of sympathisers here. Well, I think he was found out and betrayed. That's the only reason I can think for the total lack of information.'

The urge to abandon Fergal and this new marriage was overwhelming. She reminded herself it was her choice: for better for worse. Her life, (so close geographically, weren't they both from the western hemisphere, European, British, although technically Fergal was Irish) could not encompass, could not even conceive what had happened in Fergal's early life.

They made love on the big soft bed, doubts and secrets stifling passion and making sex unsatisfying, yet still unable to speak out. Briefly she slept, waking less nauseous, hungry but still uncertain what she should do. Fergal sat beside her on the bed.

'Glad you're awake,' he said as if everything was normal. Perhaps this was normal. 'Fancy something to eat? You must be starving.'

They were subdued on their way to the pub. They sat at their usual table outside as birds flitted to and fro at the bird table. So much was the same yet everything had changed in a few days. She half suspected, like Groundhog Day, the whole honeymoon would start over until they achieved a satisfactory outcome. Yet she did not even feel the same person as the Rosie who had set off on honeymoon.

Jenny was tearful when she came to take their order. 'There's a rumour that the helicopter and the ambulance were out last night. No one has the details but the word is Dermot was injured saving Driscoll. He's quite the hero.'

Rosie was glad and hoped it really was good news. She gave Fergal a bright smile. 'You'll be able to ask

Driscoll about your mother's family after all.'

'Suppose so.' Fergal did not sound overjoyed.

When Jenny arrived with breakfast Rosie asked if the hospital was far and if she'd be going to visit. 'Maybe I'll go in my time off,' Jenny said, 'as things get a bit better. The hospital's hard to get to if you've no car and no taxi.' Jenny turned her head on the way back to the bar and said wistfully, 'It could have been so much worse.'

Rosie toyed with a pastry, the wave of nausea she had felt that morning making a sudden return. 'Why don't you go shopping?' Fergal said as if struck by a bright idea. 'Buy a few things to tide you over.'

'Oh yes?'

'That pharmacy has a surprising range.'

She gave him an old-fashioned look. 'You're sounding more like a local all the time. Your accent, you know the lilt. You don't sound like that in London.'

'Maybe I'm just playing about, putting it on.'

'It sounds natural enough.'

'Why don't you go shopping? That'll cheer you up. Take my card. I'll treat you.'

'What makes you think I need cheering up?' Rosie asked.

'You seem glum and you just told me you've had a horrible time.' Fergal shrugged his shoulders.

'I don't need your card, thank you; I've my own money. And when I do want a treat it will be somewhere like Harrods, not here in the middle of nowhere.' Fergal hazarded a laugh as if uncertain whether she meant it as a joke or not. 'Anyway, I'd be surprised if Louise is open today with her father and Dermot in hospital.'

'True.'

'I suppose I'll need to wash some underwear if we're staying on. How about you?'

'No, I'm fine, I brought loads. Besides, I haven't worn anything inside out yet. Or back to front.'

She laughed reluctantly. 'Is that how it is in an orphanage? Inside, outside then back to front?'

'Yep and that's after some other boy's worn them.'

'Honestly, Fergal,' and finally she laughed freely with her head back and her resolution to go home with or without Fergal seemed almost outlandish.

Fergal went inside to pay and a small white sports car drew up, scattering small stones at the leg of the table. The door was flung open and Hugo unfolded from it, leaning back to straighten himself out. She flung herself at him. 'Hugo, you came.'

'Steady on, Rosie.' He began to pull her arms from his neck and waited patiently for her to get a grip of herself. He placed a hand on her shoulder and studied her.

'Do I look a fright?' she asked.

'No, a bit peaky maybe,' and he smiled at her, turning down the corners of his mouth to make her laugh. 'I decided, what with the situation, I might come and get you. I've been driving for hours, weeks. It's a long way and a hideous crossing. I'm parched.'

'New wheels?' Rosie looked at the sports car, barely big enough for two and thought how typical of Hugo to be so impractical.

'Sadly, not mine. Just borrowed from a friend.'

'Anyone I know?'

'Nope.' Rosie narrowed her eyes at him. She thought she knew all his friends.

Jenny hovered in the doorway, perhaps lured by the bright English voice.

'Perfect timing,' Hugo said smiling at her. 'I'll have a beer, Guinness, please, and a coffee for you, Rosie?' He looked expectantly at her. Rosie shook her head and asked for freshly squeezed orange juice instead. 'That's a bit healthy for you.' Rosie ignored him, studiously looking away from her adored brother. 'Can you bring some sandwiches too? Roast beef?' Hugo asked.

Rosie assured him the sandwiches were lovely. A little way off a woodpecker tapped. A couple walked by arm in arm, nodding a good morning, before disappearing down the lane.

'So where is he, then?' Hugo asked. Rosie did not say anything, overcome with the enormity of how much there was to tell Hugo and not trusting herself not to cry again. 'Fallen out? Hardly surprising in a place like this. Charming of course.' He waved a hand at the bijou façade of the pub with its creeper and flowering tubs. 'But not for a honeymoon. Don't suppose much happens here. Has it been that bad?' Hugo smiled at her in a big brotherly concerned sort of way then pulled a face at her till she had to smile.

'It's so good to see you,' she said, her voice wavering.

When Jenny came with the tray, Hugo asked her about the possibility of a room for at least one night.

Jenny said she would check with Mr Hennessy but she was pretty sure there was a room he could have and she could have it aired and ready soon if he didn't mind waiting.

Rosie watched him drink deeply and still not trusting herself to speak, sipped her own drink and felt it do her good. Hugo fell on the sandwiches, 'No joy with the names you gave me I'm afraid, but I've assigned a secretary to look into it,' he said between mouthfuls. Rosie wondered if he'd even bothered to look. 'I've been looking online and re-reading the back issues of the Irish Times Fergal had in the office. There's no mention of them.'

'Re-reading?' Rosie said.

'Fergal has a stash of them. His father was a well-known writer, and so there's obituaries.' Hugo gesticulated expansively with another sandwich. 'No actual details of how he died. Found dead in his home.' Hugo looked at her and smiled, with the look he used when he wanted her to believe she was a simpleton and this was all too much for her to worry about.

'Wait a minute, Hugo. Did you know Fergal's history? There is stuff online and in the newspapers and no one thought to mention it to me.' She felt as if she was part of an elaborate hoax. Not just her, but her parents, the wedding. She imagined him bamboozling clients with rhetoric but was beginning to be uneasy.

Hugo waved a hand. 'We're treating it like any other case.'

'What do you mean?' Rosie stopped her mouth from falling open.

Hugo picked up his empty glass and peered into the bottom. 'I thought you knew too.'

'I don't believe you. It was so hard to convince the parents because no one knew who Fergal was. You and Fergal deliberately kept quiet. Why?' Her mind was feverish. 'Is that why you wanted to talk to Fergal? Because you are investigating his father's death?'

'Not his death, Rosie, it's the property he's interested in.'

'Bloody hell, Hugo, what else haven't you told me? Why have you been pretending? I don't get it.'

'Fergal asked me not to say anything.'

Rosie couldn't stop her mouth falling open, preparing to emit a howl of anger, despair and sheer frustration. Hugo stood up, ignoring her, and waved at Fergal who had appeared in the doorway of the pub. He and Hugo embraced with a backslapping routine that ended in an elaborate handshake.

'You made good time,' Fergal said, kissing Rosie's cheek and immediately reaching for a sandwich. 'The food's really good here.'

Rosie felt bruised as if she'd been punched. Not only had they known Fergal's history but they had been in touch with each other during the honeymoon. Without telling her. The ability to speak or think coherently abandoned her, as her brother and husband talked across her of the journey, the weather, the sea state of the crossing, the winding roads and the inevitability of being stuck behind a slow-moving farm vehicle. There was some general office chit chat and it occurred to her they were waiting for her to go before they could say what they wanted to each other. She tried to gather her thoughts, tried to understand her situation. Of all that she had expected of married life, all the times she had defended Fergal to maiden aunts and her parents and herself, she had never doubted she was doing the right thing, till now. Fergal had duped her. She wondered had he been unfaithful to her if she would feel the betrayal as keenly.

Then she thought of Hugo. She looked at him as if he was an entirely different person. She had been wrong to trust him so implicitly. She felt his betrayal too, and the wounds ran deep. How could she have got it so wrong? She stood up slowly, 'I'm just going to the little girl's room.' She thought that expression would be a worthy decoy. 'I'll order more drinks on my way, shall I?' There was barely a response.

From the bar, there was a good view of them. She watched Hugo produce an envelope from the inside breast pocket of his jacket and hand it to Fergal, who opened it, scanned the document it contained and then signed it before handing it back to Hugo who replaced it in his inside pocket. It was this more than anything that propelled her to action. She rang the bell with a bright ping and waited for Jenny to appear. Rosie ordered another plateful of sandwiches to go with the drinks to keep them busy. She dropped her voice. 'I'm going to need a taxi,' Rosie said, 'one that doesn't mind long distances, to take me to the ferry.'

Jenny did not seem surprised by the request; in fact, she was most professional. 'Do you have a particular ferry in mind?'

'No, just the nearest port and I'll go on spec.'

'Shall I find out and tell you at the table?'

Rosie insisted she'd rather wait. She sat on a barstool, elbows resting on the bar, head in hands, her spirits sinking, concentrating on a trickle of condensation about to drip to the floor. A shadow passed over the bar and she looked up. Mr Hennessy himself smiled down from his great height. He placed a gentle hand on her shoulder. 'I was thinking of driving out to the hospital myself. Jenny wants to see her young man and I want to see him too and the old reprobate. I could take you where you want to go after that if that would be of interest to you? Go on!' he urged, with a little squeeze, 'It'll take you out of yourself.'

It took a moment for Rosie to grasp he was offering her a lift. 'Thank you,' she said, 'thank you.' Then coming back to herself she asked, 'Do you think Dermot would mind if I called in? I'd like to wish him well before I go.'

'Not at all, not at all. Tell you what,' and he glanced at his watch, 'I'll wait for you up at the crossroads. About an hour or so?' He took his hand from her shoulder and tapped the side of his nose with a finger. 'We don't need to tell anyone, do we? Leave those two myrmidons to get on with themselves.' She smiled her thanks, amazed at Hennessy's grasp of the situation. It was agreed then.

When she got back to the table Hugo's jacket was on the back of his chair and his shirt sleeves were rolled, exposing a lavish gold chain bracelet with links so thick they would need a bolt cutter to get through them. Rosie did not remember ever having seen that before as if it revealed something about Hugo that hitherto he'd kept hidden. Their mother would have commented; she hated to see men in jewels and maintained it was vulgar to openly display wealth. Their glasses were again nearly empty and one sandwich was left looking rather sorry on the plate.

'I hear congratulations are in order,' Hugo said. 'I thought there was something different about you.' He came round to hug her and she proffered her cheek for a peck from him. She did not snarl at Fergal or show any sign at all that she minded dreadfully he'd told Hugo without even consulting her.

'Well since you know, I am feeling a little tired.' She made an excuse. 'I think I'll go for a lie-down and leave you two.'

'Sure you're all right?' Fergal asked.

'Absolutely.'

'Rosie, I,' Fergal started but Rosie didn't want an explanation.

'It's all right, Fergal, I think I know. You want to uncover all there is. Hugo says you're investigating it.' Fergal put his hand round her wrist and she managed not to dash it away.

'I didn't tell you before because…'

'It's fine, Fergal.' She couldn't look at him. She thought if she had to spend another minute with either of them she would cry or shout or start hitting them.

Honeymoon

'We'll leave you in peace then,' Hugo said. 'We have one or two things to talk about and you would probably be bored.'

She looked at them for a moment, both totally oblivious, as if they belonged to some male club to which she was not invited, of whose existence she had been unaware till now, and would anyway have no wish to join. Walking away she felt light-headed. Was this love? Passionate one moment, angry or conflicting the next? The nine to five of her life before the honeymoon did not seem to belong to her anymore and trying to imagine sharing it with Fergal made her head hurt. She thought of her flat that was to have been their first home, the piles of wedding presents, the space she'd cleared in her wardrobe, folding away her possessions to make room for Fergal's. Overcome with lassitude, not entirely sure what would happen, she just knew she had to be away from Fergal, Hugo too, and a long slow journey from Ireland would give her time to work out what it was she actually felt.

It was obvious to her now that Fergal had had an agenda all along. She thought again of the trip to the cemetery. The final resting place of his father and brother were not important to him. He seemed to know or remember everything anyway. Perhaps it was confirmation of his memories that he was after. She shook her head as if to free it of thought. There was so much Fergal had not told her. One thing she knew in her bones, in spite of what Fergal and Hugo insisted, this was not simply to do with the property.

Rosie took a last look round the cottage before

leaving a note on the pillow that she hoped Fergal would not immediately see. She collected her passport, some money, her toothbrush and, as an afterthought, the brooch and put them all in her handbag.

With time to spare before the taxi, she walked to the beach, thinking to go to the secluded spot with the log where everything had seemed possible that first day. Louise was already there. How foolish to think she and Fergal had 'found' it. Perhaps Louise would object if she walked up to her, when there was the whole beach to choose from, as she had objected when Joe Kelly came to talk to her. She could at least ask after Driscoll and Dermot. 'I'm so sorry,' Rosie said and Louise looked up with a tired smile and shifted to make space for her. Rosie sat close to her and Louise laid her head on her shoulder for a while.

'The news is good. They'll both be fine. Thanks to Dermot anyway. The crazy old man thinks he must have fallen asleep with the pan still on.' She shook her head. 'He could have killed them both.' Rosie did not reply. It was comforting to be close to Louise. Louise launched into a conversation as if she was already part way through it. 'No one suspects arson, except Dermot.'

'Arson?' Rosie was uneasy. She thought of her panic in the night and Fergal's absence.

'He thinks he saw Joe Kelly round the place before the fire,' Louise continued.

Rosie breathed more easily. 'I can tell you this because you're not from here and don't really know him from Adam. The firemen have said they'll be sure to examine everything.'

Rosie could feel Louise's shoulders heaving and she tried to console her, 'I don't think Joe Kelly will have done anything like set fire to Driscoll's place. I might have misjudged him. I've spent the last few days loathing him but in the end, I feel sad for him. He's had a raw deal.'

Louise looked at her, almost surprised, 'Do you think so?"

'I think he's had love knocked out of him, one way and another.'

'You may be right. Anyway, Jenny says she arranged a taxi for Joe Kelly quite early on, so he's gone. He never even said goodbye.'

'I'm so sorry. Dermot told me a bit about him last night.'

'He just turns up out of the blue and causes havoc. How can you ruin someone's life all over again?'

Rosie stopped herself apologising again and said, 'And will you be all right?'

Louise seemed to brighten at the concern, 'I've survived worse. Maybe some good has come out of it. Driscoll will get a good dose of looking after in the hospital. He'll hate it,' she laughed, 'but it'll be good for him. Dermot will get over it and it's as well to have the truth out.' Louise sighed and blew her nose, 'whatever that is. No two versions are ever the same.'

Louise's phone rang. 'It's ludicrous, isn't it?' Louise said, 'to have the best signal here in the most secluded spot.'

Rosie said she would leave her in peace but Louise felt for her hand so she would stay where she was. 'It'll be Pat with the latest. Don't go yet.' So, Rosie settled back and waited, checking her watch discreetly, unable to avoid overhearing the clear tone of the voice at the other end of the phone.

'That's something.' Louise smiled, almost her old self. 'Guess who's been to visit? Joe Kelly. So that's one in the eye for Dermot. I guess I should go to the hospital myself, I'd feel better. In fact, I don't know why it was so important to stay here. It's always better to be doing something.' Louise stood up and squared her shoulders.

'I'll say my farewells then,' Rosie began.

'Sure, you'll be back,' Louise said. 'There's more songs to sing and there's plenty of outfits I could make your baby.'

Rosie laughed. If anything, Rosie would come back to the village just to see Louise again. 'There is something,' Rosie added and fished for the brooch Driscoll had given her from her bag. She held it out to Louise. 'I think this might belong to you.'

'I have one just like this,' Louise said, taking it with a smile. 'Unless, did you find this? Did I lose it?' As Rosie explained how she came by it, Louise was silent. Then she placed the brooch in Rosie's hand and closed her fingers over it. 'We have one each, that's all. You keep it, with my blessing. I'll be able to think of you when I wear mine – and the other way about.'

To Rosie, it felt generous, a gesture of friendship that brought tears to her eyes.

'That's really kind of you. I don't know why I'm crying unless it's the hormones everyone moans about.'

Louise patted her hand. 'Just wait till after the baby's born!' She looked quite earnest when she asked, 'You'll be sure to keep in touch and let me know about the baby?' Rosie promised.

When she enquired how Louise was to get to the hospital and Louise said she'd have to ask Hennessy, Rosie explained her own arrangement, leaving out the information about going on to the ferry. 'We'll go together then,' Louise said. 'If I dash, I'll catch Hennessy at the pub. See you at the crossroads.'

The longer Rosie waited at the crossroads, the more the insecurities of the past weeks burdened her. It wasn't that she didn't love Fergal, she was sure of that. The words of gloom from her parents replayed in her mind like a trailer for an advertisement. She did not want to prove her parents right and was on the point of retracing her steps, going back to retrieve the note and pretend that everything was fine, when she saw the taxi coming. Mr Hennessy climbed out to open the door for her. Louise smiled from the front seat and Rosie sat in the back beside Jenny and before she knew it, they were speeding away from the village.

'It's a good forty-five minutes to the hospital,' Jenny said. She had with her a small suitcase. 'I took the liberty of bringing a picnic. I've not had time for anything to eat and I didn't think you'd had much either. That new guy ate most of it with your husband.' Rosie did not say the new guy was her brother. Jenny raised her voice to include Mr Hennessy and Louise.

'You don't mind if we eat in here, do you? Or, would you like something yourselves?' Mr Hennessy said he was partial to beef sandwiches since that's what they happened to have, and didn't mind at all.

The suitcase was rammed with sandwiches and foil parcels. Rosie looked questioningly at Jenny who said softly, 'Mr Hennessy's very generous like that. He said to have enough for all of us.'

Sandwiches were passed around, handed through the dividing glass window and the taxi ride, not dissimilar to the one with Dermot that brought them from the airport, made Rosie feel so jolly she all but forgot she was leaving Fergal. She tried not to think of her cryptic note left on the pillow: *I've decided to get the ferry home*, with no explanation as to why or what she expected to happen, nor concern for how he might feel. To be honest, she neither knew nor cared much. Perhaps by the time the journey was over she would summon the energy to give it due attention. As for Hugo? She didn't know what to make of him unless her whole life had been spent in rose-tinted spectacles and she had not known him at all.

They thanked Mr Hennessy for the lift and the sandwiches then waited while he asked at reception where to find Dermot. Jenny swapped her bag from one hand to another as if it was still heavy, and smiled nervously. Visiting times were officially over it seemed but they were allowed in. Their shoes sounded out on the shining floor of the pristine new hospital as they followed an orderly down the corridor to Dermot's side room as if they were the only ones there.

There was a cheer when Louise, Rosie and Jenny entered Dermot's room followed by a round of shushing as Mr Hennessy appeared after them. Mr Hennessy had not been expected and his presence required that the general mayhem be toned down a little. Dermot seemed so overjoyed with the new arrivals that no one would guess how serious the fire had been but for his rather haunted look of one recently injured and his hands in swathes of protective bandages, fat and stiff as if he wore boxer's gloves. A bag of clear fluid was suspended over his bed with a tube disappearing into his arm under one of the bandages.

'Good day to all of you,' Hennessy said formally. He began unloading a laptop and a stash of films for Dermot from a shoulder bag. 'These'll help you while away the time till you're up and about.' Then he focused on Joe Kelly who had moved to the foot of Dermot's bed to accommodate the newcomers. 'Good to see you here, Joe; it's good you came back to face the music.'

Joe Kelly looked completely different, no longer in the smart suit they'd seen him in till now, but in a sweatshirt and jeans. If anything, it made him look much younger. He also looked more ordinary. Joe's face was blank as if he was stuck somewhere in no man's land and didn't quite know what to make of everything. Rosie kissed his cheek. 'Hello Joe,' she said softly. All the animosity she had felt for him had gone. She could have felt sorry for him but decided he wouldn't want that. She felt blank herself, undecided which was the dream, her old life or here with this new family of friends she had known only recently and yet whose lives seemed so entwined with hers.

Dermot was willing to tell his tale, repeating over and over that it was only by chance he'd found Driscoll and making light of his recent brush with death. 'Life has a way of sorting itself out,' Hennessy said cryptically. As he backed to the door he added to no one in particular, perhaps to them all, 'You're amongst friends now, you know,' and disappeared through it.

Rosie was about to apologise for coming and found herself pushed forward to the bedside. 'I was only just telling Pat I wanted to see you.' Dermot smiled at Rosie and she kissed his cheek. Jenny stood a little awkwardly and raised her suitcase of food. 'Mr Hennessy said to feed you up and not stint.'

The suitcase, still almost full with sandwiches and foil parcels was opened on Dermot's bed. Glasses were produced, and lemonade was shared. 'That's cruel,' Dermot said, as hands dipped in and helped themselves. 'Someone will have to feed it to me.' Jenny volunteered.

All the laughter flowing from Dermot's warm, small hospital room into the rest of the ward did not seem to bother anyone. In fact, when a nurse came to attend to Dermot she ended up laughing and joking with all the rest, tucking into the sandwiches and adding to the gaiety. Others stuck their heads into his room to see what was going on and to stay awhile themselves. 'Any excuse for a party here,' Rosie thought, gazing from face to face. Perhaps they believed laughter had a healing effect. She didn't ever remember fun like this. She saw the possibility of happiness, a fleeting glimpse of what happiness was and it was within her grasp. As if she were dreaming, she saw herself in years to come, as she would like to be with an extended family, perhaps this extended family, with Dermot, Louise, Pat, even Joe Kelly and Jenny.

The fire had brought this community together. It had given Joe Kelly an excuse to stay. Not that she knew this as fact, but she could see that in spite of what he told Fergal the night before, this was where he wanted to be. Finding he had a son was a source of happiness for him.

She spoke to one of the nurses. 'Is this a slack time for you? I mean, is there no one too seriously ill here?'

The nurse laughed. 'It's this hospital, brand new, funded by private investment, only now they can't afford to run it so half the wards are closed. We'll be redeployed or laid off.' Rosie asked the nurse what she would do and the nurse shrugged. 'Oh, one of the two, you know. I'll be redeployed or laid off.'

In her shoes, Rosie knew she would go to pieces. Any set back left her weepy and incompetent. Maybe the nurse, all the staff, had already done that and now were accepting and prepared to find a solution. She should stand up to Fergal and Hugo. How could they be expected to guess what she was thinking? Perhaps her own family were all so anxious not to hurt anyone's feelings they never got round to having any feelings at all. Perhaps all the laughter was good for her too.

Dermot raised his voice above them. 'Can you hold off a minute? I have something I'd like to say to Rosie in private so perhaps you would all like to give Driscoll some of the attention you're lavishing on me. Only for ten minutes or so, I don't want to relinquish it entirely.'

Rosie was snapped out of her daydream, not wanting it to end or to put everyone to so much trouble. Dermot assured her it was no trouble, and besides, it was time for a progress report on the old man.

~ * ~

Hennessy stood near the door of Driscoll's room, head slightly bowed, and did not venture closer to the bed. He'd imagined Driscoll, near death, swathed in white bandages with only peepholes for his eyes, yet there were no bandages and he looked as peaceful as if he was lying in his own bed at home, but for the tell-tale bag of clear fluid attached by a tube to his arm.

Driscoll turned his head, 'Hello Hennessy.' His face was wan against the pillows, his voice no more than a whisper, his breathing rather laboured.

This moment was not as Hennessy expected and had so often rehearsed. Of all the things Driscoll could have said, 'get out', not least among them, 'Hello Hennessy' came as a surprise. Hennessy had ostracised his friend, a decision not taken lightly but one he had not reversed for twenty years, even though he'd thought about it and wondered at the wisdom of it every single day. 'I didn't want to wake you,' Hennessy said finally.

'You didn't.' Driscoll's voice was hoarse.

Hennessy cleared his throat a few times as if an inconvenient lump made it hard to speak. The day Hennessy banned Driscoll from the pub, Driscoll's life had begun to unravel in a way that would have destroyed many men but had been salvation of a kind for Driscoll. Hennessy had been reliably informed, as on most matters concerning those in the village, and had pieced together this story for himself. Driscoll had renounced drunkenness for a start and had released his wife from any obligation to him, accepting her solution to Louise's predicament with the baby. Louise had disowned him. Perhaps Driscoll deserved no better, who was he to judge? 'I thought you'd gone to your grave with this still between us,' Hennessy said at last.

'I thought I would too.' Driscoll's eyes glittered in his white face. 'But, thanks to Dermot.'

'Ah, Dermot,' Hennessy said with a smile. Dermot had saved him too, and become both consolation and joy. Their saving grace, Hennessy liked to think. Ever since Dermot's trouble with the police, some while ago, Hennessy had let himself meddle, favouring him with the job, humouring him with the taxi, even though he had rather wanted a fast little number but what would be the point here, a solid taxi cab was far more the thing. As it turned out, it was more than a whim.

'I should have lifted the ban,' Hennessy said tentatively.

'Let's say we dealt with it in our own way,' Driscoll said wearily.

Hearing this, Hennessy ventured closer, desperate to explain himself. 'I forbade you the pub because looking at you would remind me. How can you look in someone's eyes and know, know they know you know, and not do or say anything about it?'

'Just don't look anyone in the eye,' Driscoll said then

relented and twisted his mouth into a smile. Hennessy smiled too and took Driscoll's hand and gently shook it.

'You've no home to go to. You can stay in the pub for as long as you need, for the rest of your days for all I care.' Hennessy waved a hand expansively. Driscoll shrank back.

'I'm here for a while they tell me. Louise has persuaded them I need tests. But thanks,' Driscoll wheezed, 'I appreciate it.'

'It was a close thing, so I understand.' Hennessy was lugubrious then brightened. 'There must be unfinished business. You were spared because there is still something you must do in this world.'

'Do you believe that?' Driscoll closed his eyes.

Hennessy collapsed onto the chair. 'I have often thought, if I'd come as agreed, I could have done something and the man and the boy would still be alive. I have blamed myself as well as you.' Driscoll moved his head on the pillow to get a better look at Hennessy. They stared at each other for a long time. 'The guilt has changed us,' Hennessy said at last.

He leaned forward, shaking his head from side to side. 'Did we really think that by keeping silent it would matter less? What did we think back then? A tissue of lies is just that, paper-thin, see-through and easily destroyed.'

'This is not a tissue,' Driscoll said. 'It's a vein buried deep in our core.'

Hennessy sighed. 'It had to happen, of course, some little catalyst to upset and undo it all. Perhaps every year around this time for the past twenty years we have been

on edge, more taciturn. Not just one visitor, either.'
Again, they were silent. Driscoll barely moved. Hennessy looked at his old friend and sighed, 'There's an eerie calm over the village.' Then, as if he could not help the indelicate question, 'Why a fire? Why now? Phoenix from the ashes, was that it?'

Driscoll gave him a long cold look, 'Enough horse pills to see me out and set fire to my own place, is that what you think?'

'So, it was an accident?'

'You think I'd let Dermot risk his life getting me out?' Driscoll tutted. 'I wish I'd thought to torch the old place, you know.'

Hennessy grew restless. 'There's a lot of detritus still needs clearing, clogged with it, do you know what I'm saying?'

'No,' Driscoll said, 'sounds like bollocks to me.'

'Ghosts walk amongst us even though none would admit to feeling them or believing. Ghosts of men in unquiet graves; the disappeared, the accused, the innocent, the guilty all tarnished with blood, all tormented with secrets and lies.'

'For God's sake, Hennessy! I certainly haven't missed your carry on.'

Hennessy laughed, 'You might be right.'

Driscoll had a habit of swallowing his lips and worrying them and at the same time frowning so his head appeared misshapen, that Hennessy had forgotten but had always found fascinating. 'Don't you get it?' Hennessy said, 'a fissure's opened up and is shaking loose the secrets we locked in our hearts or buried in the ground. All shaking loose their ancient binding.'

'I'm too tired for riddles, Hennessy. Say what you mean, or don't say it at all.'

'I mean, it's time to set the record straight.'

'But the culprits are dead and gone. What would be the point now?'

'Duty perhaps, for this next generation coming up, atonement?'

'I've persuaded the boy his father wasn't to blame. The last he wants to hear is his grandfather was in cahoots with them.'

'We don't know that for a fact, though. Whoever it was in cahoots with them, it was Aidan Pierce who got killed.' A look of anguish passed across Hennessy's face. He straightened his back and breathed in sharply. 'I've seen you with flowers at the graveside. Perhaps I could take them for you while you're in here.'

There was a tap at the door and Pat, Jenny and Louise, turned out from Dermot's bedside, began to shuffle in.

'Something worth thinking about,' Hennessy said. He took Driscoll's hand in his, bade him good luck and left him to it.

~ * ~

Rosie sat on Dermot's bed and could see that he was exhausted. 'I'm surprised the nurses haven't chucked everyone out,' Rosie said.

'Why would they do that?' Dermot sounded truly puzzled. 'Anyway, they've told me I can come home soon if I stay with Louise and Pat. I may need to keep coming back for a while.' Rosie nodded sympathetically. 'So, while we have the reprieve. I've been thinking. Plenty of time for thinking, till the whole world came to see me.'

Dermot babbled away and Rosie wondered if maybe he was feverish. 'I'm sorry I took the books from the house and that one's gone astray.' She opened her mouth to tell him not to worry, but Dermot lifted his hands off the bed as if to stop her interrupting. 'I have a book your man should have. It's kid's stuff, a lot of it handwritten. I've dipped into it but to be honest with you, it was too personal; it felt like I was intruding.' He told a rambling story of a stray cat that had found its way inside the old house, frightening the life out of him with its glittering eyes, or he might never have looked inside the dresser at all. Even then, it hadn't been obvious, tucked away inside the wall. He reckoned that anything hidden so carefully must be important. Rosie's heart thudded as if it had galloped into her throat. So loud she wondered if Dermot could hear it

'I had too much on my mind last night or I might have told you then. I'd almost forgotten. It's funny the way the mind works, don't you think? I think I already knew the story,' he said. 'I just didn't know I knew it, and I bet that's why you're here, all of you.' Driscoll had told him about the boy who'd starved to death. 'At first, I thought it was a fairy story, one of those stories they frighten naughty children with, a this-is-what-happens-if you-don't-do as-I-say story.

'I've been with Driscoll several times to put flowers on the grave. Atonement, Driscoll called it. He didn't tell me what he had to atone for exactly. While there's breath in my body I'll put flowers on that child's grave. He made me agree, should anything happen to him that I'd make sure the little grave was tended. He didn't know it would be something that happened to the both of us, obviously. I always thought it was Driscoll's association with the family that made him want to, but I think it's more complicated. I think this whole story is long and complicated. Ireland's like that. We're never half-hearted.'

Rosie began to stare, dumbfounded by Dermot's corroboration of her own misgivings.

'I hereby give you – but only you – permission to go and get the book. My container is not locked. You can even make yourself a cup of tea.' He told her how to find his container, where to find the lamps and what to expect. 'I think it's only fair,' Dermot finished with a flourish, 'it's your story now.'

She smiled wanly and did not mention Hennessy's offer of a lift to the ferry or her bid for freedom. There was no escape. She thanked him for trusting her with his container, wished him a speedy recovery and did not wait for the others to come back. She would, in all probability, see them over the next few days. 'Will you tell them I had to go?' She leaned forward to kiss his cheek and Dermot said into her ear in a stage whisper, 'Go easy on that man of yours.'

She gave him an old-fashioned look, 'Why d'you say that?'

'Well,' Dermot began, 'You were pretty cross with him that day I gave you the lift.'

'Believe me, it's not been easy,' Rosie was defensive and Dermot laughed.

'It takes time to get to know a person and even then, they keep surprising you.'

'What are you trying to say?'

'People need loads of second chances.'

She opened her mouth to say more but could not formulate the words. That one so young could have realised this truth and that it applied to her in spades. How strange life is indeed, she thought. The fire and now this, to say nothing of the volcano, had all kept her back. She knew now she would return to the village and to Fergal.

~*~

Joe Kelly was sitting alone outside the room. He looked so dejected that her heart sank for him. She did not know his full story, but seeing him she knew it was not a happy one.

'I'm glad I've seen you on your own,' he said. 'I wanted to give you this to give to Fergal.' He produced a plastic bag from his inside pocket and held it out. She guessed it was the stolen book she'd seen in the pharmacy, making its way back.

'Am I allowed to know what it is?' she asked, taking it and turning it over, feeling the weight of it like an added responsibility.

'Sure. There's been enough secrets and there's a few facts that might be of interest. We have history. I don't know if Fergal told you that?'

'He did say he remembered you.' She smiled briefly.

Joe Kelly looked glum. 'Is that so? Nothing good, I don't suppose.'

She sat down with him on the hard chairs in the corridor. 'Why don't you give it to him yourself?'

'Well, I'm going for the ferry.'

'I was going to get the ferry, too.' She shrugged. 'Give up on Fergal as a bad lot.' She laughed. 'Only I've decided not to run away after all.' The dim lights of the corridor suddenly brightened exposing the two of them and then dimmed again leaving them to their quiet talk. 'It must be something to discover you've a grown-up son,' Rosie said.

'It's taking some getting used to.' His voice lisped in the now quiet corridor. 'I never thought I'd be so lucky, you know. I didn't know what I'd find, certainly not a grown-up son and to be honest, I don't want to miss another moment of it.

'Is there something urgent you need to get back to? Why don't you stay? Stay for Dermot, he'll need help for a while.'

Joe Kelly appeared to brighten. 'Dermot might take a bit of persuading though.'

'Oh, I don't know. He's very charming and affable.' Rosie began to feel bold. 'Did you come back to find Louise?'

Joe Kelly nodded, 'But that was only part of it. I've been hiding from my past all my life and coming back to Ireland was the first major step. I nearly denied it all over again. Then I just thought, what's the worst that can happen?'

She handed him back the book. 'You keep it,' said

Honeymoon

Joe, pushing it back towards her.

'Ok,' She smiled. 'I'll give it to him. You can see Fergal yourself, later.'

~*~

Rosie found Mr Hennessy outside by his taxi and quietly broke the news to him that she would not now be going for the ferry. He was overjoyed. 'It's a long run,' he said. He agreed to take her back straight away and invited her to sit beside him at the front of the cab. 'More comfortable,' he added patting the seat. She had wanted only to gaze out of the window on the way home and be quiet. She thought of Dermot's offer and wondered why she had been honoured with access to his container. Fate perhaps. She wondered if in years to come when Fergal was telling future Pierce generations of the auspicious volcanic eruption on their honeymoon if she would ever say how close she had come to leaving him.

'I'm glad you're not running off on your own.' Rosie did not comment. She had ceased to be surprised Hennessy knew everything about everyone. 'He needs you, you know. It was a very rocky start for him, and you look a steady kind of girl.' She thought of her mother's description of her, a butterfly, and decided she liked Hennessey's estimation better. She nodded, aware too of her added responsibilities. She thanked him prettily and asked to be dropped at the crossroads. Hennessy did not ask her why. Perhaps he already knew.

The beach was deserted and drizzle blew in on a

stiff, chill wind. She turned her face into it. The wreckage of Driscoll's house, now black and almost cold, where only hours before flames still sparked to life, reeked with the smell of burning. She concentrated on her mission of finding the container to quell the maelstrom of leaving or staying, staying or leaving that had occupied her so completely and made her so miserable earlier.

The dunes were steep and at the top of the first, she stood to get her breath and admire the jagged ranks of rocks along this wild stretch of beach before slithering down and up the next to discover the odd sight of the container.

The heavy metal door hung open as it had been left the night of the fire. She lit the lamps as Dermot had instructed, surprised how cosy the inside seemed. It made her think of a hobbit's home. It took no time to find the notebook, hidden in the drawer where Dermott said it would be, wrapped in plastic and carefully placed between his neatly folded shirts. Small and fat and precious, the red silk cover burnished under lamplight and convinced her this must be the one Fergal wanted. She flicked through seeing inkblots and little sketches. The childish writing, though faded, was in two distinct hands. Typed pages had been folded and inserted between the handwritten ones, making the book bulge. Opening one of these she read a list of words without fully understanding. Then she opened more, gradually piecing a story together, picturing Fergal and Lorcan as the little boys in the photograph with their belts tied high over big round tummies, even hearing them quarrel.

Fact: Our mother was long gone before we knew her.
Fact: There are no photographs of her known to exist.

She laid the book on the table by the door with a sense of completeness. Whatever else happened, Fergal would have the notebook he was searching for. The rest of the books that lined the walls of the container seemed to beckon, like ghosts of Fergal's family. She ran her fingers along their spines surprised to find them warm to the touch. They had been saved. Dermot, Driscoll and the rest had actually done them a favour. They would surely have been destroyed by the elements in the wreckage of the house. She picked a book at random just to have it in her hands not realising it was not a book but a writing case held together with an elastic band that disintegrated limply. A sheaf of letters spilled from the covers and floated to the floor. She stooped to gather them, noting the old-fashioned pen and ink that had blurred with age as the paper became damp; one was near transparent.

Dear Father.

Her sigh exhaled with the ghosts of other sighs faced by sudden sadness. Her hand did not tremble as perhaps it should have. She squatted on a low wooden stool that acted as a bedside table and held the lamp nearer.

There seems no point explaining that as yet I have committed no crime. I certainly intended to. I've been taken for a fool and the gobbet of information that I thought would relieve our financial embarrassment, was a trap. Informers play a dangerous game whatever side they are on.

I should have suspected Malachi. I am sorry for that because I know he has been a friend to you for many years, perhaps even a consolation. He has the knack of materialising wherever there's trouble and boys are doing something they shouldn't, with a cuff round the head and 'That's Father Malachi to you, my boy'. Somehow, I can't picture him ever having been a child. Born in the same black cassock that has slowly accumulated the reek of tobacco. Even as a confessor he induced terror in his seven-year-old victims. I'm glad the twins have not yet had that pleasure, and trust since I may not be there to protect them, that you too will forebear.

When I said, I'm afraid my father is not at home, Malachi looked over my shoulder into the house. 'It is you I have come to see,' and crushed me to one side like a wavering blade of grass. He left wet footprints on the wooden floor and I thought perhaps he did live in subterranean places after all as he did in my boyhood nightmares. He told me he passed you and the boys by the lake. Maybe you even saw him pass.

He helped himself to whisky, draining the first glass and pouring himself another then offered one to me. I took it even though as you know I do not like the stuff and for a moment the sound of liquid filling cut glass was the only sound, and the world was tinted through the amber liquid.

'We'll wait for the men,' Malachi said, then offered to hear my confession so I could die in a state of grace. I told him to go to hell, although I didn't feel brave.

Honeymoon

'I dare say I will,' he said, 'but there is no need for us all to meet up.' He laughed till his jowls shook like the persistent bulldog he is. I laughed too in spite of everything.

I have a grudging respect for the man; a veritable pillar of the community whom no one ever questioned let alone suspected. But I have never liked him or his henchmen or that large boy he would like to insinuate into the house who insists on torturing the boys.

I shall be eternally glad that he did not marry us and that Margaret and I were married in the mellow stone church turned to pale gold in the sunshine of an English village with her people near us.

Malachi has left me to my own devices, to retreat to my own quarters and, till I hear him come, I will write and it calms me to write, then I will hide it amid the books. There is no chance of escape, no chance of reprieve. I know that. Better today than some other day when the boys are with me, better this way while they are safe and out of the way.

The day wears on. I wonder you have not come in, pinched and hungry with the boys zipping through the house to find me. I can think of only one explanation: you have arranged this with Malachi. I can only hope you expected a punishment and not as Malachi has threatened repeatedly, an execution.

The words settled like snowflakes on her consciousness with a new white light and a deeper understanding of loss and love, betrayal and despair. She felt she grasped the enormity of what had happened to Fergal, how it had shaped him and made him wary and unable to trust even her; unable to trust that she loved him. In the quiet soft light suffused with shadows she wept for all that had gone before, all that was to come and was stronger for the tears. It was, she realised, as if she had come of age. As if she understood a world of feeling outside her narrow experience that rather than threaten her, enriched as it stripped away her narrow view. A view that changed inexorably as she read as snow blankets the world and at the same time reveals a new truth, a new beauty.

A decision came to her, not deceit exactly, but a conscious decision to tell a white lie. Perhaps those lies are like snow and simply reveal a different truth. Fergal did not have to see this letter. A letter that suggested his own Grandfather might be implicated in his father's death. She did not have to destroy it, nor yet did she have to reveal it. She would simply put it back where she'd found it. Better for Fergal to have Driscoll's explanation. It would be like a betrayal to let Fergal see this.

She thought of Malachi, almost a pantomime villain, had he not been so treacherous. What if he was still alive and lived out his old age in relative peace? More likely, he was dead now and his premonition that he would go to hell had come to pass. She hoped his misdemeanours had revealed themselves in other ways and he'd had his comeuppance.

As she tried to put the secret back in its place on the bookcase she met with resistance as if the gap had sealed over. She used the stool to help and saw that a picture frame had pushed to the back. She pulled it out and the writing case slid in with ease. The small wooden photograph frame fitted her hand so comfortably that she stepped down from the stool to hold it closer to the light. This time her gasp sucked up sadness, lessened it and replaced it with joy. She gazed for some time at the classic studio portrait of a young woman. Fergal's mother, she assumed. The resemblance was striking, the same profile and strong chin. With different hair, it could have been him.

Her fingers felt the ridge of a small label on the back of the frame, a photographer's mark she thought and turned it over. Not surprised to see the brown paper mottled with mould spores she squinted at the tiny print on the label. It was not as she'd expected, nothing here ever was: Colonel and Lady Gopsill and an address in Gloucestershire. She hugged the picture to her. 'Thank you, thank you, thank you,' she whispered out loud, not sure whom she addressed: God, guardian angels, or the grandparents themselves, wherever they might still be. She knew the word serendipity. This photograph wanted to be found. Of course, it might already be too late, his grandparents could have moved, or worse, but she felt it was significant. The what-ifs and if-onlys of Fergal's life gathered in her mind. There could have been any number of explanations why they had not adopted him or been to see him or even written; there were any number of possibilities. She felt bright at the prospect with a feeling of satisfaction. She had gathered evidence herself and besides, Fergal might have a family after all. She stood at the door ready to return to Fergal, ready to meet him and give him the notebook he wanted. As she turned out the lamps the rose silk cover of the notebook glowed like buried treasure.

She swung the container door to with a deep metallic

clang. It must have been raining hard while she was inside but she hadn't heard it. Now it had stopped and the sand was wet and pockmarked. Wind blew about her face, sweet smelling and refreshing. She bounced back over the sand as if she was dancing.

~*~

There was a light on in their cottage as she pushed the door open. Hugo sat at the table with his hand wrapped around a mug. When he looked up he was not smiling. 'We thought you'd gone home,' he said.

'As you see, I'm still here.' They eyed each other.

'Fergal's borrowed the sports car and gone to the hospital to see Driscoll,' Hugo looked at his watch. 'He should be back in half an hour or so.' Rosie nodded. 'That note gave him quite a scare,' Hugo sounded stern. 'What are you playing at?'

Rosie sniffed, 'I could ask you the same question.' She tripped upstairs with the notebooks and photograph safely in her bag. 'I'll be down in a minute. You can make me a cup of tea.' Hugo made a scoffing sound, but she heard him get up and fill the kettle. She laid the books and the photo in the lid of her suitcase. She locked herself in the bathroom and studied her face in the mirror, surprised that she still looked the same. Hugo called up to her, 'Your cup of tea's here.'

They sat without talking as if a gulf had opened between them. She felt a frisson of excitement. Hugo gave her arm a little squeeze, 'Someone walk over your grave?'

'Just thinking, I guess.' She smiled briefly. At least

the story unfolding was unique. She thought of the coming months. Talking of her honeymoon to her colleagues, telling her parents of the baby, maternity leave; those normal things that happened to other women who were always leaving or coming back with photos for the office to paw over. Her turn, she supposed, to join the great sorority. She imagined the future billowing with hope and sweet, free air, not sunk in a quagmire of deceit with the past.

When Fergal wandered in dispirited from the street, his face lit up at the sight of Rosie. He wrapped her in his arms. Neither of them spoke, they just clung to each other as if they had survived some ordeal.

Hugo broke the spell and said brightly, 'Fergal has plans for the house, has he told you?' Rosie took a deep breath to stop herself being sarcastic. 'Why would he confide in me when he has you'? Then said it anyway.

'I thought you were sulking about something,' Hugo said and pretend-punched her shoulder.

'Darned right.' She looked sternly at the pair of them.

Hugo threw his head back and laughed, 'Is that your sternest look, Rosie?'

Fergal shot him a warning glance. 'I suppose you're used to teasing,' he said.

'I can only take so much. Hugo will vouch for that.' Hugo nodded vigorously.

'I thought you'd left me, after this disaster of a honeymoon.'

'It was close Fergal, believe me, baby or no baby.' She laughed mirthlessly, 'I think we should have called this a fact-finding mission and not a honeymoon and then it would have been simpler. No one would've had wrong expectations. It's as if we've had different agendas.'

'Told you it wasn't your best idea,' Hugo said and Fergal grimaced.

'What really got me was you knew enough about your father to make a case.'

'It's not a case exactly,' Fergal was sheepish. 'I just want facts, I feel I owe it to my brother and to myself.'

This was the aspect she had dimly understood. The house was not Fergal's only concern, in spite of the talk. Rosie was thoughtful. 'So, you've found no proof so far and that is one reason we're here?' Fergal nodded.

'I knew you'd understand Rosie,' Fergal kissed her gently.

'Yes, but you didn't trust me, did you?'

Fergal apologised, 'Sorry Rosie, I really didn't know what I'd find, I just knew I wanted you with me.'

Rosie looked searchingly from one to the other.

'I want to know everything you know,' she said.

'How long have you got?' Hugo asked, and began to bluster.

'I'm not letting you off the hook so easily. I've got as long as it takes.' Rosie felt a steady kind of girl with every right to know. 'That's another thing,' Rosie said, believing it as she said it. 'Dishonesty. Lies are so damaging. Even untruthful silences.'

'A bit philosophical,' Hugo said.

Rosie glared at him. 'It's never too late for the truth. That way there's a kind of justice for the dead,' she said.

'That's important too, don't you think?' Hugo smiled appreciation for her valid point.

'On the one hand, if there's anything to be salvaged from the past, it could be the property, right?' He looked to Fergal for corroboration.

Fergal drew her to the couch and took her hands in his. 'I wanted to find out who killed Aidan and why. Everything pointed to a cover-up. Hugo agreed to help me search but we've not been able to find specifics. Everyone was very good at going to ground. So, I decided, since property is my field, to look into the house as well. That's basically it.'

None of them spoke for a while but Rosie still felt there must be more. The night before, Fergal intimated that from a small boy he'd known he would study property law. Rosie looked searchingly from one to the other. 'Why didn't you tell me?'

Hugo moved to the window and gazed out at the street. Fergal groaned and rested his head in his hands, weighty with details his father's case.

'It all seemed too complicated.'

Rosie relented but there was another line of enquiry that troubled her.

'Fergal, why were you never adopted?'

Fergal's head shot up in surprise. As Rosie continued, he stood up and moved away to stand nearer to Hugo.

'Didn't your family, any family, want to scoop you up in their arms and sweep you away?'

'Nope.' Fergal shrugged, glancing briefly at Hugo.

'There must be some reason.' Rosie would not let it drop.

Fergal's eyelids drooped. Hugo clapped him on the back with a smile and said, 'He had issues with anger. That's what they call it these days, isn't it Fergal?' Rosie waited, looking expectantly from one to the other. 'He used to destroy things,' Hugo volunteered. Fergal smiled thinly.

'What kind of things?' Rosie asked more gently, directing her question to Fergal.

'Possessions,' Hugo said.

'Shut up, Hugo,' Rosie snapped, rising from the couch to stand with them. Hugo saluted her and she put her tongue out. 'I don't know why I don't hate you, Hugo.' She stood facing Fergal, looking up at him expectantly.

'I used to torch things,' Fergal said quietly. 'Set fire to them and watch the flames consume them. And before you ask, I have been in trouble with the police, but that was all a long time ago.'

'Stop, Fergal.' She put her hand over his lips and pulled him to her. 'It's ok.' Her instinct was to comfort him, rescue him, but she shuddered.

'You're shivering.' Fergal kissed her head.

'I was remembering last night when I was so frightened.'

'We'll look after you,' Fergal said.

'That's what I was afraid of,' Rosie said and Hugo laughed. 'It wasn't you Fergal, was it? Tell me it wasn't you.'

'No, Rosie, I never did anything awful and I

wouldn't now, I've too much to lose.' Fergal was still clinging to her, stifling her with a surge of heat. She fought him off so she could stand alone.

'I didn't really doubt you, Fergal. It's just with all these secrets, and even Hugo at it.'

Hugo touched his forelock. 'I just do as I'm told.'

'Since when?' Rosie said realising she was no longer in awe of her big brother and no longer besotted with Fergal. She still loved them, of course, but felt her expectation of them was more realistic now. Perhaps her naivety invited them to dupe her.

'Have you anything to add, Hugo?'

'No,' Hugo looked sheepish. 'That seems to be the strength of it.'

'Right then, Hugo. It's late and I'm tired. I suggest you make your way back to the pub and we'll see you in the morning. Breakfast half eight?'

Hugo looked too astonished to offer any resistance. 'I'll say goodnight then,' he said.

When they were alone in the bedroom, Rosie produced the two notebooks and held them out to Fergal. He didn't take them. He simply stared, first at the notebooks and then at Rosie. She began to explain briefly how she had come by them and worried he was going to cry.

'Thank you,' he breathed, his mouth all pulled out of shape. 'Thank you for everything.' He took the books and laying the brown one aside, he held the red book to his face and inhaled deeply. He didn't even open it and when she asked him he said, 'I probably know it by heart. Having it is what I wanted.'

Rosie hesitated. 'This other notebook belonged to your father, I think. Joe Kelly asked me to give it to you.'

'Did he? Ah yes, Dermot's missing property. I'm amazed that you've found them both.'

She shrugged but was pleased with herself. 'I hoped you might find some consolation. Peace, perhaps, or do they call it closure?'

'It has been difficult, but I'm glad I,' he corrected himself, 'I don't think I could have done it without you, Rosie.' He cleared his throat as if preparing to say something important but said nothing.

'There's one more thing,' she said. Fergal collapsed on the bed. Perhaps like her the day before, he had reached a saturation point, and simply did not want, and could not take any more. 'There is something else you should see,' she said, retrieving the photograph before flopping beside him.

He took it from her and studied it. 'This is exactly how I pictured my mother. She was lovely. I've thought about her often since I met you, and realise how lonely Aidan must have been after she died. I don't think Aidan ever got over her.' He shook his head.

'Check the back, Fergal,' Rosie urged. 'We might have a way to find your mother's family. That would be amazing, wouldn't it?'

'How can I ever thank you?' He laid aside the photograph and hugged Rosie. 'I knew I needed you to be with me.'

'Did you think you'd be angry?' Rosie asked, thinking of the troubled boy who burned things.

'Maybe.' Fergal looked stern, then looked expectantly at Rosie as if seeking permission to keep talking. 'I remember my father as gentle, kind and loving, if rather absent-minded. My grandfather was crotchety and so arthritic he walked with difficulty and two sticks. He was also kind and very loving. Our childhood was idyllic, but that ended so abruptly that I was off kilter for years. I truly believe if the good memories hadn't persisted, even if only in my dreams, I would not have survived. What I wanted most in the world for quite some time was some kind of vengeance. I determined on law as a career and then I met Hugo and you and gradually it became obvious that it was justice I wanted, not vengeance. Closure, yes perhaps that's it. I had a long chat with Joe Kelly last night and he advised me to let it go. That's what he's managed to do. Sometimes someone else's story can put your own in a different light. Besides, now there's you and the baby and I know I'm very lucky.'

Rosie did not fall instantly asleep, as Fergal did. The past days of the honeymoon, the visit to Ireland, so many changes in so short a space of time, to say nothing of Fergal's reaction to the notebooks, all conspired to keep her awake. She couldn't understand why he wasn't curious. Why he hadn't slavishly read every last word of his father's notebook – a diary perhaps, with intimate details. Restless, after what seemed hours, she crept downstairs taking Aidan's notebook with her. She made herself a cup of tea, carefully turning pages as she waited for the kettle to boil, then settled on the settee. A twinge of guilt that she should read it first, and without

Fergal, was soon forgotten as she began to scan the first page. Almost immediately she heard Fergal get out of bed and start to come downstairs and she closed the notebook, tucking it close to her on the settee.

'Can't you sleep either?' Fergal said.

Rosie offered Fergal tea. 'No, thanks,' he said and settled down beside her.

'How's Driscoll, by the way?' Rosie asked.

'Not bad, considering.' He shifted uneasily and glanced at her.

'What?' Rosie asked, prepared to be exasperated.

'Have you read this stuff?' Fergal picked up the notebook lying beside her.

'No, not yet.'

'We could both look now if you want. And then perhaps we'll sleep.'

Snuggled together, Rosie turned the scant, badly mottled pages and they released their secret, underground smell.

'Wait,' Fergal said. 'I should tell you first, I was investigating all the wrong things.'

'Oh?' Rosie asked, still intent on the book.

'Joe told me Driscoll was there when Aidan died and his death was…' Fergal faltered.

'Oh, my God.' Rosie shifted so she could see his face, pale and drawn. 'Driscoll?'

'And Joe Kelly.'

Rosie felt sick. 'I don't understand.'

'Aidan's death was an accident. I wanted there to be a cause, something important enough for all the heartache.'

Rosie still didn't understand. She would have liked to absorb the heartache herself, seeing Fergal wipe tears from his eyes.

'I truly believed Aidan's death was political,' Fergal sniffed. 'The year he died IRA bombings tumbled out of Northern Ireland into Europe, like the explosion at the British army base in Germany and everyone was desperate for information and informers both sides of the border. I believed he was targeted as a likely collaborator, perhaps because he'd had an English wife, perhaps because he was an intellectual.'

'But it wasn't politics,' Rosie said.

'No. It was a tiff, a beating, according to Joe Kelly. It ruined his life too, from what he told me.'

'Only part of his life, perhaps the best is yet to come.' She gave him a bright smile and he laughed.

'The best part of mine has already started.' He kissed her nose.

'Perhaps this notebook will explain,' Rosie suggested.

~ * ~

'I think you're a dreamer, Aidan Pierce.' Margaret disappeared out of the lecture hall in the sea of other students. 'Pub lunch?' she mouthed and beckoned. I bolted over rows of seats like a colt. In the pub, her closeness blurred everything.

'I have to go home to England for my mother's birthday, Aidan. I wondered if you'd like to come?'

It was a key, an open sesame that unlocked the whole sequence. Her car and the ferry, the wind in our hair and feeling seasick, leaving Ireland and the boat's wake trailing all the way back to port, laughing with her in my arms.

'Will it always be like this?' I asked as her hair blew into my mouth in the wind. 'Of course,' she said, a slippery eel wriggling to be free.

The party was unlike any party I had known: no singing, no dancing, just little trills of conversation in the afternoon like a spray of roses petering out with a pleasant smell and a disintegration of petals. The coldness of it blighted, like frost nipping fingers and toes. But that night she came to my room, slipped between the cold sheets and wrapped me in her limbs till I sank into her, and saved myself from drowning.

In my dreams, I fold and refold my arms about her till we are one and not to have her in my arms leaves a dull ache where she should be.

Rosie's chest felt tight and she struggled to breathe. This was a love story that had not ended happily. She thought of the grave and the bright flowers and the date, the day they were all found, Fergal had said.

"Twins, Aidan, just think of it: a family.'

I kissed her fingertips and put my rough fingers over them on her belly, not a belly yet, no sign of the lives growing there. Her flesh was warm to the touch, fertile like land in sunshine.

We wore a groove in the same old ground for nearly nine months but made no headway. I knew I was losing; I would give in to whatever she asked; it is always the ties that bind.

'You're such a worry boots. There's a midwife in the village; she'll come. It's not the Middle Ages.' A trickle of her laugh.

'You'll be safer in England.'

'Aidan, please don't go over it again. I'll be safer in my own home. I am where I want to be, where I belong.'

'I can work just as easily over there. Better, in fact, because there won't be the worry. I would be with you, that is what matters don't you think?'

'And then there's your father. What would he do without us?'

Rosie thought of the new life in her and the life described in the musty pages, all part of the same story: past, present and future, a continuum and hoped she and Fergal would love each other like that. She turned her face up to Fergal and smiled. How childish it seemed now to have wanted to run away. 'It's a love story,' she said.

She closed the book and asked gently, 'Shall we just let it go and not read anymore?'

His mouth was a half-smile. 'Maybe. Read the rest tomorrow, you mean?'

'Or not read it at all. Maybe we know enough of the truth already. If we stop now, we have an inkling of the love affair and that they were happy.'

'I want to know,' Fergal said.

One Sunday I went to the pub. Or, as Father would say, took it upon myself to go, as if I had no right to enjoy a drink with the rest of them. 'The fellows', as Father called them, ignored me for the main part except for one who sought me out. It was not something that happened often, that I should be sought out. He even offered to buy me a drink, so that the one usual, infrequent drink became two, then three and before long I had lost count and was unaccountably jolly. I remember some backslapping, and feeling well-disposed towards him, Mountjoy, a ruddy-faced Englishman, as out of place in the pub as I was.

I meandered home a little light-headed, and was nearly at the gates deciding whether to follow the sweep of the drive or to take the shortcut across the field, about to croak into song as a full and generous moon slipped from behind clouds to light my way as bright as day, when Mountjoy appeared. He must have followed me all the way and never let on. Mountjoy with something urgent to say that could not have been said before in the full pub.

'It was hardly full, two or three old boys round a table.'

'There was the other room,' Mountjoy replied, but I couldn't picture this other room, and wanted to be rid of Mountjoy. There followed ridiculous Boy's Own whispering, with the heat of Mountjoy's face in mine, and something rank in the clouds of his breath. 'All you have to do is leave three pebbles in the crevice of the wall,' and Mountjoy thrust white pebbles like bird's eggs in my hand and showed me where. 'If you want to meet again for a drink or whatever, I'm often out this way so I'll soon see them.'

I laughed out loud. It felt unreal. How would that ever get us anywhere? Did Mountjoy think me a careless man who would let fall all I knew over a drink? Did he think that a man who'd had an English wife would be a willing sympathiser? Mountjoy mentioned money. Damp seeped through the soles of my shoes and as the moon slid back behind clouds, Mountjoy was gone.

The pebbles sat on my desk slowly disappearing under a mound of paper but money was on my mind, waking and sleeping. Money was paid for information.

It was one Sunday morning, ambling home from Mass with the boys, listening to their way of finishing off the other's sentences. There had been the usual courtesies asked after Father, God love him, and how is he? And the boys growing so tall and so like their —and then the usual pause, unsure whether to mention Margaret by name or whether not to mention her at all was more refined in the circumstances. A few glances exchanged and then, the gauntlet run, we were ahead of them all. I could hear low voices but not see whose. Men were concealed behind a hedge, crouching maybe. They identified a murderer. A trickle of sweat ran down my back. A careless snippet that might prove valuable, whispered on the wind, on the way home from Mass with my sons.

I refused to dwell on thirty pieces of silver counted into a waiting hand. Who knows the community might well be grateful? Relieved at least, if the ever-present threat of this man was removed. What would happen? Just desserts. A man who invoked fear, a bully reputed to dole out rough justice. Suspicion always fell on this man in the flurry of whispers that followed a sudden disappearance. Surely the authorities knew this? Or, were they always short of vital information? No one willing to stand against tradition and speak up. I know the code of ethics instilled since childhood. 'You keep your eyes open and your trap shut, if you know what's good.' Some days I'm quite rational about this; my concerns are simply financial. It all boils down to survival in the end.

They paused. 'That's it, isn't it?' Fergal said, 'Confirmation. He was prepared to sell information. People got killed for doing that. He risked his life - for what? Nothing?' He sounded disappointed.

Rosie inhaled deeply. 'Perhaps it's a novel he was working on. Or, if we do accept this is what happened, it shows how desperate Aidan was.'

Fergal stroked her hair. 'You may be right on both counts. This is not necessarily fact and, yes, perhaps he was desperate.'

Trees blew down in the high winds, enough to keep us in firewood for weeks. I think of days of hard work, blisters to my hands, breaking back and aching shoulders, involved in keeping my father warm; all of them I suppose, but mostly him, blinking now in the firelight, oblivious that the record has ended and the needle of the gramophone player is scraping the paper in the middle of the disc. It sets my teeth on edge. He does not look up when I switch it off. He could be dead in his chair and I wouldn't even know it. If he were to die here now, tonight, my life would not be worth living anyway. I'm not sure who depends most on the other.

'Father do you hear me? I need a favour,' feeling churlish to have to rely on him. 'Will you take the boys in the morning; I've some business.'

He looks at me, suddenly alert, 'Will you be away long?'

'Well, only overnight, two at the most. It might not even involve a stay away. I wouldn't ask, only.'

'I don't need your thanks,' he is gruff. 'Not for this anyway. You be careful.' He catches hold of my hand and holds my gaze, 'You hear?' We stay like that for some moments and I wonder if he knows. Some instinct, some parental bond gives insight when an only son is about to betray his fellows for money. How could he know? The old man never leaves the grounds now and the only regular visitor is the priest, Malachi, come to hear his confession and growl at the boys. The whole country could be blowing itself to bits and we'd not know till a week later when I walk the boys to Mass and some tittle-tattle would be pleased to break any news with a smug smile. Glad, no doubt, that the family are no longer so grand, no longer to be looked up to.

Does betrayal make me less of a man? No doubt it's a sin of the first order and Malachi would be glad to shrive me. When everyone is at pains to pretend and falsify, it's anyone's guess who's telling the truth. Certainly no one speaks out, and no one ever speaks plainly.

Dappled sunlight dances on the ceiling. Wind whispers through trees. A consoling backdrop keeps the house alive; low bickering from the boys' room and the sporadic tap of the typewriter; the rhythmic rumble of Father's radio, unless he's reciting poetry to the cat which I wouldn't put past him. The cat, an emissary from Father, jumps up on my bed and begins to purr. 'All right Mystique, I'm getting my lazy arse out of bed.' The cat winds round my bare ankles as I fish for my slippers. 'You know Mystique, you are the easiest to get along with in the whole house,' and I pick him up to carry him downstairs. They all look up expectantly when I come into the kitchen.

'Who's for porridge?' There's no reply.

'Are you going away, Da?' the boys ask. How could the boys know that? There's an almost imperceptible shake of Father's head.

'Just overnight, maybe,' and I turn quickly to the stove so no one sees the flush rising on my cheeks. I have no idea how the information will be passed. I might not even go through with it. I'm to expect a visitor, that's all I've been told and I don't want the boys or Father around.

'Granda's taking us exploring today. We're having a picnic.'

'That's grand.' I do not turn around.

Latterly, a brisk walk into the grounds to forage for anything edible counts as exploring. In the old days, we went further afield, Father on his hunter and me trotting along behind on a dappled, Connemara pony, long since sold off. How terrified I used to be after the sweep of the drive on turning into the lane in case we should meet anyone. I never told and Father never seemed to notice the mockery of the village lads lying in wait. Now the grounds are *as God-forsaken as I am and no matter how often I repeat Malachi's recommended mantra for times of deep need, 'Come Holy Spirit, come Holy Spirit, come Holy Spirit,' nothing ever comes.*

With the ghost of a smile, Father said there would be a swim in the lake and when I convey this to the boys they whoop with delight.

'Come hell or high water it's time for a bath; come hail or come shine that's what we'll do,' the boys chant, banging their spoons on the wooden table.

I watch them set off, my identical boys with their knapsacks of packed picnic; not much I'm afraid, and their towels in a roll under their arms. Even Father had his togs. The memory of those swims makes me shudder: Father's: 'Make a man of yourself, dive in,' shouted encouragingly. Making a man of myself seemed as impossible as total immersion in freezing water, and as undesirable. I still can't bring myself to go near the lake, never mind wash in it and would rather boil kettles at the range and bathe in stealth at night. There was never the money to put in a bathroom and after Margaret died, I hadn't the heart. It's a minor betrayal that I don't extend this luxury of hot water to the boys. But then perhaps they are more adept at making men of themselves.

I prowl the house waiting for the visitor, perhaps Mountjoy himself. In the boys' room I sink on the double bed, its springs gone, and remember unbearable sleepless nights with the empty space beside me. I have the straight and narrow, the penance of a single bed now. After today, everything will be different. The question asked a thousand, thousand times, what else could I have done?

'It seems too much of a coincidence for it all to be fiction,' Fergal said. He closed the book.

'I'm so sorry,' Rosie said. She ran her fingers over the leather cover, spoiled by damp but still quite beautiful, resisting the urge to hold it to her nose.

When finally they went back to bed, sleep was instant, as if their bodies simply shut down.

~*~

Breakfast in the pub was subdued. Mr Hennessy served them himself and service was slow but friendly. Joe Kelly came to join them as they finished eating. They spoke in general terms of grandiose plans for the house renovation, foreign investment, a golf course, a grand hotel, a family home. Out of the discussions, a consensus was reached. Regeneration for the village would be grand. Hugo was certain he had several eager businessmen lined up and then Mr Hennessy said he would back them all the way. Joe Kelly too seemed to think regeneration was the way to go and offered his building expertise.

Rosie imagined the old house done up, even living in a part of it. She couldn't say if they would ever come back, yet she hoped all the hope-fuelled plans would come to something.

She felt the permanence and the fragility of the village clinging to this far-flung coast. She thought of further trips to the hospital, Driscoll getting better, Dermot going back to his container. The community had survived betrayal and brutality. She remembered something Fergal had said about being an infinitesimal speck in the universe and felt she understood.

ACKNOWLEDGEMENTS

My thanks to all who have helped and encouraged the final version of Honeymoon, especially my family who liked the story from the outset; the delightful reading group in Pieces for Places whose encouragement finally gave me confidence to self-publish, and not least Team Author UK (TAUK), who do as they suggest on their website, and so much more.

I would also like to thank the artist Lateefa Spiker for use of her picture for the front cover.

ABOUT THE AUTHOR

Mary J Howell was born and brought up in the West Midlands with her mother, two sisters, a tabby cat and an accent to die for. She now lives in North West Wales with a view of sunsets over the sea.

Milestones she counts as achievements and vice versa:

- ❖ Surviving to be a grandmother
- ❖ Walking solo 500 miles across Northern Spain to Santiago along the pilgrim route the Camino de Santiago de Compostela.
- ❖ Writing a second book

www. maryjhowell.co.uk
Facebook: @AuthorMaryJHowell

Made in the USA
Columbia, SC
09 December 2017